PRAISE FOR *The One*

'If you are looking for a read-in-one dash of mystery then this has it all... train or beach-side holiday.' —Reading, Writing and...

'I absolutely couldn't put *The One That Got Away* down . . . it had me totally consumed . . .' —Mrs G's Bookshelf

'Both tender and tragic, heartbreaking and triumphant . . . A wonderful life-affirming story I highly recommend—another riveting read from Karly Lane!' —Cindy L. Spear

PRAISE FOR *For Once In My Life*

'There is something special about Karly Lane's novels. She inspires, uplifts, encourages, advises and even provides a heavenly escape through her fictional worlds where characters come alive and become friends we never want to say goodbye to . . . *For Once in My Life* is no exception.' —Cindy L. Spear

'Lane's engaging storytelling instantly draws us into Jenny's world . . . a compelling, fast-paced and engaging read with heart and substance, perfect for summer reading.' —Better Reading

'If you are looking for a good holiday read, then definitely choose *For Once In My Life* . . . sit back and relax and enjoy the characters.' —Blue Wolf Reviews

PRAISE FOR *Time After Time*

'*Time After Time* moves from a small country town in Australia to the red carpet of London and Karly Lane has woven a story of dreams, fashion, fame and second chances.' —The Burgeoning Bookshelf

'With a stunning second chance love story, a picturesque country backdrop, pressing rural community themes and characters that grow on you, *Time After Time* is another warmly told read from one of my favourite writers.' —Mrs B's Book Reviews

'Proving herself once again top of the game in this genre, Karly Lane brings us a tale that juxtaposes the high-end London fashion industry and a small-town community.' —Living Arts Canberra

'Heart-warming . . . an enjoyable read that will be warmly welcomed by fans of Australian romance writing.' —*Canberra Weekly*

'Karly Lane has a way of dragging you in and making you feel like you are a part of the story . . . It is a wonderful read.' —Beauty and Lace

'Lane vividly evokes Australian rural communities, and gives due recognition to its challenges, especially for farmers. Written with the warmth, humour and heart for which Lane's rural romances are known, *Time After Time* is an engaging read.' —Book'd Out

PRAISE FOR *Wish You Were Here*

'A comely rural romance that encapsulates the heart and emotions of Australian country life . . . You can't go wrong with a Karly Lane novel and this latest one was no exception.' —Mrs B's Book Reviews

'It's always a great day when a new Karly Lane book is released . . . *Wish You Were Here* has all the small town country vibes you could want in a closed door romance with a whole lot of heart.' —Noveltea Corner

'. . . a fabulous rural romance, the perfect book to snuggle up with on the recliner! Loved it.' —Mrs G's Bookshelf

'With the magic of country atmosphere, a cast of incredible characters . . . true community spirit and a relatable romance, it has all the contents of an engaging read. You can smell the way of life, feel the weather and breathe in the fresh air as Karly's inviting storytelling comes to life from the pages.' —HappyValley BooksRead

PRAISE FOR *A Stone's Throw Away*

'Fans will not be disappointed and new readers are likely to be converted . . . those looking for romance, suspense or contemporary novels will all find something to enjoy.' —Beauty and Lace

'With its appealing characters, well-crafted setting and layered storyline, *A Stone's Throw Away* is an entertaining read.' —Book'd Out

'Karly Lane has delivered a wonderfully immersive novel with a highly engaging plot, gripping suspense and compelling twists. *A Stone's Throw Away* is a story of courage, resilience and a passion for the truth.' —The Burgeoning Bookshelf

'I'm always highly impressed by Lane's ability to write compelling, entertaining and emotional storylines and weave some of Australia's history through her stories . . . an absolute treat.' —Noveltea Corner

PRAISE FOR *Once Burnt, Twice Shy*

'Well written, and bravely done . . . *Once Burnt, Twice Shy* is Karly Lane's best yet, celebrating the power of community working to support one another in terrible calamity.' —Blue Wolf Reviews

'Karly Lane gives it her all in *Once Burnt, Twice Shy* . . . a story of faith, courage, strength and future prospects, Lane's eighteenth novel is a sizzling summer read.' —Mrs B's Book Reviews

'This book has a huge amount of hope after loss, a wonderful read.' —Noveltea Corner

'Heart in mouth stuff, readers. You won't be able to put the book down till you know what happens to Jack and Sam.' —Australian Romance Readers

PRAISE FOR *Take Me Home*

'Full of romance, humour and a touch of the supernatural, this is another engaging tale by the reliable Karly Lane.' —*Canberra Weekly Magazine*

'Such a fun read . . . Karly has smashed the contemporary fiction genre with *Take Me Home*.' —Beauty and Lace

'*Take Me Home* is a delight to read. I loved the change of scenery while still enjoying Karly Lane's wonderful, familiar storytelling.' —Book'd Out

Karly Lane lives on the beautiful mid-North Coast of New South Wales, and she is the proud mum of four children and an assortment of four-legged animals.

Before becoming an author, Karly worked as a pathology collector. Now, after surviving three teenage children and with one more to go, she's confident she can add referee, hostage negotiator, law enforcer, peacekeeper, ruiner-of-social-lives, driving instructor and expert-at-silently-counting-to-ten to her resume.

When she isn't at her keyboard, Karly can be found hanging out with her beloved horses and dogs, happily ignoring the housework.

Karly writes Rural and Women's Fiction set in small country towns, blending contemporary stories with historical heritage. She is a passionate advocate for rural Australia, with a focus on rural communities and the issues currently affecting them. She has published more than twenty books with Allen & Unwin.

Twist of Fate

KARLY LANE

Twist of Fate

ALLEN&UNWIN
SYDNEY·MELBOURNE·AUCKLAND·LONDON

This is a work of fiction. Names, characters, places and incidents are products of the author's imagination or are used fictitiously. Any resemblance to actual events, locales or persons, living or dead, is entirely coincidental.

First published in 2024

Copyright © Karlene Lane 2024

All rights reserved. No part of this book may be reproduced or transmitted in any form or by any means, electronic or mechanical, including photocopying, recording or by any information storage and retrieval system, without prior permission in writing from the publisher. The Australian *Copyright Act 1968* (the Act) allows a maximum of one chapter or 10 per cent of this book, whichever is the greater, to be photocopied by any educational institution for its educational purposes provided that the educational institution (or body that administers it) has given a remuneration notice to the Copyright Agency (Australia) under the Act.

Allen & Unwin
Cammeraygal Country
83 Alexander Street
Crows Nest NSW 2065
Australia
Phone: (61 2) 8425 0100
Email: info@allenandunwin.com
Web: www.allenandunwin.com

Allen & Unwin acknowledges the Traditional Owners of the Country on which we live and work. We pay our respects to all Aboriginal and Torres Strait Islander Elders, past and present.

 A catalogue record for this book is available from the National Library of Australia

ISBN 978 1 76106 933 8

Set in 12.4/19.6 pt Simoncini Garamond Std by Bookhouse, Sydney
Printed and bound in Australia by the Opus Group

10 9 8 7 6 5 4 3 2

 The paper in this book is FSC® certified. FSC® promotes environmentally responsible, socially beneficial and economically viable management of the world's forests.

To Nanna May and the others, who continue to watch over me and try their best to stop me making stupid mistakes, this one is for you.

Soulmate [sohl-meyt], noun: The person destiny has chosen for us. Our missing piece. The one with whom we experience a connection of minds and an unconditional, effortless, never-ending love.

Prologue

How to Manifest Your Soulmate
Step One. Write a list.
Step Two. Be specific.
Step Three. Release it to the universe.

Bel put down her phone after checking the instructions and picked up her pen, looking at the blank piece of paper thoughtfully. Then she started writing.

My Soulmate List
BY MABEL BUCKLEY

He will be brave
He will have a chiselled jaw
He will be intelligent

He must be someone who understands me
He loves excitement and has hero qualities
He must be handsome
He will have beautiful eyes
I surrender with heart, truth and absolute trust that you will make this so for me.

Bel carefully read over what she'd written in the beautifully ornate notebook. It was specific without being nitpicky, unlike her last two lists. Her first attempt at manifesting a soulmate had resulted in a five-page list particular to the point of ridiculousness. There was no way the universe was going to be able to find a man with a list *that* complicated, so she'd refined it. It was easy once she'd realised exactly what it *was* she wanted. The answer had been sitting right there on her bedside table: Jax Lexington.

Bel folded the list carefully and slid it into the front pages, giving the man on the cover one last longing look as she put the book back on the table, before turning off her lamp and falling asleep.

One

Bel Buckley stifled a sigh as a car pulled up at the bowsers. *Just when I was getting to the exciting part.* She hated when her work life got in the way of her reading life. The latest book in Alison Gatsby's Lexington Millionaires series had finally come out and Bel was desperate to start reading it. She'd promised herself she'd wait until she got home from work so she could settle into bed with a glass of wine and devour, uninterrupted, the whole book in one sitting, only the temptation was too strong . . . like the jawline of Jax Lexington, who posed shirtless on the front cover, lazily resting one hip against the side of a very expensive sports car, a pair of dark sunglasses resting low on his perfect Roman nose as he stared straight into her soul.

'Bel! I ain't got all day!' an impatient voice bellowed from outside, snapping her out of her daydream in an instant as she quickly hit the button to activate the pump. She gave one last, disheartened glance at the cover and slid the book under the front counter. She pushed her thick-rimmed glasses back up her nose as she waited for Bill Matheson to finish filling up his battered old ute.

Bel watched his faithful old kelpie, Meg, drop her head over the side of the ute while Bill meandered across to the fridge and selected his usual sixpack of beer, then a packet of cashews, a *Take 5* magazine and a bag of dog treats before heading to the counter, where Bel was already ripping off his five dollars' worth of scratchies.

'Any sign of that rain they said was coming?' Bel asked after informing him of the total. She listened to his usual rant about bloody government taxes and greedy politicians in bed with fuel companies for the billionth time—it was the same thing, like a record playing on repeat, every single Tuesday.

'Nope. Won't rain till the twenty-sixth.'

'I hope not. There'll be a lot of unhappy people around here if it does.' Surely even Mother Nature wouldn't dare risk the wrath of Larkin Buckley, bridezilla incarnate.

Bill shrugged one skinny shoulder beneath his dusty flannelette shirt—she was pretty sure it was his *only* shirt, as he wore it into town every week. It had a small rip underneath the front pocket. 'Rain don't care who it upsets.'

'See you next week, Bill,' she called out after him.

'Maybe. Unless I'm dead.'

She should be used to his usual farewell, but it still made her wince every time he said it. She had no idea how old he was, but one day he wouldn't be in on a Tuesday, and she wasn't sure she was going to be ready to cope with that day. As grumpy as he was, she'd grown fond of him. Underneath that gruff exterior was a kind man. He never left his farm without Meg and always bought her treats, and after he stopped in to get his fuel he would drop in at the nursing home to sit with his former neighbour, Mary, who had gone into care twelve months earlier. He always made sure to bring her a *Take 5* magazine so she could do her puzzles.

Bel listened to the ute drive away and heard her phone ping: 'I hope you're all wearing your shoes in!' She groaned and reached for her book only for the door to open and set off the jingle of bells. She placed the book on the counter with exaggerated patience. Couldn't she get just one minute of peace and quiet?

'And no lollipops. I need to talk to Aunt Bel for a minute.'

Bel's irritation passed and she smiled at the woman and toddler who entered. Then she walked around the counter, snagging a wrapped lollipop from its jar and slipping it into the little girl's hand. 'Shh,' she said with an exaggerated wink, getting a conspiratorial nod in return.

'Mabel Rose Buckley!' Emma said, causing Bel to straighten and narrow her eyes. Emma was the only person who ever called her by her full name and lived, and that was only due to the fact they'd been best friends since childhood.

'Oh, come on, you and I both know Lucy would have used that cheeky grin to get a lollipop out of one of us before you left anyway.'

'I know which one of us that would be.'

'Well, you shouldn't make such irresistible children.' Bel watched Lucy's cherub-like face smiling around the lollipop as she settled herself comfortably on the chair behind the counter.

'Come over at dinnertime and tell me how irresistible they are then,' Emma said. 'Which reminds me, come over tonight. You haven't been over for ages.'

'I can't. I have a date tonight,' Bel said.

'What! When? With who?' her friend asked, staring at her.

'With Jax Lexington,' Bel said, wiggling her eyebrows as she leaned an elbow on the counter and gave her book a gentle pat.

'Oh, for goodness' sake,' Emma snapped. 'I thought you'd found someone.'

'It's the one I've been waiting six weeks for. There was a hold-up in the pre-orders. I told you about it,' Bel prodded.

'Yes, I know. You've been complaining about nothing else. I seriously worry about you, you know.'

'I don't know why. I'm perfectly happy.' Bel tucked a stray strand that had fallen out of the messy bun she'd pulled her hair into on her way out the door that morning.

'Sure you are.'

Okay, so maybe that was a slight exaggeration. She may not be *perfectly* happy . . . but she wasn't *un*happy. She was embracing positivity and abundance this year. It had all started with a book, titled *Mindfulness and Manifesting a New You—Love, Wealth and Career*. She'd been drawn to the book while she'd been browsing in the bookshop, waiting for Larkin to buy napkins for the wedding. The self-help aisle wasn't one she normally ventured down, but that day the bright gold and pink cover had caught her eye. New year, new me, she reminded herself.

And it wasn't as though she didn't *want* to find some nice guy to go out on a date with but come on—this was Wessex. In the middle of nowhere and the back of beyond. The pickings were pretty slim at best. Hence the need to take drastic action with the whole manifesting thing.

Bel pulled herself up. That wasn't the kind of energy to be putting out there. She took a breath, remembering her list. *Trust in the universe.*

'Your fictional boyfriend isn't going to keep you warm in bed at night.'

'Clearly you haven't read any of these books,' Bel said dryly.

'I'm being serious, Bel. You need to start looking for a real man.'

'And where do you suppose I start looking? It's easy for you, Miss I-married-my-high-school-sweetheart. You got the last eligible male within a hundred kilometres who still has all his own teeth.'

'There are lots of eligible men around,' Emma said.

'Like who?'

'Well . . . there's . . . Terry O'Shea,' she said.

'He's in prison.'

'Oh, yeah. I forgot about that. Well, what about his brother—Mitch?'

'He's in prison too—remember? They were *both* in the tow truck dragging the ATM down the main street.' To their house . . . where the police found it after following the scrape marks down the road. Not the brightest gene pool, clearly.

'Tex . . . whatever his name is. You know the one who works at Stumpy Richardson's workshop.'

'The one who got Kylie Smith pregnant and already has a baby with her older sister?'

'He did? How come I didn't hear about that?'

'Because you don't work in Dwyers' general store and hear *all* the gossip.'

'Wow. I'm really out of the loop.'

The bell dinged as the door opened and both women turned to see the newcomer. Emma gasped, drawing his attention.

'Emma. Bel,' he said, nodding briefly at them before heading for the aisle of groceries the small store stocked.

'Dean Preston,' Emma said in a loud side whisper. Her eyes lit up as she swung back around and stared at Bel with growing excitement.

'Absolutely not,' Bel hissed back, horrified.

'Why not?'

'Are you kidding me? He made my life a living hell in primary *and* high school.'

'That was a hundred years ago.'

'Still not long enough to forget,' Bel snapped. Dean Preston's return to town a few months earlier had only been the topic of general conversation for a few days, which said a lot for how boring the bloke must be now. There was absolutely nothing of interest for anyone to gossip about.

'I can't believe I didn't think of this sooner,' Emma said, ignoring her friend's warning glare. 'He's perfect.'

'He's *not* perfect.'

'Did you see his butt in those jeans? When did *that* happen?'

Bel rolled her eyes. 'Would you keep your voice down?' she said in a low voice as she tried to keep an eye on the man in question, praying he was far enough away not to overhear. A nice butt in jeans wasn't exactly an oddity around here—jeans were, after all, the main wardrobe staple of the majority of the population, although Bel could admit that some men wore them a little better than others. Dean Preston was possibly one of those men. His dark brown hair was a little long around the ears and on the top, a clear testament to the fact he was too snowed under to have found time for a haircut recently, and his dark beard was probably not grown as any kind of fashion statement but because it was easier than shaving every day.

'Ask him out.'

'What?' Bel immediately clamped her lips closed as her voice almost echoed off the walls. 'You are out of your freaking mind,' she added in a hushed but furious tone.

'Everything okay?'

Both women immediately straightened. 'Yep, fine. I haven't seen you around in ages, Dean. How have you been?' Emma asked sweetly, ignoring Bel's warning glance.

'Yeah. You know. Working, sleeping . . . working.'

'Oh yeah, I hear ya. Craig's the same. Sometimes I almost forget I'm married, I haven't seen him in so long.'

'How's he doing?'

'Yeah good, he's still doing the mine thing. Just for a couple more years, we hope. Then he'll be back to full-time farmer.'

'Gotcha. I did it for a while. Must be tough with kids, though.'

'It can be, but I've been a farmer's wife for a long time now. I'm kind of used to being a single mum,' she said with an easy grin that would fool most people. Bel knew she was covering up the stress of the bad years of battling to hold on to their property. It was still a struggle with Craig having to work away and still see to the farm when he was back.

'So what about you?' Emma asked. 'Are you married? Divorced?'

'Gay?' Bel piped up.

Dean eyed her oddly before looking back at Emma. 'None of the above,' he said.

'So, single?' Emma prodded.

'I guess so.'

'You guess so? What's to guess about it? You either are or you're not,' Bel said with a slight scoff before realising she wasn't even interested in his answer. She slid her old glasses back up her nose. *I really need to get new glasses.*

'I am,' he said, looking at Bel with a frown.

She pulled a slight face and reached out for the milk and bread he held. 'Is that all you're after today?'

He seemed slightly distracted as he nodded and pulled his wallet from his back pocket. She rang up the items and waited for him to tap his card.

'It was nice to see you again, Dean,' Emma said.

'Yeah. You too. Say g'day to Craig for me.'

As soon as the door shut behind him, Emma grabbed Bel's hand and gave a strangled squeal. 'He's perfect!'

'A perfect *dick*,' Bel replied, shaking off her friend's grip.

'He is not.'

'Are you forgetting the time he stuck chewing gum in my hair?'

'We were ten, Bel.'

'Give him time,' Bel said, her eyes following his vehicle as he drove away. 'A leopard doesn't change his spots.'

'Okay, David Attenborough,' Emma said making fun of her. 'Once you realise he's not that kid you remember, you'll see.'

'I'll date Bill Matheson first,' she said, crossing her arms defiantly.

'Now there's an image I won't be able to unsee for a while,' Emma said, holding her hand out as she waited for her daughter to climb back down off the chair. 'Tomorrow night, dinner at my place. No excuses.'

'Fine,' Bel agreed. She'd have tonight to read. She sent a longing look at the book on the counter and felt her resolve stiffen. Until she found a man who could make her quiver and swoon the way Jax did, she was happy to stay single. Dean Preston crossed her mind quickly and she gave a small chuckle. If he was her only option, her heart was more than safe.

In the midst of the masquerade ball's opulent splendour, the air crackled with anticipation and hidden desires. Masks concealed identities while whispers of intrigue danced around the room like a forbidden waltz. Jax moved through the crowd with the grace of a predator stalking its prey.

Then, through the crowd, he saw her—Corrine—her eyes wide with fear, cornered by a man wearing a leering jester's mask. With a silent promise in his heart, he stepped forward, a dark and enigmatic figure. In one swift motion, he whisked her away from her tormentor, his touch gentle yet possessive as he guided her through the maze of dancers.

Finding sanctuary in a secluded alcove, they were sheltered from the prying eyes of the ballroom. Alone in their hidden haven, their masks fell away, revealing the raw vulnerability beneath.

Their eyes met, sparking a firestorm of desire that consumed them both. Without a word, Jax drew her close, his lips capturing hers in a hungry kiss that left them both gasping for air. The world around them faded into oblivion as they surrendered to the intoxicating passion that pulsed between them.

Clothes were torn at with urgency, each touch igniting a wildfire of sensation that threatened to consume them whole. In the flickering candlelight, their bodies moved as one, a symphony of longing and pleasure that echoed through the night.

And as the masquerade ball raged on, they surrendered to the undeniable pull of fate, their love transcending the boundaries of time and space.

Bel closed her eyes and gave a small sigh as she hugged the open book to her chest. 'Oh, Jax,' she whispered as she immersed herself back in the world where Jax was always there to save the day and be the kind of hero every woman dreamed of finding.

Bel set up her phone on her desk and did a quick check behind her to make sure there was nothing embarrassing that might show up in the video. It was her worst nightmare that she would post a video on her BookTok account and have viewers pointing out something she'd missed, like that horrific video of the woman in a Zoom meeting with a massive dildo in plain view on the bookcase behind her. Of course, that was an extreme example. Bel was more concerned it would be something awkward like a pair of undies or a bra, which, to her mind, would be bad enough.

Happy that everything was as it was meant to be, she began filming.

She'd fallen into the whole social media thing by accident. She'd always followed her favourite authors and was part of a reviewers' network within the romance readers' circle, but making her own videos was not something she'd ever thought she'd be doing. Then one day, after reading a book that had angered her so intensely because it had been such a blatant copy of her most-loved series—and a completely crap-house one at that—she'd decided to have a rant, as you do. It probably hadn't been the best idea after a few glasses of wine, but then again, had she not had that Dutch courage under her belt, she most likely wouldn't have ever posted the video, which went viral and ended up earning her a rather hefty following on social media. Her new side hustle also earned her a small income, thanks to display advertising and affiliate marketing.

She loved her little romance community. She'd made so many friends over the last few years; this was the one place she could be herself in, talking about books to her heart's content, surrounded by other romance readers and book lovers.

Not that she didn't talk about her books to Emma. She did. A lot. But Emma had never gotten into romances the way Bel had and she knew her best friend was only humouring her when she let Bel rave on about one of her recent reads. Since starting her channel, though, Bel no longer felt like she'd burst if she didn't tell someone about the exciting books she'd found. She had an outlet.

She hit the record button and she was in another world— her favourite one.

Two

Bel pulled into her driveway. *Home.* The day had dragged on forever, and she was already picturing a long, hot soak in the tub, then a hot date in bed with her book. After devouring the latest Lexington Millionaires book, she always went back to the beginning of the series to reread her favourites; it helped dull the pain of realising she now had to wait over a year until the next release.

A text message sounded. 'Please make sure you read over your wedding-day timetable.' Followed immediately by upbeat, emoji-filled replies from some of Larkin's other bridesmaids.

Bel rolled her eyes as her phone pinged again, but this one was from Emma. 'See you soon!' *Shit. Bugger. Bum!* The dinner thing. She'd forgotten all about it.

The image of her bubble bath faded from her mind. She dragged herself inside, dumping her handbag on the hall table with a low curse. She hated socialising with a passion. She dealt with people all day, and the last thing she wanted to do after work was go out and be all chatty, even if it was with her best friend and her family. She just wanted to read her book. Was that too much to ask?

Emma and Craig's property, Fernvale, was only a half-hour drive, but it felt like an eternity tonight, when she would rather be at home. Still, she thought as she started the car up again, it was always a nice drive out their way, the wide-open paddocks stretching for miles either side of the narrow bitumen road before it turned to dirt for the last five or so kilometres of her journey to her friend's front gate.

Her faithful old Subaru rattled and shook her about as it crossed the cattle grid that led to the long driveway lined with Japanese maple trees, which would put on the most amazing show of red, orange and yellow leaves come autumn, and eventually led to a ramshackle brick and fibro farmhouse. It had started as a small cottage and grown to a sprawling monstrosity over the last five generations. Emma and Craig, along with their four children, had lived there since Craig's parents had retired to the coast three years ago.

Bel glanced at the dusty ute in the driveway as she pulled up and narrowed her eyes. Why was Dean Preston's vehicle here? Before she could think any further, the screen door opened and Emma came out, followed by her brood of children and a very excited Blue Heeler.

'Jack! Get down!' Emma yelled among the chaos of children running with a chorus of 'Aunt Bel's here,' and 'Come and see my bedroom,' from the older kids, and 'Pick me up!' from Lucy.

With her displeasure at discovering she had been set up effectively defused by strategically placed children, Bel had no option but to be carried inside by a wave of small bodies with smiling faces. It was nearly impossible to stay mad around them, but she sent her friend a look that promised they'd be talking later.

It was close to twenty minutes later by the time Bel had successfully inspected said bedrooms with new doona covers and been presented with an array of artwork done for her at preschool and been given a personal introduction to Ben's new stick insect pets, which she would be having nightmares about for the next week at least. By the time she came out, Emma and Craig were sitting out on the back deck with Dean, drinking beer.

'They let you escape?' Craig said, standing up to get her a drink.

'For now,' Bel said. Her gaze briefly went to Dean as she greeted him with a nod.

'Now we're all here, I'll put the barbie on,' Craig said as he handed Bel a glass of wine. The beauty of having been friends with the same people all your life is they know you so well. The downside to having been friends with the same people all your life is that, well . . . they know you so well . . .

'Before you get mad,' Emma said as soon as the two men headed for the opposite end of the deck to start cooking, 'Craig invited him without telling me. I couldn't very well uninvite him, could I?'

'You could have mentioned it to me,' Bel pointed out.

'And have you make up some convenient excuse not to come? I don't think so. Relax. Craig will keep him occupied and you won't have to say a word to each other.'

Half an hour and another wedding-related text later, this one saying 'Remember to drink lots of water, ladies! Keep that complexion fresh and those fine lines away!', Bel was seated at the long table on the verandah, happily surrounded by the kids. She let Emma and Craig carry the majority of the adult conversation.

'So, fill us in, Dean,' Emma said as she finished cutting a slice of meat into smaller pieces for her youngest. 'You've been gone a while.'

'About ten years or so.'

'Where have you been and what have you been doing since you left town? We don't get many people coming back once they've made the great escape.'

'I went away to ag college down south, then worked for a few years on some big properties in the Northern Territory and Central Queensland. Then some mine work for a bit.'

He shrugged. 'Then decided to come back to work the old man's place.'

'I was sorry to hear about your dad passing. That must have been a bit of a shock?' Emma asked.

'Yeah, it was. He was a stubborn old bastard, I guess it shouldn't have been a surprise that he'd ignored the doctors and kept pushing himself,' Dean said, declining the sauce bottle that was being passed around the table.

'Does that mean you're home for good, or are you planning on selling?' Emma asked.

'For good, I suppose. Dad and I never really got along—he was still pissed off that I left in the first place, so I wasn't expecting to come back any time soon. But now, I guess all the stuff I went away to learn will finally come in handy, even if he isn't here to see it. I've got some big plans to upgrade the systems we use and do things differently.'

Bel suspected he was underplaying the significance of his father's passing in favour of the typical, she'll-be-right bravado used by a lot of the men she knew. There was being strong and manly, and there was being emotionally stunted. A real man knew it was healthy to show emotion—like Jax, when his Marine Corp father figure/mentor was thrown from a helicopter by that bastard Jenner in book two. Jax had openly wept, showing a strength of character that had been far more powerful than simply burying his grief and taking it out on a rampage of murder and revenge . . . which, admittedly, he *had* done by the end of the book. But still. Bel felt her eyes threaten to water at the memory. Poor Jax.

'And you haven't been married?'

'Jesus, Em, we didn't invite him over to be interviewed. Give the poor bastard a break.'

'What? I'm only going to be asking *you* all this after he leaves anyway, and you'll just say, "I don't know, I didn't ask," so I'm cutting out the middleman.'

Bel bit back a grin. She couldn't fault Emma's logic.

Dean gave a surprised chuckle. 'It's okay, I haven't got anything too interesting to tell you about. Never married. Came close. She was a top sort, but she didn't want to live on a farm, so that ended that.'

Emma leaned forward slightly in her seat and Bel knew she was about to dig a little deeper into this new information, but just then a fight broke out between Ben and Ivy over the tomato sauce bottle, effectively derailing further questioning as Emma was forced to play referee.

'What about you, Bel?' Dean asked after a short pause. 'How come you're still here?'

Bel glanced up, surprised to be drawn into the conversation. 'Where else would I be?'

'I don't know, maybe *anywhere* else? There can't be that much to do out here.'

'Bel took care of her gran for a long time,' Emma cut in smoothly when Bel didn't immediately answer.

'I like it here,' Bel said, wondering why she felt so defensive all of a sudden.

'Not that there's anything wrong with working in a service station, but I always thought you wanted to do more,' Dean said.

Bel had a memory of her younger self declaring she couldn't wait to leave this place and *do something amazing.* Thinking back on it now, she had a funny feeling she'd actually said that to Dean one time, after he'd said something stupid to her in class. And here they were, years later, and *he'd* been the one who'd left town and had experiences and come back full of adventures, while she was . . . working at Dwyers'. 'Life doesn't always work out the way we planned,' Bel mumbled, lowering her eyes from his.

'So, Dean, have you picked a side?' Emma asked.

'Sorry?' he said, tearing his gaze from Bel.

'I assume you've heard about the current issue that's dividing the town? Which mascot we want for the town's statue. Have you voted?' Emma asked.

'Voted?' Dean echoed.

'On which mascot we're choosing.'

Dean looked across at Craig and shook his head. 'I don't know anything about it.'

'Are you serious? It's the *only* thing people are talking about,' Emma said.

'I don't really stay in town long when I come in.'

'Well, we need everyone's input, so next time you're in town, drop into the tourist information kiosk in the foyer of the pub and vote for which "big thing" you'd prefer.'

'Big thing?' he asked, kinking an eyebrow.

'Yeah. For the mascot. You know—big things that make towns famous. The Big Banana, the Big Pineapple,' Emma explained. 'We've been raising money to go along with a grant we received to build a statue of ours in town.'

'What are our choices?'

'It's been narrowed down to two. The Big Burger, after the famous line of hamburgers Bob Baxter serves at the truck stop on the road out of town.'

'Or the Big Cock,' Craig jumped in with a grin.

'The big what?' Dean asked, his eyes widening, which made Bel smirk slightly.

'*Rooster*,' Emma corrected her husband. 'Elvis Peckley. Clement Rhodes bred him back in the fifties. He's officially in the *Guinness Book of World Records* as the biggest rooster ever recorded. I think it's pretty amazing that little old Wessex has a world record.'

'Seriously?' Dean said, eyeing the others as though waiting for the joke.

'Yep. Still unbeaten,' Craig nodded.

'Must be some big rooster.'

'He's on display in the museum,' Emma informed him.

'They stuffed the poor bastard,' Craig said, shaking his head.

'How come I've never heard of this?' Dean asked, frowning.

'None of us had until about eighteen months ago, when Elvis was donated to the museum by the Rhodes family and the historical society did some research on it,' Emma said.

'I'm leaning towards the burger myself,' Craig informed his friend.

'As long as you'll be okay sleeping out in the shed if you do,' Emma said lightly, reaching across her husband for the salt shaker.

'Oh, come on. Tourists like burgers.'

'And just how are we supposed to promote said burgers, with names like the "Ring Burner" and the "Heart Attack"?'

'It's hilarious,' Craig chuckled. 'Trust me, the tourists will flock here to try one.'

'The tourists can discover Bob Baxter's burgers when they come out to see Elvis,' Emma said.

'I think you're missing out on a winning drawcard,' Craig said, tucking back into his meal.

'Elvis has been around a lot longer than Bob Baxter,' Emma said, closing the subject.

'I'll make sure I check it out next time I'm in town,' Dean promised.

After the meal, Emma went to put the younger kids to bed and Bel started packing the dishwasher. She didn't know how her friend did it, running a household with four kids under seven, as well as the farm work that needed doing when Craig was away working off property. Bel came out occasionally for a sleepover to keep her company and do what she could to help out, but Emma managed to run a tight ship. The kids all had their routines and she was one of the most organised people Bel knew—always cooking and prepping meals and school lunches. It was exhausting just watching her some days. But her friend seemed to thrive on it. For as long as Bel could remember, Emma had said she couldn't wait to be a mum. Bel on the other hand still had no clue what she wanted. Sometimes she felt like a colossal failure, twenty-nine years old and still living in the same town she'd grown up in.

It hadn't been the plan. She'd been ready to leave a few times over the years, and felt the urge to maybe go to university and do something different . . . marketing or promoting, maybe even get into advertising, writing or . . .

Well, there'd been endless possibilities, but then her gran's health had declined, and—despite Gran telling her she didn't want Bel staying for her sake—there was no way Bel was leaving her. Her uncle and aunt were never going to be any comfort. If they'd had to, they probably would have hired someone to sit with her or clean the house now and then, but Bel couldn't think of a more depressing or lonely life for Gran. So she had stayed and she hadn't regretted it, not ever.

By the time Gran had passed, Bel's burning ambition to go explore the world dimmed. If she were being completely honest with herself, she'd gotten to the point where the thought of leaving everything she was familiar with scared her.

It was stupid. Logically, she knew there was nothing to be afraid of, but there just wasn't anything she wanted to do badly enough to compel her to step outside her comfort zone. She didn't need much. She'd inherited Gran's little brick cottage, she had a job and a reliable car. She could afford to shop whenever she felt the need to splurge a little, but honestly, she really didn't *want* anything. Except books—they were her only real passion. She'd always been okay with things the way they were. At least, until lately.

It was when she'd look at Emma and Craig together that she'd sometimes get a pang of loneliness in the pit of her stomach. Sure, it would be nice to have someone of her own, to love her and look at her the way Craig looked at Emma, but she wasn't going to find that here in Wessex—and leaving what she had here for the off-chance she might find that out there, somewhere? That was a big risk, and she was no longer the starry-eyed teenager who thought heading out into the big wide world was some exciting adventure. Did she really want to look for a new job? Meet new friends? After all, she already had friends here, and what if she discovered that it wasn't really any more exciting *out there* than it was here?

It wasn't that she hadn't started opening her mind to new possibilities either, she had. Over the last few years, the desire to leave to find adventure had been pushed to one side, but the desire to find that special someone to share her life with had become stronger with each romance novel she read. She wanted to feel *that* excitement—that heady love-at-first-sight thing.

That's where the soulmate list came into it. She'd taken what she'd learned from *Mindfulness and Manifesting a New You* to heart—the whole attracting-what-you-put-out thing made sense to her. Gran had been a big believer in it, even if she hadn't read a single book about manifesting. She'd always said, 'If you smile, people will smile back at you, but if you walk into a room with a sour look on your face . . . well, everyone's going to avoid you, aren't they?' It was pretty much the same principle—you attract the vibration you send out. So Bel had written her list and sent it out to the universe to bring her a soulmate. So far, the universe was working slowly, but that suited the part of her that was a little bit afraid that meeting her soulmate would mean leaving Wessex. But if that was what the universe had in store for her, then she supposed it would give her an opportunity or sign. Bel just hoped that when that day came, she'd be ready.

She glanced up from placing a dinner plate in the dishwasher to find Dean carrying in more dirty cups and cutlery.

'Thanks. Put them down anywhere,' Bel said, gesturing towards the countertop.

'I've been meaning to say hello and catch up properly when I've been in the shop, but you've always been busy.'

Bel looked up at him again, wondering why he was so fidgety. 'Yeah, it gets a bit hectic sometimes.'

'I didn't want you thinking that I was being unfriendly or . . . anything,' he said, handing her a glass tumbler.

'It's okay,' Bel said. 'We weren't close or anything at school.'

'I guess not. That's probably my fault. I was talking to Craig earlier, and we were reminiscing about the old days . . . we were little shits back then, to be honest,' he said, sending her an off-centre kind of grin.

For a moment his smile caught her off guard. 'You *were*,' Bel agreed, ignoring the strange moment. 'You used to make fun of me reading at lunchtime and play keep-away with my books whenever you got the chance. Then there was the frog-in-my-lunch-box incident.'

He chuckled. 'That was kinda funny . . . your face when you opened the box and it was sitting there, looking up at you. But it wasn't just me,' he protested.

She gave an involuntary shudder at the memory. Still to this day, she hated frogs. 'No, I suppose not.' Now that she thought about it, she did recall that Craig and a few of the other boys they'd hung around with back then had been equally annoying. Funny that she'd mostly only remembered Dean.

'I was surprised to see you still in town, though.'

'I don't know why. There's a fair proportion of other kids you went through school with who never left town.'

'Yeah, but they're mostly guys who stayed on the family property, or a few girls who married local blokes, like Emma. I guess I figured there was something about you even back then.' He hesitated before hurriedly continuing, 'You always had this faraway look in your eyes, like you could see some kind of big future. Or maybe,' he continued with a hint of a smile, 'it was because you'd get all high and mighty and stare down your nose at me when you got angry. I remember you telling me that I should try reading a book so I'd know there was more to the world than stupid sheep and tractors.'

Bel felt a twinge of shame. She did recall saying something like that to him, which was rather condescending of her, even if he probably *had* deserved it at the time.

'I always thought you'd head off into the big city and do something exciting with your life.'

Bel stared at him, irritated afresh. 'As opposed to staying here and doing absolutely nothing with my life?'

'I didn't mean it like that,' he started.

'Just because I chose to stay and take care of my gran instead of going away to university or ag college or whatever doesn't mean I've wasted my life.'

'No, of course—'

'You've barely been back five minutes and you think you have the right to look down your nose at me? You don't know anything about me.'

'I didn't mean to—'

'What? Tell me how pathetic my life is?'

'That's not what I—'

Bel shut the dishwasher door and dried her hands on a tea towel, which she then tossed onto the now clean bench. 'I really don't care. Goodnight,' she snapped, walking down the hall. She waved at Emma as she passed the doorway of the bedroom where her friend was in the process of detangling herself from a sleeping child. It was perfectly timed, because she knew Emma would have tried to talk her out of leaving. 'I'll call you tomorrow,' she whispered from the door.

The moon hung low, casting a silvery glow upon the choppy waters as Jax and Angelica, their faces etched with determination, sped across the darkened expanse of water in a sleek speedboat. Behind them, the menacing silhouette of the drug cartel's vessel loomed, its engines roaring as they gave chase through the labyrinthine waterways.

With every pulse of the engine, the tension in the air mounted. Adrenaline coursed through Jax's veins as he pushed the speedboat to its limits. The wind whipped through their hair, their eyes fixed on the distant horizon, their every sense on high alert for signs of danger.

As they raced along the narrow channels and hidden inlets, the cartel's pursuit grew ever more relentless, coming closer with each passing moment. But Jax was undeterred, his steely gaze locked on the path ahead as he navigated the treacherous waters with unwavering skill.

The cartel's vessel drew near, its searchlights piercing the darkness as they closed in. Jax, using every ounce of strength and cunning he possessed, pushed the speedboat to the brink.

As they raced into the open sea, the cartel's vessel fell behind, its engines no match for the speed of Jax's boat. With a surge of triumph, they disappeared into the darkness, their mission far from over, but their spirits unbroken.

As she read, Bel ignored her phone ringing. She wasn't in the mood to talk. All she wanted was to stay curled up and lost in this alternate universe where she could be swept up in romance and a little bit of danger, all the while knowing that she'd be fine by the end of the book and get her happily-ever-after. Why couldn't real life be like that?

Three

To say nothing really happened in Wessex would normally be to speak the truth. However, something pretty big had been brewing for the last twelve months, and it was due to hit town in exactly one week: the wedding of the century.

It might not be a celebrity or royal wedding, but did involve Wessex royalty—Bel's cousin, Larkin. In most families, being the cousin of royalty would make you royalty too, but not in this case. Due to her failure to make something of herself, Bel was the embarrassing black sheep who her aunt and uncle didn't talk about. So when Larkin had asked her to be a bridesmaid, it had not sat well with Aunt Lois which, of course, was the only silver lining in Bel accepting.

Lois was the only daughter of the district's wealthiest grazier family, the Ramseys, pioneers in the region with ties back to the original settling families.

Bel's family, the Buckleys, were from a more modest mixed-crop farming background; their land was primarily run by her grandparents and their two sons: her father, Robert, and her uncle, Stanley. That is, until her father had met her mother and decided to move to South Australia. Meanwhile, Uncle Stan had set his sights on the local heiress, Lois Ramsey, along with pretty much every other eligible bachelor in the state. When her wealthy father suddenly took ill and passed away, leaving the enormous estate to his only child, the competition grew fiercer.

Sadly for Bel's family, when Stanley threw everything at his pursuit of his future bride, it was literally *everything*. Behind his parents' backs, he ran up enormous debts, using the family property as collateral, and almost sent them into bankruptcy. Luckily, Stan's gamble paid off and he won the hand of the fair Lois and they were promptly married. Stan managed to pay back his parents and save the family farm, but it was too late. His triumph had come at a cost to his elderly parents' health, and they eventually sold the farm and moved into town for a quieter life. Of course, all that had been covered up. The only reason Bel knew about it was because when she'd been nursing Gran, who had suffered dementia, she'd started talking about it when she mistook Bel for Vera, Gran's younger sister.

Gran had been Bel's world, having taken her in after Bel's parents had died in a car accident when she'd been ten years old. It had been a horrible time in her young life—losing her parents and being torn away from friends and everything she loved to move to another state, surrounded by people she didn't know. Her grandparents had been a refuge from the harsh new world.

Her uncle and aunt had offered to pay for her to go away to the boarding school Larkin attended, but thankfully Gran had stepped in and decided she needed nurturing and a home more than an elite school. So instead she'd gone to Wessex Primary School, which was where she'd met Emma. The two had instantly bonded and been pretty near inseparable ever since.

Larkin had to be the most spoiled person she'd ever met, but despite having had everything she'd ever wanted handed to her on a silver platter, Bel had always thought her cousin must have been the loneliest kid in the world. Her parents had hounded her day and night about her appearance and grades and behaviour. It had been relentless, and Bel had often felt sorry for her. She'd never once seen her aunt cuddle Larkin, and, if it wasn't for Gran, she doubted her cousin would have known what affection was.

Bel and Larkin were chalk and cheese, with nothing in common other than a surname and a handful of DNA, yet, for all their differences, they had grown up to be surprisingly close.

Larkin was tall and willowy, as graceful as a feline, with long, silky blonde hair and big blue eyes. She was always impeccably made-up and spent a fortune on creating her flawless beauty, looking like she'd stepped out of the pages of a fashion magazine on any given day.

Bel, on the other hand, usually looked like she'd stepped out of a month-long hibernation, complete with bed hair. Long, plain and mud-brown, her locks had an annoying kink that meant they were neither curly nor straight, and she couldn't quite remember the last time she'd been to a proper hairdresser. She usually trimmed her fringe herself whenever it got in her eyes, much to her cousin's dismay. She'd missed out on her cousin's baby blue eyes too, instead ending up with brown ones, and not even a pretty chocolate brown or coffee brown, but a weird, light orange-brown. She'd worn glasses since she was eight and hated them, but had never bothered trying contacts despite Larkin's encouraging her to since high school. She wasn't sure why she'd always resisted Larkin's attempts to 'fix' her appearance. Maybe because she didn't want to be compared to her beautiful cousin. There was no way she could ever compete. Bel preferred to stay out of the spotlight and do her own thing, and she'd been allowed to do that, until she was pushed into this whole bridesmaid debacle.

'You can't be serious,' Bel had said when Larkin had rung her twelve months earlier to tell her she was going to be in the wedding party.

'Of course I'm serious.'

'But . . . why? You've got plenty of people you can ask.' *Beautiful, stylish, A-list friends.*

'You're my cousin, Bel. Please? I love my friends to death, but none of them know me like you do. I need you there with me on the day.'

Her cousin's words had caught her off guard and Bel had felt her resolve weaken. 'What does your mother say about it?'

'This is *my* wedding,' Larkin said firmly.

So . . . Aunt Lois does not approve.

It was going to be the biggest wedding the district had seen in years. Aunt Lois would be out to impress the city guests after her daughter had managed to snag the most eligible bachelor of Sydney's social set. There was a lot at stake here, and already Lois's headstrong daughter had messed up all her well-laid plans by insisting the wedding be held at the estate.

A grand, somewhat imposing homestead with a rich cultural heritage, Glentoberon was nothing to sneeze at, but it had been beginning to show signs of its age after a few decades of mismanagement paired with a handful of natural disasters and the odd bad season. As a result, Larkin's parents had spent a not-so-small fortune giving the entire place a facelift.

Now, suddenly, the wedding was here, and Bel had to work out how she was going to get through the whole ordeal. She could not wait for it to be over so life could go back to normal.

With a quick glance at the general store's clock, Bel pulled out her book and decided she could fit in one more chapter before the afternoon school pick-up rush descended. What she needed in order to forget about all the upcoming stress was some Jax Lexington. Book three, set in Las Vegas, was always a favourite.

In the heart of Las Vegas, where the neon lights dance across the night sky and the air thrums with excitement, Jax strides, his piercing blue eyes gleaming beneath the glitz of the Strip.

With each confident step, Jax commands attention, his chiselled jawline cutting a striking figure against the backdrop of the bustling casinos and dazzling marquees.

Though the city pulses with energy, Jax moves with a calm assurance, his every movement calculated and precise. He is a man of action, unafraid to take risks in pursuit of justice and honour.

As he navigates the casino layout, the unrelenting poker machine tunes trilling in the background, Jax's mind—always one step ahead, his keen intellect and street-smart instincts honed by years of clandestine operations—remains on alert. A woman dressed in a red, slinky silk evening gown smiles seductively at him. Despite the dangers that lurk in the shadows, there is always room for a little excitement.

In a city where fortunes are won and lost on the roll of a dice, Jax remains a steadfast beacon of strength and resolve—a hero for whom no challenge is too great, and no danger too daunting.

As the lights of Las Vegas twinkle in the background, there's no doubt that his next adventure is just beginning.

The tinkle of bells sounded and Bel inwardly groaned, reading faster to squeeze in the last paragraph before she had to serve whoever had the audacity to interrupt her and Jax. But when she finally looked up everything around her ceased to exist. It felt as though the air had been sucked out of the room. All she could do was stare at this magnificent specimen of manhood.

'Jax,' she breathed, gaping. She had to be hallucinating. She shook her head and blinked, but when she opened her eyes, he was still standing there. Staring at her . . . like she had grown a second head.

'Are you all right?' he asked, his deep voice running over her like aged whiskey. 'Should I call an ambulance or something?'

The jarring sound of a needle being dragged across an old record album rudely interrupted her daydreaming as she realised he was staring at her mouth not with longing but a look of grave concern.

She lifted her hand to tentatively brush it across her lips. *Oh God! Is that . . . drool?*

Bel straightened abruptly, knocking her cup of coffee, which flew across the counter and splattered across the front of his crisp white shirt. 'Oh God!' She grabbed a fistful of tissues, raced around the counter and began to wipe furiously at the brown stain spreading across the expensive fabric that covered a firm, flat torso.

He grabbed her wrist to still her frantic rubbing. Her skin burned beneath his touch. 'It's fine. Thank you.'

'I'm so sorry.' She stared at him, utterly mortified and mesmerised. Jax Lexington was standing in front of her, in real life.

Then it hit her like a bolt of lightning. The list. She'd manifested him. *Holy crap! It worked!* 'I can't believe you're here,' she said, swallowing hard.

'I, uh . . . Do I know you?' he asked, looking up from his shirt, which he'd taken over trying to dab clean.

'I'm Bel,' she said, thrusting out her hand and making him flinch.

'Tate,' he said, reaching forward to give her hand a brief shake.

'Tate?'

'Yes. Look, I was just after some directions,' he said hesitantly.

'Oh. Okay,' Bel said, belatedly noticing her hand had oil or something on it from when she'd been cleaning up around the bowsers earlier. She rubbed it as inconspicuously as she could on the thigh of her baggy jeans and gesticulated awkwardly towards the road with her other hand to distract him. 'Where were you headed?'

'Glentoberon. Apparently it's a property around here somewhere? I think I missed the turn.'

Bel's eyes widened. 'You know the Buckleys?'

'I'm here for a wedding.'

'Larkin's wedding?' she asked, as her heart rate picked up.

'Yes,' he answered cautiously. 'I'm Tristan's best man.'

'Get out of *town*!' Bel said, pushing his chest, then immediately staring in horror as he stumbled slightly and knocked into a stand of sunglasses, sending a number clattering to the floor. He quickly righted the stand and cleared his throat.

'I'm so sorry,' Bel said, horrified. 'No, please, don't worry about that,' she added as he moved to pick up the glasses on the floor.

'Uh, so, directions to . . . ?' he started uncertainly.

'Oh. Yes. Of course. Head down the main street and then turn right at the intersection. Follow that road for about fifteen kilometres and you'll see the big gates with Glentoberon written on them. You can't miss it.' The enormous new gates had been installed a few months earlier. The only thing it needed now was uniformed guards standing out the front.

'Right. Okay. Thanks. Uh, is there anywhere around here I can grab a quick bite to eat?'

'There's a cafe across the road. If you're quick, you might catch them before they close.'

'It's not even two o'clock,' he said, glancing over his shoulder to search for the cafe.

'They close up at two.' Much to every out-of-towner's disbelief, and something Bel hoped would be addressed at the next progress committee meeting in preparation for the tourist boom they were hoping the much-debated statue would usher in.

'Right. Thanks.' He nodded, turned and walked out of the store, leaving Bel to stare after him as she released a long, unsteady breath. *Holy. Crap.* She'd gone and conjured up her dream guy.

Grabbing the phone, she called Emma, tapping her fingers on the countertop as she waited for her to answer.

'Hey.'

'Are you in the car?'

'Yes, I'm on my way in to pick up the kids from school.'

'You need to get over to the store.'

'Why? What's wrong? Are you okay?'

'Jax Lexington just appeared in town! I swear to God, he was just here.'

'Who?'

'The guy from the book.'

The line went quiet for a moment then Emma started speaking slowly. 'Bel . . . have you been drinking?'

'What? No! Oh, for goodness' sake. I'm telling you, this guy walked into the store a minute ago and he is the spitting image of Jax Lexington. Get over here. Pronto.'

No more than five minutes later, Emma's car pulled up outside.

'He's *here*,' Bel said, putting her fists to her mouth in an attempt to contain her excitement.

'I still have no idea what you're talking about. Who's here?'

Bel whipped out the book from under the desk and slammed it on the counter. 'Him. Look!' she said, pointing past her friend to the cafe across the road, where the man in question sat sipping from a mug. 'It's Jax Lexington. He's right here in Wessex!'

'*That's* him?' Emma asked, her dubious expression echoing in her equally doubtful tone.

'Look,' Bel said, holding the cover closer to Emma's face and tapping the image urgently. 'It's *him*.'

'It's not him.'

'Well, obviously it's not *him*,' Bel said impatiently, 'but it's who he would be, if he were a real-life person.'

Emma stared at her silently for a few moments. 'I am officially worried about you,' she said with a shake of her head.

'He has the same rugged good looks and chiselled jawline that makes women's nether regions quiver,' Bel said.

'Nether regions?' Emma repeated.

'He's easily six foot and has blue eyes,' Bel continued, ignoring her friend's cynicism.

'And you're saying that this fictional creature has magically appeared right here in Wessex?'

'Kind of. I brought him here,' Bel announced matter-of-factly.

'Of course you did.'

'I manifested him.'

'Bel, I love you like a sister, and you know that I would literally die . . .' Emma paused briefly. 'Well, not die, but take a minor . . . somewhat painful . . . but ultimately superficial injury for you, right? But I'm beginning to think that you need to be committed for your own safety. You can't "manifest" a person, fictional or otherwise.'

Bel rolled her eyes. 'I've been practising this manifesting stuff—you know, putting out good vibes, law of attraction and all that,' she said. 'I made a soulmate list and wrote down everything I wanted in my perfect man.' She stopped, and lifted her gaze back to the man across the road. 'And there he is.'

'Riiiiight.'

And this was exactly why she'd never told her best friend about the soulmate list. She knew Emma would make fun of it. 'I don't care if you don't believe me.'

'Okay, whatever,' Emma said, throwing her hands up. 'It doesn't matter how he got here . . . I'm excited for you. Now, go over and talk to him.'

'What? No!'

'What do you mean? You just said he's your dream guy.'

'I can't talk to him,' Bel said.

'But you manifested him, remember?'

'Yes, but . . . I didn't really think past that bit. I'm not sure what to do with him now that he's here.'

'Well, for starters, you could go talk to him,' Emma said.

'I can't. I tried, and I made a complete fool of myself.' She reluctantly gave a summary of the earlier encounter and felt the mortification return.

'Oh, dear,' Emma sympathised. 'Okay, well that was . . . *unfortunate*,' she said, seeming to select her words carefully.

'But you can't give up. I mean, how often does a guy like that, or *any guy*, to be completely honest, turn up in Wessex? It may never happen again in our lifetime. Like Halley's Comet or something.'

That was a fair point, but it didn't change the fact that she was a walking disaster and he was . . . perfect.

'Come to think of it, what *is* a guy like that doing in town?'

'He's here for the wedding. He's Tristan's best man.'

Emma's eyes lit up and a smile replaced her frown. 'That's *perfect*. He'll be here all week. That's plenty of time.'

'For what?'

'For Operation Soulmate.'

'Operation what?'

'Look, you can believe in your manifesting thing, but I'm suggesting something a little more practical. You've got a guy stuck out here for a wedding—he's literally a captive audience. All you need to do is catch his attention.'

'Captive' sounds a little desperate, but then again, who am I to get nitpicky over details?

'You're going to win that man over by the night of the wedding,' Emma said firmly.

'I am?' Bel felt a tiny spark of hope reigniting at her friend's confident words.

'You are. You manifested him,' Emma said, turning back to face Bel and clasping her upper arms decisively. 'You can do this.'

'I *can*.'

'You *will* do this,' Emma continued.

'I will!' Bel repeated, feeling like a State of Origin player about to head out after half-time.

'Thatta girl.' Emma grinned. 'Now, go wipe off that streak of grease, or whatever the hell it is that you've had on your face since I got here, and let's make a plan!'

'What!' Bel ran out the back and stared in horror at the smudge across her cheek. What hope did she seriously have with a guy like that? No wonder he'd fled.

She took off her glasses and scooped a handful of water from beneath the tap, letting the cool water soothe her flushed cheeks. When she looked back in the small mirror above the sink, she blinked at the blurry woman staring back. If she wanted a man like that, she was going to need to make some pretty big changes.

Four

The next day, Bel was restocking the grocery shelves for the final time before her leave for the wedding. She'd taken a week off and her boss, Doreen, had been grumbling ever since she'd put in her request a whole two months earlier.

As far as bosses went, the Dwyers were okay. They'd owned the service station and general store for years and were now both in their early sixties. They'd made Bel the manager six years earlier and were pretty much retired, heading off on long trips in their motorhome and taking up hobbies they'd never had the time to do before. It was a good arrangement and Bel was a great employee, rarely taking time off, so asking for a week leading up to the wedding shouldn't have been a big deal. Only Doreen wasn't the warm fuzzy kind, and she had been getting used to her retirement. She wasn't overly thrilled to be called in to work.

When Doreen had asked, 'Do you really need to take this time off?', it had taken a lot of nerve, and the thought of dealing with a disappointed Larkin, for Bel to hold her ground.

The door opened and the relative peace and quiet of the little store was broken as the bride herself blew in like a category four cyclone.

'It's a disaster! The wedding's ruined!' Larkin announced, her big blue eyes filling with tears. She walked past Bel to the freezer section and pulled out a one-litre tub of cookie dough ice cream.

Bel bit back a sigh as she removed the container from Larkin's hands, replacing it with a small bag of pistachios from the nearby healthy snack rack.

'Your dress,' Bel reminded her with a wry grimace. Ice cream would also be her own go-to remedy in a crisis, however only last week it had taken Bel the entire drive home from a dress fitting to talk a sobbing Larkin down after the zipper on her wedding dress hadn't been able to do all the way up. Bel had been under strict instructions not to allow anything fattening to pass her cousin's lips until after the wedding day.

'I won't even need a wedding dress if we can't find napkins!' Larkin said, raising her voice as she ripped open the small packet of nuts.

It had been twelve months of crises, each with the potential to *ruin* the big day, and Bel had become an expert at defusing these situations. Bel now chose her words with all the skill and caution of a seasoned bomb technician.

'What's happened to the napkins we already chose?' After walking around three Sydney suburbs and looking at hundreds of white napkins until they found the *right* white . . .

'There aren't enough and they don't have any more. We'll never match them exactly! It's a disaster,' Larkin said, shoving more nuts into her mouth as fresh tears began to flow. Only her cousin could cry and still look beautiful, Bel thought absently as she struggled to find enough patience to deal with this crap at the end of a long day.

'Can we maybe go with a different white?'

'It's not *white,* it's *salt.* And it was expertly matched by my interior décor expert. Now nothing matches!'

How hard can it be to match freaking white napkins? 'Can you maybe ask your interior décor person to find another shade we can use?'

'It's too late! The entire colour scheme will have to be changed!'

'That sounds a bit extreme—' Bel stopped as her cousin glared. She quickly searched for something constructive to say but was saved by the door. This time, when Bel glanced up, she knew she wouldn't be uttering another sensible word as her tongue seemed to swell inside her mouth and her brain scrambled.

He had returned.

'Larkin? Is everything okay? What's happened?'

'Oh, Tate! No! Nothing's okay. Everything's a mess,' Larkin simpered as she reached out to put her hand on his arm and tell him about the great napkin debacle.

Bel simply stood there and soaked him in. He was so close that she could smell whatever divine manly scent he was wearing, bringing to her mind a big, tough lumberjack cutting down enormous trees in a Canadian forest. Bel's eyes were glued to his face—that finely chiselled, Greek god-like face that was focused intently on Larkin. *A man who listened.*

When Larkin finished, Tate smiled and Bel swooned so heavily that she thought one of her ovaries actually exploded.

'Everything is going to be fine,' he said gently. 'Leave it with me. I know a guy. He's a professional event organiser. He owes me a favour.'

'Oh, Tate. Really?' Larkin gasped, looking up at him in complete awe.

'Absolutely. I'll go call him right now.'

'You're a lifesaver.'

Bel caught her breath at his impossibly ocean-like blue eyes, which crinkled slightly at the corners.

Glancing across to her cousin—who was now smiling brightly at Tate as he turned and walked away to make his call, all traces of her earlier tears gone—Bel's giddy excitement came crashing down. What was she thinking? That next to her gorgeous, bouncy, blonde-haired, blue-eyed cousin someone like Tate would honestly give her, with her big glasses and muddy brown hair, a second look? She would never have Larkin's charisma—or the confidence that came with belonging to that class of society Tate so obviously belonged to.

Emma was wrong. There was no way someone like her was going to ever get a guy like him. She'd have to stick to reading about romance in her books. Which suited her fine. Inside books, she could be whoever she wanted to be. When she read a book, she wasn't plain old Mabel Buckley. She was a runaway bride, or a billionaire's personal secretary who steals his hardened heart to become the love of his life, or a nanny to some rich oil sheikh's children in a far-off exotic foreign land, who he falls madly in love with.

She'd stick to books. The ordinary, quiet girls always triumphed in books.

'Attention, please,' Betty Miller raised her voice from the head of the long table and gave a sharp clap of her hands, waiting for the conversations around her to stop.

'Did she just clap her hands at us like a bunch of kindergarten kids?' Emma murmured to Bel from where they sat further down the table.

Betty was the president of the progress committee, as well as a number of other groups in town, and was one of those amazing people who thrived on overcommitting themselves.

Although, in all fairness, without people like Betty driving them, most of the organisations would have probably folded.

'This is the last meeting before the market and movie night, so I'm going over the list and confirming with everyone that they have their schedules and know the times they'll be needed to man the committee's fundraising stall. Just a reminder that all baked items and goods for sale need to be dropped off before the day and we will need people to help with pricing and packaging,' she said, staring pointedly over the top of the reading glasses perched on the end of her nose.

Bel had known Betty for most of her life—her gran had been on some of the same committees over the years—and the woman didn't seem to age. She also didn't seem to get any less intimidating. Bel always felt the urge to squirm in her seat whenever the woman stared at her. Even now, as she listened to Betty speaking, she felt the same way she had when she was ten and Betty had turned up at Gran's house in a tizzy because Bel and Emma had picked Betty's prize roses to make their own range of perfume with the perfume factory kit Emma had gotten for Christmas.

The meeting had dragged on for another forty-five minutes when a disagreement broke out over who was the original tenant in the old cordial factory, which had nothing whatsoever to do with finalising the event.

Bel swallowed her frustration. She just wanted to go home.

Finally, the meeting drew to a close and Emma and Bel wasted no time on their farewells.

'Dear Lord, I thought that would never end,' Emma said as they stepped out into the cooler night air.

'I know. Thank goodness that was the last meeting for a while.'

'So?' Emma said as they walked towards their cars.

'So . . . what?'

'How goes the great soulmate quest?'

'It doesn't. I blew it. I ruined my chance at a great first impression and now he doesn't even notice me.' She recalled how he hadn't even seemed to be aware there'd been anyone else in the room because Larkin had outshone everything else around her as usual.

'Look, I know you believe in all this manifestation stuff, but maybe this wasn't a sign? Maybe he isn't the one?'

'He's exactly what I put on my list,' Bel said, shaking her head.

'But is he? You don't really know him well enough to say that for sure though, do you?' Emma replied.

'I wanted my own real-life Jax Lexington,' Bel said stubbornly. 'The universe sent him but I missed my opportunity.'

'Well, if it *is* meant to be, don't you think you're giving up a little too easily? I mean, nothing worthwhile is supposed to get handed to you, right? Maybe this is the universe testing you?'

Bel frowned a little as she considered her friend's words.

'All I'm saying is don't give up if this is what you really believe in. Men don't just drop out of the sky around here.'

Bel grinned. 'Wow. Careful, you sound like you almost believe in it too.'

Emma shrugged, clicking her key remote. 'Who am I to say manifesation isn't real? People believe in much stranger things than this. I just want you to be happy,' she said, leaning in to hug Bel lightly.

Bel watched as her friend climbed into her car. Maybe she *had* given up too easily. After all, had Edward given up on Bella in *Twilight*? Jamie would never give up on Claire in *Outlander*, and Romeo and Juliet . . . well, that probably wasn't a great example, but still. Maybe she shouldn't throw in the towel just yet.

As she sat on her bed later that night, Bel took her soulmate list from inside the book and smoothed it out. She closed her eyes and repeated the words on the paper until she felt the same sense of peace and determination that she'd felt all those months earlier when she'd first written them.

Letting out a long breath, Bel put the list away and slid down in between her freshly washed sheets, enjoying the feel of crisp linen and the delicate smell of sunshine she imagined still lingered on them. Drifting off to sleep, she dreamed of Jax Lexington smiling at her across a Black Jack table . . . or was it Tate? She wasn't sure and, to be honest, she didn't really care. All she wanted was to be swept away into a life far more exciting than the one she was currently in.

'Morning, Bel,' Larrisa greeted her as she walked into the cafe.

Larrisa was a few years younger than Bel and a single mum to two young boys. She'd been working in the bakery ever since she'd left high school and had recently bought out her old boss to become the owner. 'Morning,' said Bel. 'How's things?'

'Not too bad, had a little extra traffic. I'm hoping Larkin's wedding will bring in a heap of out-of-towners over the next few days.'

'It should.' Bel smiled. 'The guest list is a mile long.'

'How's it all going?'

'About as crazy as you'd imagine.'

As Bel waited for her coffee, she checked the bridal group chat. 'Have you checked in on your bride today? Remember your duty as a bridesmaid is to reassure her!'

She closed the app again immediately and glanced up to see Dean walk inside. She hadn't seen him since the other night at Emma and Craig's. She bit back an irritated huff and braced herself.

'Hi,' he said, eyeing her warily. A part of her was happy that he seemed unsure of his reception after their last conversation.

'Hello.'

'I ... uh,' he started, shifting his weight slightly. 'About the other night.'

Bel raised her eyebrows slightly.

'What I said came out wrong. I wasn't having a go at you. I was ... I don't know ...'

'Was astonished that someone could still be living here all this time?' she asked.

'No,' he said, shaking his head. 'Surprised, yeah, but . . . if you want to know the truth, pleasantly surprised.'

Huh?

'Pleasantly?' she repeated, as she eyed him uncertainly.

He shrugged and shoved his hands in the pockets of his faded fleece-lined jacket. 'I wasn't expecting anyone I knew to still be out here. Figured it'd be kinda lonely. Plus, most of the people around here are married and have a tribe of kids.'

His shy reply took away some of her earlier irritation. 'Yeah. Me too. But it's not so bad. There may not be a lot of nightlife, but we've got a pretty decent progress committee. And the local hall is always hosting get-togethers and events,' she told him. 'You just have to get involved.'

'I saw a few flyers up around the place for the movie night and markets. Are you going?'

'Yeah. I'm kind of obligated since I'm on the committee. But it should be fun.'

'Sounds good.'

Bel was starting to concede that Dean might no longer be much like the fourteen-year-old jerk who'd stolen her bra and hung it from the flagpole in high school. 'Well, I better keep going, I suppose. I'll have to face Larkin's wrath if I'm late for my dress fitting.'

'Ah, the Wedding of the Year.' Dean nodded sagely. 'Is it true they're bringing in that celebrity chef from the TV to cater it?'

'Is that the rumour going around this week?'

'Heard it down at the pub.'

'Interesting. No, I don't believe so. There *is* a reality TV star invited, but I have no idea which show they're from.'

'Sounds like a major production.'

'It's going to be something, all right.'

Larrisa called to Bel and handed over her flat white.

'Well, good luck,' he said.

'Thanks. See you around.' Bel waved and headed out, taking a fortifying breath as she walked back to her car.

She dreaded these stupid fittings. She had no idea why there had to be so many, but thankfully, this was the final one. There was added stress today—the possibility of running into Tate had been sending her into alternating fits of anxiety and excitement. She couldn't wait to see him again, yet every time she thought about it, a wave of nausea instantly followed. She was a complete mess.

She tried to distract herself during the drive by turning up the playlist of love ballads and drowning out all rational thought, which did help somewhat until she arrived at the imposing gates and could no longer put off the inevitable.

Pulling her car to a stop, she took out her phone and began to record. 'Well, here we are at Glentoberon,' she said, zooming in on the gates. 'It's the final bridesmaid fitting before the big event. I imagine tensions will be running high inside. Wish me luck.'

Her followers had gone nuts over the wedding updates she'd been posting lately. It was amazing how many likes the content she posted on her hometown and daily life often garnered. People were clearly interested in how country folk lived.

'Finally!' Bel's aunt called out in lieu of a proper greeting, taking her arm and leading her towards the drawing room, where a group of women were already gathered. 'You're next. Quickly, now.'

Yes, so nice to see you too, Aunt Lois.

'Right. Undress,' Gisele said as Bel entered, clapping her hands briskly. Apparently wedding planners extraordinaire even oversaw the final dress fitting before the wedding.

'Here?' Bel asked, looking around for a private corner.

'Yes, yes. Don't be shy, it's only us girls here,' the snippety wedding planner added.

Across the room, Kelly, another bridesmaid, was stepping out of her dress with the help of the seamstress, Leslie, the same woman Bel had met at the last dress fitting in Sydney. Bel noticed Kelly's pretty matching bra and underwear set in cream lace and felt her cheeks getting warm. After the first dress fitting, when she'd realised she would be semi-naked as she stepped in and out of her dress, Bel had purchased a few new sets, but they were just the department store ones, not the designer lingerie kind the other girls favoured. And when she'd gotten dressed earlier, the only matching set she'd had left in the drawers were her hot pink ones, probably not the ideal selection for a dress fitting.

The drawing room was a massive area that could easily fit a hundred people or more, as it had often done for the various charity events her aunt and uncle had hosted over the years. Light streamed in from the huge windows overlooking the front driveway and gardens, which was obviously why they were using the room. It felt incredibly . . . open. Anyone could look in through the windows or walk in.

Bel was feeling more than a little uncomfortable at this thought as she hesitantly unzipped her jeans and dropped them to the ground.

'It's okay, Bel,' Larkin said, coming up behind her. 'All the men have gone to play golf—a bonding session of sorts.' Bel glanced across at Lisa, the other bridesmaid who was there, lounging comfortably in a light robe which barely covered her undergarments. She and Kelly, the matching blondes, laughed and drank champagne without a hint of self-consciousness.

'That pink is great on you,' Larkin added, holding out a wheat-coloured robe for her.

Taking off her top, Bel accepted the wrap and quickly slipped into it as she was bundled over to the impatiently waiting Leslie.

The dressmaker was an odd-looking woman, tall and thin and always dressed impeccably in a pencil skirt and button-up blouse. The style had been the same each time Bel had seen her, but the colour changed. Today, she wore navy blue. Her dark eyes were almost black, but it was hard to tell their exact shade as she was always squinting or sizing something up. Bel had to concentrate to not keep staring at Leslie's beak-like nose, which was incredibly hard since the more she tried to ignore it, the more she found herself focused on it.

Today, Leslie's emotions seemed to be running high. Never exactly warm or welcoming, the bird-like woman was even more abrupt than usual. Bel wasn't one to be easily offended and put it down to being under enormous pressure to have all the dresses, including Larkin's, perfect for the big day. There was a lot riding on this wedding. For Leslie, her reputation—and the business that would come her way from the social elites if everyone was gobsmacked by her designs—was on the line.

Bel kept her mouth shut as she was turned this way and that, and did what she was told. She was greatly relieved when the zipper at the side did up without resistance and hoped Larkin appreciated the month-long ice cream ban she'd imposed on herself.

'You may take it off now,' Leslie snapped. Bel had been trying to figure out the woman's slight accent for months. Sometimes, when she listened extra hard, it didn't sound like there was one at all, and other times there was the faintest hint of something . . . Russian maybe? She wasn't sure and, judging from the woman's tightly pursed lips, today was probably not the day to ask.

Her aunt stopped to ask Leslie something and Bel carefully undid the zip and began to pull her arms out of the sleeves to step out, the same way she'd stepped into it earlier. Only Leslie had made a few alterations and now it was too tight to free herself. She reached down and gathered up the long skirt to try taking it off over her head but found out halfway through the process that she wasn't quite tall enough to pull it all the way off. Now, dress pulled over her head, Bel realised she was effectively stuck.

'No! Wait!' Leslie exclaimed, giving an irritated click of her tongue as she attempted to carefully pull the dress the rest of the way over Bel's head.

A sharp pain tugged at Bel's scalp and she yelped. 'My hair's caught,' she said, trying not to give in to the rising panic of being smothered alive in a sea of pink baronet satin.

'Well, well, well, what do we have here?' a deep voice boomed.

Bel stiffened and heard Larkin shriek, 'Get out!' followed by more high-pitched, coy feminine protests. 'You're supposed to be away all day, Tristan. What are you doing back so early?'

'We got sick of golf,' Bel heard him explain.

A low wolf-whistle floated through the room followed by a chorus of male chuckling. Bel heard Larkin raise her voice again. 'Out! Now. All of you!'

All of you? The cool air against her scantily clad body reminded Bel how much of her was on show, even if her head was still bured in satin, and she instinctively began to struggle against the restrictive fabric, desperate to cover herself.

'Stop squirming,' Leslie grunted, then gave a triumphant, 'There!'

Bel heard an irritated mutter of, 'Oh, for goodness sake!' from her aunt and realised she had yet again lived up to her reputation as a disappointment. The dress fell to her feet in a puddle of harmless glistening satin. Bel grabbed for the wrap she'd worn earlier, shoving her arms into the sleeves and securing it across her tightly. When she dared to look up, she caught the briefest glimpse of one very tall, extremely good-looking romance hero lookalike as he disappeared through the door. Bel squeezed her eyes shut, completely mortified. It was bad enough that Tristan had barged in and had seen her in her underwear, half-swallowed by a bridesmaid's dress, but for Tate to have also witnessed it? She wouldn't be able to face him. She couldn't.

Bel grabbed her clothes from the chair across the room and pulled them on. She sat down and tugged on her work boots, feeling her face burn with delayed embarrassment.

'We're going to have drinks out by the pool now,' Larkin said, coming to stand by her side.

'I'm going home.'

'What? No! You can't.'

'I'm not staying here after . . . *that*,' she said, throwing her hand out towards where Leslie was carefully hanging the dress that had tried to eat her. 'You said no one was here!'

'They weren't supposed to be. But who cares? They barely saw anything.'

'They would have seen plenty,' Bel snapped.

'Bel, I'm pretty sure they've seen steamier things than a woman in her underwear. It wasn't like you were naked.'

'I practically was!'

Larkin rolled her eyes. 'You're the only one making a big deal. No one else will think twice about it. Trust me. It's not the drama you're making it out to be.'

Bel stared at her cousin and bit down hard on her tongue. This from Larkin, the drama queen of the Central West? 'I am not going out there with a bunch of men who just ogled me. It's humiliating.'

'I'm sorry it happened, but seriously, they won't bat an eyelid. By the end of the night, they'll probably all be skinny-dipping in the pool. No one cares.'

She knew her cousin was trying to put her at ease, but it wasn't working. 'Well I do. I'm not up to a pool party tonight.'

'Okay,' Larkin said with a resigned huff. 'But you'd better be back for the spa day.'

Oh God.

Five

Ever since Larkin had asked her to be a bridesmaid, Bel had been dreading this day: the bridal spa day, which she'd been warned she would be forcefully dragged along to if need be. She'd glanced briefly at the itinerary when it had been sent out months earlier. It was, in fact, going to be a mini makeover. Which, up until recently, Bel had been underwhelmed about.

But now, she found herself wanting to do this. Not for her cousin's wedding but for herself. Emma was right. She would never have another chance like this again, and if the universe had decided to throw her a life raft in the form of Tate, then she bloody well better take hold of it.

The dress fitting ordeal was still fresh in her mind and although the sting of humiliation had not quite faded, it had been put into perspective. Sort of. She'd called Emma and replayed the whole sorry tale, and her friend had been full of sympathetic noises and enough comforting outrage to take away some of the pain. She'd decided to try her best to pretend the whole thing had never happened and, true to Larkin's word, no one had mentioned it on the ninety-minute drive to Toormanlee, the large regional town that served as the once-a-month, big-day-out location for Wessex residents. It was a nice town, settled on the banks of a wide river that carried water from further inland towards the mountains and then down to the coastal regions.

Larkin had been beside herself when Bel had told her she was ready to accept her style guidance, and she hadn't given Bel any time to rethink her decision, thrusting her into the hairdresser's chair and flicking through magazines until she found a look she was happy with. After a brief glance at the image, Bel sent a doubtful look at the hairdresser and shrugged. 'If you think you can pull that off with this,' she said, lifting a strand of her limp hair up, 'then go for it.'

'Marcel can work miracles,' Larkin said with a knowing smile, her own freshly blow-dried hair gleaming luxuriously.

Three and a half hours later, Bel could only stare at the reflection in the mirror in stunned silence. *Holy. Cow.*

'What did I tell you?' Larkin grinned from behind her.

'I . . . I can't believe it,' Bel said, hesitantly lifting a hand to touch the now shimmering locks, highlighted with cinnamon and caramel, falling in soft cascades of bouncy curls to her shoulders.

'Come on. Next stop, Beauty by Celine. Facials and waxing!'

Bel had no more time to admire her beautiful new do before being whisked from her chair and hurried along the street to the next port of call.

'Ouch!' Bel yelled as the young woman ripped another chunk of hair from her eyebrows. 'Surely there can't be any more hair left?' she muttered as the pain continued to throb and she began to wonder if there was any skin left behind.

Over the previous hour, she'd had her eyebrows waxed, her eyelashes tinted and a number of blackheads forcefully removed from her face—all after being lulled into a false sense of security following the most glorious facial she'd ever experienced. Also the *only* facial she'd ever experienced.

'Almost done now,' the elegant young beautician assured her. 'Are you sure you don't want the bikini and Brazilian wax the others are having?'

Are you freaking kidding me? It was bad enough having hair ripped from your face. 'No thanks,' she said quickly.

'All done,' the beautician announced after delicately spreading something she promised would help take away the redness from her face. Bel took one look in the mirror held up for her and gasped. Her entire face was one big, splotchy, red disaster. Although she did pause to admire the fact her eyebrows did indeed now have a remarkable shape. Who would have thought it could make so much difference?

She was in the process of putting her glasses back on when Larkin walked out, followed by Lisa and Kelly. All of them stopped in their tracks and stared at her.

'Your brows look amazing,' Larkin said, quickly covering up the awkwardness. 'The redness is normal,' she assured her, even as Bel noticed the others didn't have the same swollen red blotches on their perfect faces. 'I'd like to take you to one more appointment,' she said, linking her arm through Bel's.

While the others went ahead to have a make-up trial, Larkin and Bel walked across the road and into another store.

'What are we doing here?' Bel asked as they waited at the counter of the optometrist.

'I know you've always baulked at contacts,' Larkin started, 'but I was hoping if you tried them—'

'Larkin, I don't—'

'You look so amazing when you aren't wearing those big, heavy frames,' her cousin continued as though she hadn't spoken. 'I swear, it's like you're hiding behind them. If you're absolutely against contacts, then at least let me help you find some frames that don't make you look like you're some little old lady. You're so pretty, Bel. You just don't let anyone see it.'

'I'm not, though,' Bel said. 'I've always been invisible, and I'm fine with that. You and I are different, Larkin. You like people looking at you. I prefer to stay in the background.'

'It's only because you've never been brave enough to try stepping out of it,' Larkin retorted, and Bel wondered when her cousin had become so astute. 'I don't want to use the wedding-day card, but I will if you force me to,' she warned.

'Oh no. Not the you'll-ruin-my-wedding-photos threat,' Bel said, rolling her eyes. They both knew that was something Lois would say—not Larkin. They shared a smile. 'Fine. I'll try the contacts. For you, and because I know how long you've been wanting me to do it.'

'Only because I hate seeing you try to cover up the real you.'

Bel swallowed hard over a lump. For all her spoiled princess ways, Larkin had a kind soul, even if she was delusional about whatever it was she imagined Bel was trying to hide.

With the quick examination done, the optometrist showed Bel how to put the contacts in and, after a few tries, she managed to master it. She blinked a few times and looked around the room. It felt . . . *wonderful*. She felt almost weightless without her glasses.

As Bel walked out of the examination room, Larkin looked up from the magazine she'd been flicking through and a smile spread across her face. 'There you are,' she said simply. '*Now* we can see you.'

Bel blinked back the rush of emotion her cousin's soft words triggered and gave a tiny smile in return.

Armed with a trial pack of contacts, they left the shop and headed back to find the others.

Over lunch at an upscale pub, Bel listened as the others gossiped about people they knew and places they went that Bel had no idea about. Lisa and Kelly were friends from

Larkin's boarding school days. There was only four years' difference between them and Bel, but as she listened to their conversations, Bel felt considerably older. All they seemed interested in discussing was how much money they thought someone was worth and where they'd last been on holidays overseas.

'What about you, Bel? Lisa asked, taking a breath after spending the previous twenty minutes or so recounting her most recent spiritual retreat in Ubud, from which she'd just returned. 'Have you been anywhere interesting lately?'

'Uh, no. Not really.'

'So, you actually live out here? Like, all the time?' Kelly asked.

'Yep. I do,' Bel answered, trying not to shift uncomfortably in her seat.

'But . . . *why?*' Kelly crinkled her nose slightly. 'I mean, what do you *do* out here?'

'I work,' Bel said, glancing across at her cousin, who was busy cutting up her salad.

'I couldn't do it. I mean, it's nice for a little, you know . . . getaway, I suppose, but to live out here?'

'So have you *ever* left town? Like travelled? Have you been to Paris?' Lisa asked.

'No. I haven't. I grew up in South Australia until I was ten. And I've been to Sydney.'

The two women stared.

'The others will be here tomorrow,' Larkin cut in, smiling.

'Oh, thank *God*,' Kelly said, dragging the words like she was in pain. 'Gigi and Niki will definitely shake things up a bit.'

'Yes, but I won't like giving up all the one-on-one time we've had with Tate,' Lisa pouted. 'You know what they're like, always trying to steal the attention away from everyone else in the room.'

At the mention of Tate, Bel's interest instantly spiked.

'We're having a cocktail party at Glentoberon tomorrow night. A kind of pre-rehearsal rehearsal for the bridal party,' Larkin informed her.

'It's going to be so much fun. I love cocktail parties,' Kelly said, clapping her hands together. 'I have the most divine dress. It's sure to drag Tate's attention away from Gigi and Niki.'

Bel's spirits plummeted. She'd been excited by the prospect of seeing Tate again, but now she remembered she'd be in a room full of glamorous socialites in designer label outfits and she'd be wearing—Bel mentally ran through her wardrobe options—absolutely nothing. She'd known there would be a number of stupid events leading up to the Wedding of the Century, but until now, she truly hadn't cared what she'd be wearing. Now she was regretting her earlier rebellion. Big time.

As they left the table after finishing their meal, Bel discreetly pulled her cousin aside. 'Small problem,' she started, 'I don't have anything to wear to a cocktail party.'

Bel wasn't sure if she was relieved or mildly insulted by the smile Larkin gave her as she patted her arm in a there, there fashion. 'I figured as much. Which is why I've packed you a suitcase with some outfits you can have. Lucky we're the same size.' She leaned back slightly and ran an expert eye up and down Bel and added, 'More or less.' She gave her cousin a smile that didn't quite give as much encouragement as she'd probably intended. Still, at least that was one problem down. Maybe she wouldn't make a complete idiot of herself.

'Bel!' Emma cried as she gaped at her friend later that afternoon. 'Oh my God . . .'

'Is it too much? It's too much, isn't it,' Bel said, touching her hair, still feeling luxuriously soft and bouncy.

'No!' Emma said, shaking her head as she continued to stare. 'It's . . . perfect.'

'I feel a bit ridiculous.'

'Well, don't. They didn't change anything. This is all you, girlfriend,' Emma said, snapping out of her initial surprise. 'I *am* a little pissy that I've been trying to get you to do something with your hair for years and you've always refused, though.'

'I know,' Bel agreed wearily. 'And I would have said no to Larkin too except that it's for her wedding. And the fact Tate would never actually see me with all those other eligible women around if I didn't do something drastic,' she added.

'I wouldn't say drastic, but it's definitely dramatic. I think I need a trip to Toormanlee. So, anyway,' Emma continued, 'what's next on the bridal party itinerary?'

'The cocktail party.'

'That sounds fun,' Emma said encouragingly.

'It's one thing to have all this stuff done,' Bel said. 'But it's another thing entirely to fit in. Inside, I'm still the same old boring Bel.'

'You are not boring. You look amazing and you deserve to be there just as much as they all do. You'll be all right.'

That night, Bel stared at her reflection in the bathroom mirror and found herself contemplating the massive changes that had taken place. She felt like the same person . . . until she saw her reflection, and then it was like a stranger was staring back at her. Who was this new version of Bel Buckley? She certainly looked more exciting than the old one. This Bel looked like she was ready to take on the world. She didn't look like she belonged in Wessex. *This is crazy*, she thought with an irritable shake of her head.

Not as crazy as letting a chance to have your real-life version of Jax Lexington pass by.

Bel chewed on her lip as she examined the woman in the mirror.

Embrace this new version. New me. New beginning.

The cocktail evening arrived and Bel was *not* all right.

True to her word, Larkin had left her a suitcase full of clothing as well as everything she could possibly need to accessorise—including a couple of pairs of shoes and jewellery. The problem was that they'd been made for Larkin, Sydney socialite, not Bel, Wessex non-socialite. The dresses were beautiful—probably designer, although Bel didn't know one label from another. However, while she and Larkin were pretty much the same clothes size, they weren't the same build. Larkin was tall and graceful. Bel was . . . not. She was shorter and had curves in places Larkin didn't. She also had boobs. And this was the current dilemma. The cocktail dress Larkin had packed her for tonight—a beautiful shimmering blood-red stretchy number—had a rather low neckline that Bel was currently exploding out of. She'd been forced to call in reinforcements and, thank goodness, Emma had come through.

'This is impossible!' Bel said as Emma stood back to study the issue at hand. 'I've got straps showing everywhere. How on earth are you supposed to wear this bloody thing?'

Emma tapped a finger against her lips, tilting her head slightly sideways. 'I don't think you're supposed to wear a bra with it,' she concluded. 'I mean, Larkin wouldn't need to, would she? She missed out on the Buckley cleavage.'

'Yeah, well, I wish I had too.' Throughout high school she'd been self-conscious about her breasts, so much so that she'd always tended to wear baggy clothing to hide them while most other girls in her year were proudly showing theirs off. Nowadays, it wasn't such a drama, except when they refused to fit into the only cocktail dress she had to wear to an evening that was rapidly approaching. 'I can't *not* wear a bra,' Bel said irritably as she imagined her uncooperative breasts suddenly realising they had the freedom to swing in any direction—and not necessarily in the same direction at that.

Emma crossed to the open suitcase on the bed and dug through it. 'Ah-ha! Here you go. Trust Larkin to be prepared.' She held up a plastic bag.

'What is that?' Bel asked, stepping closer to accept the small bag. 'Silicon adhesive bra cups?' she read, grimacing.

'It's a stick-on bra. I've seen these, but never tried them.'

Bel took one of the cups from the bag and grimaced. 'There's no way these things are going to support a large boob. Look at it,' Bel said holding the jelly-like mould up and watching as it flopped about.

'Well, if you're going to wear this dress, and I'm guessing you don't have anything else to wear, then you'll have to give them a go.'

'This is so stupid,' Bel sighed.

'This is fashion, my love. Welcome to the high life.'

'Why would anyone buy a dress you couldn't wear a normal bra under?'

'Just try it,' Emma said.

Bel finally managed to wrestle the girls into a vague imitation of the photo she'd found in an online tutorial. Emma helped her slip the dress over her head and stood back to admire their handiwork.

'Is the left side higher than the right?' Bel asked, examining her breasts.

'No, I think it's okay. I don't think we should try adjusting them again in case they lose their stickiness.'

'Em, I am not feeling supported. At all.'

'It'll be fine. Just . . . don't run, maybe,' Emma added, eyeing Bel's chest critically. 'Or jump too much.'

'I'll try to contain myself.'

'Then we're good!' Emma declared with a bright smile. 'You look amazing.'

'I feel like an imposter,' Bel said, eyeing her reflection. The person looking back at her was a stranger. With no thick-rimmed glasses, her eyes seemed to dominate her face—she'd never seen them looking quite so dramatic. Emma had helped her with make-up and the neutral tones she'd used enhanced her eyes, making them seem almost golden. She had to admit, she did love her new hair. The base was pretty much her own colour, a dark brownish tone, but the highlights they'd added shimmered attractively. With the weight of the dead ends pulling her hair down gone, and a little bit of layering and artful feathering, her natural curls now bounced healthily. She felt like a brand-new person.

She understood why people had been staring at her today. They couldn't believe it was the same person. *Bel* couldn't even believe she was the same person.

'This has *always* been you,' Emma said, catching her gaze in the mirror. 'You've just been hiding for a very long time. Get out there and own it.'

'But these people aren't like us. I don't fit in.'

'They're the ones who don't fit in here,' Emma pointed out. 'What would a character in one of your books do in this situation? Be her. This is your moment to step into a storyline. Jax is waiting. Go get him!'

Six

With Emma's heartfelt speech still ringing in her ears, Bel arrived at Glentoberon and parked, carefully wiggling out of the driver's seat in her tight dress and taking one last glance in the side mirror to make sure everything was still in place.

On a normal visit, she rarely entered through the front door, but tonight, everything was lit up and the front of the house glowed with a welcoming light.

The old house was grand—there was no other word for it. It boasted a wide, tiled verandah that circled the lower floor of the house, and a covered balcony on top that led out from the bedrooms on the second storey.

She walked into the huge open foyer, admiring the sweeping staircase leading to the second floor.

There was an audible gasp to her left and Bel turned to find her aunt blinking at her. 'Bel, you look . . . so different,' she said, forcibly regaining her composure.

'Hello, Aunt Lois. Yes, it was time for a bit of a change.'

'Well after time,' Lois corrected, lifting her eyebrows pointedly. 'It's a *big* improvement.'

Gee, thanks, Bel thought, inwardly rolling her eyes as she followed her aunt into the enormous sitting room to the left of the foyer and took a moment to appreciate how beautiful it looked. The whole house had been repainted, and the sitting room had undergone a massive facelift—much like herself. There was a feature wall with delicate pale blue flowers on one side and the furniture had all been reupholstered in varying shades of blues, creams, whites and yellows. A small table was loaded up with nibblies and a bar stretched along the back of the enormous room.

'You made it! I knew that dress would be perfect on you!' Larkin squealed, coming across to greet her.

'Thank you for the lend. You were a lifesaver.'

'Keep it. I never really liked it on me. Come and meet everyone,' she said, pulling Bel along behind her. 'Everyone, this is my cousin, Bel. Bel, this is Gigi and Niki. And Tristan's groomsmen, Henry, Oliver, Elijah, Leo and Tate. And you know Kelly and Lisa, of course.'

Bel registered how disconcertingly similar they all dressed and spoke, even if they were set apart by different hair colours and heights. They all had the same perfectly white straight teeth and well-manicured hands. Bel swallowed nervously as her eyes fell on Tate. Was it possible he'd somehow gotten even more handsome in the past few days?

'Bel?' Larkin said, making her jump guiltily.

'Sorry?' she stammered slightly.

'What would you like to drink?'

'Oh. Um . . . whatever. Wine? Anything is fine.'

'Look at that, an easily pleased woman. Who knew they existed?' said Leo, a tall blond-haired variant, as he left to get Bel her drink.

'How have you managed to keep this little gem a secret for so long, Larkin?' Elijah asked as his gaze shifted from Bel's face to her chest.

'Bel rarely comes to the city, despite my best attempts to drag her there,' Larkin said.

'You really should come and visit. I'd be more than happy to show you around,' Elijah continued. Bel suppressed a frown. He wasn't even trying to hide the fact he was ogling her.

'Here you go,' Leo said, cutting in smoothly. He stepped closer to hand her the drink, brushing his arm against the side of her breast.

Surely that hadn't been on purpose? It was hard to tell. She held her glass awkwardly and took a sip, looking around for a seat somewhere quieter, but the men were still trying to make small talk.

'So, you're a Buckley too?' Henry said. Bel tried not to shift uncomfortably under the weight of their sudden interest. This was the exact reason she preferred to be at the back of the room, ignored.

'Yep.'

'Did you grow up here at Glentoberon?'

'Ah, no. I lived in town.'

'So not a farm girl like Larkin, then?' Oliver said.

Bel was grateful she hadn't taken another sip of her wine or she would have spat it all over the front of Oliver's shirt. Larkin was about as far removed from being a farm girl as you could get. 'No.'

'What a shame. I have a thing for country girls.'

'Since when?' Niki asked, sidling up to Oliver and sliding an arm through his.

'Since arriving.'

'I doubt you'd know one end of a cow from another,' she teased.

'It's not the cows I'm interested in.'

'It's more sheep,' Bel found herself saying. She glanced around and noticed Tate had joined the little group and was watching her with a faint grin.

'Excuse me?' Oliver said while the others chuckled and made rude remarks about his being overly affectionate with sheep. 'What, because my parents are from New Zealand? Is that what you're trying to say?'

'What? No,' Bel stammered. How the hell was she supposed to know where his parents had come from? 'I meant, out here, it's more sheep than cattle.'

Oliver flounced away, taking Niki with him. It seemed Bel had unintentionally made fun of poor Oliver on a touchy subject.

'That's hilarious, Bel,' Elijah said, still chuckling.

'I didn't mean . . .' she started to explain, but he'd walked away.

'He'll be fine,' Tate said lightly. 'The sheep thing's been a bit of an ongoing in-joke. Don't worry about it. So, you're the Bel that Larkin's been talking about.'

Bel lifted a dubious eyebrow. She couldn't think of any situation where Larkin would have been talking about her.

'We went on a bit of a tour of the area earlier and she mentioned her cousin Bel in a number of stories.'

Bel smiled at that, although she would be surprised if Larkin had told any of these people the more normal childhood things they'd gotten up to. When Larkin would come into town to stay at Gran's, she'd always reverted back to an ordinary country kid who liked going to the public pool to cool off and staying up late with Bel, giggling and planning their futures when they were supposed to be asleep.

'That's me,' she said.

'It's nice to meet you,' he said.

Bel went to remind him that they'd already met but was interrupted when Gigi walked up and placed a hand on Tate's arm, looking up at him with sultry eyes. 'My drink's empty.'

Bel resisted the urge to roll her eyes at the simpering female. It was so blatantly coy, surely men saw right through it?

'Then allow me to remedy the situation. I'll be right back,' he said, taking Gigi's empty champagne flute and turning away. He had the same suave, sophisticated air about him that Jax was famous for, and Bel found herself catching her breath.

'I'll come with you,' Gigi said quickly, leaving Bel to stand by herself, feeling more than a little self-conscious. Thankfully, dinner was announced and the crowd began to migrate into the dining room. Much to her delight, as she carefully eased into her seat, Tate appeared beside her. She sent him a nervous smile, silently praying she wouldn't make a fool of herself.

She'd sat in this room on numerous occasions growing up, mostly for important events like Christmas dinner and birthday celebrations. It was everything a stately Edwardian manor house dining room should be—opulent and rather posh. She'd always felt intimidated by the regal-looking room, but tonight, she was distracted by the man sitting beside her. They weren't touching, but she swore she could feel his warmth radiating. She listened to the stories being told around the table—none of them having any great meaning to her, as they all related to places and people she didn't know, but she wasn't bored in the slightest. She was overly aware of every move Tate made. The tapping of a lean finger on the table, the shifting of his body in his chair, a shuffle of his foot. Her gaze fell to the delicate way he held the shiny silver cutlery in his large hands.

'Bel?'

She jumped, startled from her thoughts as she blinked up at her cousin.

'You okay?' Larkin asked, staring at her with no small degree of concern.

'Yep. I'm fine. Everything's fine,' she stammered, scooting her chair back.

'We're all heading into the drawing room. You coming?'

'Absolutely.' Bel spoke with forced cheer to cover the fact she'd been lost in rather steamy thoughts.

Larkin hooked her arm through Bel's as they left the dining room. 'I know this is a lot,' she said, lowering her voice, 'but I really am glad you're part of all this. It means a lot to me.'

It was easy to forget Larkin's bridezilla tendencies in these moments, when Bel caught glimpses of the person she knew her cousin was deep down. 'It's going to be a beautiful wedding and you will be an utterly stunning bride.'

'Oh, I know,' Larkin said lightly.

Annnnnnnd now it's gone.

A dessert buffet had been laid out, and Bel collected a plate and served herself a piece of pavlova. She carried it past the other bridesmaids, holding her head high as she ignored the pursed lips. *She* fitted into her dress. If they were worried about eating for the next few days, then that was on them.

Bel sat on the sofa, eating her dessert and ignoring the fact she was once again left hanging like a shag on a rock as the others laughed, drank and danced around her. As she reached to place her empty plate on the table, Bel suddenly felt something snap. *Oh no.*

She forced herself not to instantly grab hold of the top of the dress and risk drawing attention. *Stupid silicon thingies.* She could feel her right boob slowly beginning to slide downwards, the sticky cup surrendering what little support it had been giving.

This is not happening. She had to get to the bathroom to try to salvage the situation, but she didn't want to stand up and make things worse.

'Is everything okay?' Bel looked up into a pair of curious blue eyes.

Her gaze roamed across Tate's broad face and perfectly sculpted cheekbones. *Christ, he is beautiful.*

'Bel?' he asked, sounding slightly more concerned. It was enough to snap her from her trance.

'I'm fine . . . I just—' *Do not tell this man that your bra has given out under the weight of your stupid boobs.* '—have a slight wardrobe malfunction situation.'

'I see,' he said, lifting an eyebrow slightly as his eyes briefly dropped to where she held her arms protectively across her chest. 'Come with me.' He put a hand out and helped her to her feet, before wrapping an arm around her waist and tucking her close to his side as he led her across the room, to where two other couples were dancing. Tate pulled her in against his body and Bel automatically placed her arm around him and her hand into his, her chest now firmly pressed against his, effectively hiding her torso from the others.

Her previous discomfort was immediately replaced by a sizzling sensation of heat where their bodies connected, and she forgot all about her earlier dilemma. She was in Jax's freaking arms! No, she quickly amended, Tate, not Jax. This wasn't some fictional hero from a book. This was an actual, warm blooded, real man. And he was holding her in his arms, moving her across the floor as they swayed to the gentle, romantic music playing on the stereo. All of a sudden, they were close to the doorway and then, before she knew it, Tate was releasing her to walk swiftly down the hallway to a powder room. 'There you go,' he said, as she continued to stare up at him, too unable to snap out of the fairytale moment to immediately register where they now were.

'Oh,' she mananged. 'Thank you.'

'Do you want me to wait out here for you?'

'Oh. Um, no, thank you. I should be fine.' She was not fine. Her heart was pounding like she'd run a marathon and her legs felt decidedly jelly-like. Already she missed the warmth of his body.

'I'll see you back in the drawing room, then,' he said and bowed his head slightly. He actually bowed his freaking head, like some rakish hero from a Victorian romance.

Bel closed the door of the powder room and leaned her back against it, closing her eyes as she felt an idiotic grin fill her face. He was everything her foolish romantic heart could ever dream of, and he was *real*.

She opened her eyes and looked at her reflection in the mirror. Her eyes were bright and her face was flushed. She still didn't recognise the woman looking back at her with those well-shaped eyebrows and thick eyelashes that made her eyes seem extra big, an effect amplified by her lack of heavy glasses.

'New me. New beginning,' she repeated softly. She could do this. She could step into this new life and be someone else for the next few days. It wouldn't last—reality would inevitably come crashing in—but, for right now, she could embrace the change and live out a fantasy, then have something to remember once it was all over.

She managed to fix the support issue, but she feared the solution would only be temporary and decided it wasn't worth the risk of staying too much longer. The party was winding down when she returned anyway, with couples breaking off to talk quietly or dance.

Bel poured herself a coffee from the silver pot sitting on a warmer, then gave the assortment of pastries and after-dinner treats a cursory glance, selecting a dainty custard-filled tart with real flower petals scattered on top. She was trying to decide if she should pick them off when a now familiar voice spoke up from beside her.

'Apparently they're edible,' Tate said quietly. He reached across her, took a number of the tarts and placed them on his plate. 'I heard the caterer telling your aunt earlier.'

Bel glanced at the plate he was filling with sweets. 'You must be the only one here who isn't counting calories.'

'Life's too short to count calories.' He nodded down at her own plate approvingly as she added another item. 'I like a woman who isn't afraid to eat.'

'I love to eat,' she said, sounding ridiculously eager, then bit down on the inside of her cheek. *Just don't talk!* There was less chance of embarrassing herself that way.

'I figured as much. You were the only woman at the table who cleaned her plate.'

Oh God. He's been watching me eat? Has everyone else been doing the same thing?

'Like I said, I appreciate a woman who isn't afraid to eat more than a salad,' he said, as though sensing her alarm.

'I like to think that Uncle Stan's sheep didn't die for nothing,' she quipped.

His chuckle sent a pleasant trickle of warmth down her spine. 'Do you mind if I sit with you?'

Mind? She was practically jumping out of her skin at the prospect of having more time alone with him. 'Of course not.' *I want to have your babies.* The wayward thought made her start slightly, and she had to grip the coffee cup so as not to spill it. Christ, she hoped she hadn't said that out loud. A swift glance at him didn't detect any surprise or disgust on his beautiful face, so she assumed she hadn't. Then again, maybe he was used to women offering to reproduce with him. 'How are you finding Wessex?' she asked. 'I'm assuming it's a lot quieter than Sydney?'

'It's a lot quieter than anywhere,' he said drolly, 'but I live in Perth.'

'Really?' Her heart took a nosedive. She'd assumed he'd travelled out from Sydney like the others. But Western Australia? There'd be no chance of ever bumping into him after the wedding. *Bold of you to think this guy would ever see you again after the wedding, Perth or not.*

'Yeah. Been over there for the last three years. I love it. Have you ever been?'

'No,' she said, shaking her head.

'You should. The landscape is like nothing you find on this side of the country.'

'What do you do over there?'

'I'm in the mining industry, primarily iron ore.'

'You're a miner?'

He flashed her a brief smile. 'No, I'm more corporate. I deal in the business side of things.'

'Oh.' *Dumb arse*, she rebuked herself. As if those hands had ever dug in a freaking mine.

'How do you know Tristan?'

'We went to school together.'

That had put the question she'd wondered about to rest—his age. Tristan, she knew from Larkin, was almost thirty.

Which made Tate the same age as her. Thank goodness for Larkin's attraction to older men. She wasn't sure she wanted to be a cougar quite yet.

'So, you and Larkin are cousins?'

'I know, it's hard to believe. I'm the black sheep of the family.'

Tate sent her a strange look. 'Black sheep? How so?'

'I mean, Larkin is . . . well, *Larkin*. She's got the looks and the talent . . . the ambition,' Bel said. 'And I'm just . . . me.'

'You don't think you're as beautiful as Larkin?'

His question made her give him a double-take. 'No.'

'Seriously?'

Bel wanted to laugh at him, but he looked genuinely confused.

'I don't normally look like this,' she said, swallowing hard.

'How do you normally look?' he asked with a teasing glint in his eye.

He didn't recognise her. He had no idea she was the woman who'd served him and made an absolute idiot of herself that first day. Part of her was high-fiving at the realisation she now had a clean slate, but a small part of her was asking how he could not know. She hadn't changed that much, surely?

She pushed the question away and decided to take the small win. He had no idea she was that fumbling, awkward woman. His only knowledge of her was here and now, in her new, albeit somewhat temporary, skin. She was a new woman, for all intents and purposes. She didn't have to be lonely, romance-reading Bel. For a little while, she could be better-hair, nicer-clothes, more-worldly Bel instead.

She glanced at her watch and reality knocked on her door. It was almost midnight.

'I have to go,' she said, placing her empty plate on the table.

'You're not staying out here?'

'No, I have my own place in town.'

'It's still early. You can't stay and have a drink?'

'I have to drive. But there's still the practice dinner and the pre-wedding rehearsal and the pre-pre-wedding dinner.' She smiled, rolling her eyes at the ridiculous number of social functions Larkin had scheduled.

'I'll walk you out,' he said.

Bel said her goodnights to Larkin and her uncle and aunt, declining Larkin's invitation to stay, and slipped out of the room just as a debate started up about climate change, distracting everyone.

They came to a stop by her car. 'Thank you for your help earlier,' Bel mumbled, feeling the heat beginning to creep its way up her throat.

'Glad I could help,' he said, sending her a grin that made her almost forget her name.

'I better go.' She turned just as he leaned forward, managing to bang her head against his chin. 'Ouch!'

'Sorry!' They said it at the same time, as Bel rubbed her forehead. *Jesus, is his jaw made of titanium?*

'Are you okay?' he asked.

'I'm fine. Goodnight,' she said, opening her door quickly.

Had he been about to kiss her? *You absolute moron!* What if he had been? No, surely not. That would be . . .

She glanced in the rear-view mirror as she drove away. Tate was still standing, tall and broad-shouldered, watching her.

Oh. Dear. Lord.

Seven

Bel opened her eyes as the familiar ding of the daily bridesmaid text sounded—right on cue. With a reluctant sigh she reached over and picked up her phone. 'Have you stocked the wedding bathroom baskets? I've forwarded the list of items needed, please check your email.'

What on God's green earth was a wedding bathroom basket? She opened Google and searched—sadly this wasn't the first thing she'd had to look up. Who knew weddings were this bloody complicated to organise? 'A basket or a box, placed in reception venue bathrooms, full of items to help your guests with any mini emergencies they may have,' she discovered.

True to her word, Gisele had sent through the list—an enormous list—of suggested items . . . bobby pins, hand lotion, tweezers, eyedrops, sewing kits, cough drops, indigestion medication, Vaseline, lollipops and Party Feet gel cushions . . . *what the hell?*

The group chat was conspicuously quiet, she noticed, and she gave a small grunt of resignation. Clearly, *she* was going to be the one running around town today searching for everything on this stupid list.

Bel dragged back her bedcovers and looked over at the new clothes hanging in her wardrobe. She'd allowed Larkin and the girls to talk her into buying them before they'd headed home from Toormanlee, and she reminded herself that she'd promised Larkin to embrace this 'new Bel' thing. There were new jeans—tight ones, not the baggy, boyfriend style she usually preferred. Tops that hugged her torso, as opposed to her old loose-fitting ones; cropped jackets, skirts and even a couple of sundresses. She couldn't remember the last time she'd worn a dress before last night.

After a quick breakfast she grabbed her keys and headed out, determined to get the shopping over and done with as quickly as possible.

She'd already received a few comments about her new hair and the absence of her bulky glasses, and she was expecting a few more. As soon as she entered the chemist she was proved right by a twitter of 'nice hair' comments from the girls. But she had underestimated the older locals, who seemed to think their age excused them from the bounds of social politeness. Mrs Fortescue squinted and stared at her for a solid five minutes before declaring, 'I don't like it! Makes you look all washed out.' Twenty minutes later, in the bread aisle of the supermarket, Bill Woodstock let her know he thought she looked like 'one of them Kardashian women'. Bel wondered what was more alarming: his announcement or the fact that he knew who the Kardashians were. And then, minutes later, while she stood in line at the check-out, Carol Connelly, the local CWA vice president, shook her head and tsked something about young women these days and their Botox and implants. By the time Bel had finished checking off the list and headed home, she was feeling drained.

She had only just sunk down on her gran's comfy floral-patterned sofa when there was a knock at the front door. She considered ignoring it and letting whoever it was believe she wasn't home, but that was pointless when her car was parked in the driveway. Dragging herself upright, she opened the door to the last person she'd ever expected to find on her doorstep.

'Dean,' she said, unable to disguise her surprise.

'Wow. They weren't kidding,' he replied.

'Pardon?' Bel asked, frowning at him as he continued to stare.

'I heard you'd had a bit of work done,' he said.

What the hell? 'I had a haircut and I got rid of my glasses. I didn't exactly go under the knife.'

'If you believe what everyone else is saying, you've undergone radical surgery and lost fifteen kilos.'

'What?'

'Wouldn't say fifteen, but losing the overalls and baggy jeans, I reckon it'd be close to ten maybe,' he said thoughtfully as he studied her legs in the new jeans.

'I have not lost any weight, and I've definitely not had any surgery,' she snapped, fighting the urge to shuffle her feet under his scrutiny. 'What are you doing here? Or have you just swung by to lend your two cents' worth?'

'Emma asked me to drop this into you,' he said, remembering the plastic container under his arm which he now held out to her.

Bel eyed the container she'd used to take the salad to Emma and Craig's for dinner. 'Thanks. You didn't need to drive all the way in here to drop it off, though.'

He shrugged and her gaze went over the blue flannel checked shirt he wore open over a black T-shirt. 'I was coming into town anyway. I had to, uh, pick up some . . . groceries and stuff,' he said vaguely, before clearing his throat.

He seriously acts so weird sometimes.

'I did take your advice, though,' he said, shoving his hands into his pockets.

'My advice?'

'About joining in. The whole community thing.'

'Oh. Right.'

'Dad was a unit commander with the State Emergency Service when I was in high school, so I was a member as a kid, and I've done a bit of firefighting in the Northern

Territory. So I joined the Rural Fire Service and the local SES. Figured that would keep me busy for a while.'

'I should think so.' Though she hoped they wouldn't be having another fire season like the one that had just taken out a number of local properties. 'That must be pretty special, joining the same unit your dad used to be in.'

He seemed a little surprised by her comment, and Bel briefly wondered if she'd said the wrong thing.

'Yeah. I guess it is. Most of the older guys worked with him at some stage.'

'Does it make it easier or harder? Having people around who talk about him? You said the other day that you two didn't get along?'

'To be honest, it's a bit strange. The way he was with his mates in the SES, he was a different person to the one he was at home. He never wanted to be a farmer, but he grew up in a time where you took over from your dad, the way he took over from his, and you didn't really get a choice. You were a farmer and that was that. I think he found his true calling with the SES. That was where his heart was.'

'But you chose to stay in farming?'

'Yeah. I guess I inherited the love of the land from my granddad. I always wanted to work the property, I just couldn't do it under Dad. We rubbed each other the wrong way. I regret not making a bigger effort to get back and see him more often, though. I guess we were the same in that way, both stubborn.'

'I'm sorry you didn't get the chance to make things right,' Bel said, and she realised she truly was. The old Dean might have been a little a-hole to her, but she could see losing his dad had been hard and she genuinely felt sorry for him.

'Thanks,' he said, giving her a tight smile.

'Okay, well . . .' Bel let the sentence dangle between them. 'I shouldn't hold you up.'

'Yeah,' he said, straightening. 'I better keep going. I guess I'll see you at the movie night?'

'I'll be there.'

'See you then.' He hesitated before adding, 'I like your new look.' Then he quickly headed to his ute.

Bel closed the door with a small frown. *What on earth was that about?*

Later that evening, Bel glanced over at her phone on the bedside table and saw 'Unknown caller' flash across the screen. She ignored it because . . . well, only psychopaths answered unknown numbers. A ping sounded, indicating a message, and she tipped the phone towards her to see who it was from. Only reading the first line, she floundered about trying to sit up and almost dropped the phone. 'Hey Bel, it's Tate.'

How had he gotten her number? Obviously from Larkin. She opened the message to read it in full. 'We're heading into town to go to some markets. Larkin thinks we all need some country culture. Just wondering if you're going? Hope to see you there tonight.'

The markets? Yes! The prospect of going was suddenly far more exciting.

She'd been thinking about Tate since the previous night. The almost kiss had been playing over and over on her mind. Tonight, she'd be super careful. Clumsy clod Mabel would be replaced by cool, calm and collected Bel, bridesmaid extraordinaire—and this time she'd be wearing a proper bloody bra.

Other places had festivals or another major yearly highlight, where the community came together as a whole and celebrated their town. But Wessex had never really had any defining event in its two hundred-and-six-year history. It had slipped through all the festival nonsense and plodded along to its own special beat. It wasn't on any major highways, and it took a considerable drive from the nearest exit on Newell Highway, about sixty kilometres or so, to reach their little town. For years, the only real traffic was livestock road trains and trucks carting grain to the silos along the train route.

Times had changed, though, as had the population, and tourism was a new industry with a lot of potential. Over the last few years, with the grey nomad revolution and the vast number of younger families choosing to live on the land, visitors had been trickling into places like Wessex. That's why the progress committee had decided they needed to do something to help encourage the spike in tourism, with the idea of getting a grant for the 'big thing' concocted over beers and chicken schnitzels at the pub almost twelve months earlier. The progress committee had since lifted its game and become a lot more professional, with meetings given an allocated time, in the conference room at the pub, prior to the snooker and schnitty night.

Emma was a driving force behind the new and improved committee. She was a doer—she got things done—and under her leadership, big things had been slowly beginning to take shape, quite literally in this case. The debate about which 'big thing' should be the town's tourism icon—the Big Rooster or the Big Burger—had led to many a heated meeting, with various members walking out during discussions more than once. But the time had come to make a decision.

Today, people would vote, and tonight, the announcement would be made. There was a lot riding on the outcome. There had been rumours floating about that Bob Baxter had been trying to coerce votes from people, but the committee was confident that the appointment of Betty Miller as the chief electoral officer had ensured there was no funny business going on. Betty took her position very seriously.

The markets and movie night were a biannual fundraiser that had been a huge success over the last few years. It had been started to help pay for a number of town-beautication projects, and it had grown considerably since the inaugural event. Now they had enough stalls to line both sides of the main street for its entire length. Stallholders came from as far away as Dubbo and Orange—they'd even had enquiries from a few who did the Sydney markets. It was quite the event.

Bel glanced up at the heavy grey clouds that had begun to gather throughout the afternoon. No one was allowed to mention the R-word around Larkin but, on more than one occasion over the last few days, Bel had heard the odd whisper asking what would happen if it rained. She never managed to hear any answers to the dreaded question and had decided that Larkin must have had it worked out. She hoped. Surely it would hold off anyway?

Grabbing her fold-up chair from the back of her car, Bel set off to get a good place in the park to watch the movie. Having the ideal vantage point was critical when it came to the open-air movie experience. Too close and you couldn't see the screen; too far and you couldn't hear anything. Locals tended to get there early to set up their chairs and blankets and bag the best spots. She'd already done her shift at the bake stall earlier in the afternoon, where she'd smiled her way through a few more surprised looks and the odd gape at her new appearance. She'd been thrilled to hand over her apron and escape.

Bel searched the already impressive gathering of people for a glimpse of Emma then, spotting her friend's frantic waving, weaved her way in between blankets to reach her.

'Great position,' she said, nodding as she eyed the enormous white screen set up at the front.

She smiled at Craig and faltered slightly as her gaze moved to the other man seated in a camping chair next to him. 'Dean.'

'Bel,' he greeted her easily.

'Dump your gear,' Emma ordered. 'We have to get to the pub for the official close of the voting poll. You know how Betty will get if we're late.'

'Heaven forbid.'

Bel unfolded her chair, helped Lucy scramble up and get comfy then left strict instructions that the three-year-old must guard it with her life. She and Emma left the park to head across the street.

'Are you sure Craig will be okay?' Bel asked.

'He'll be fine. They'll convince him to take them to the jumping castle soon. Sucker,' Emma said with an evil chuckle. 'I had to bring out the negotiation skills earlier in the week to get them off the playground equipment and into the car when we went into Toormanlee. It'll be interesting to see how successful Mr I Would Have Had Them In The Car In Five Minutes will go. Anyway, he has backup with Dean. It'll be fine.'

The close of voting was only supposed to be a mild, superficial ceremony. However, Betty had managed to turn it into something of a theatrical extravaganza. Dressed in a purple velvet robe, complete with fluffy collar, and wearing white gloves, Betty gave a heartfelt speech to rival any royal ceremonial closing. The crowd of seven swapped awkward glances as the speech came to an end, the scattering of applause clearly not the thunderous ovation Betty had been hoping for. With an indignant sniff, she left the stage, snapping her fingers for Sid the bartender to bring the box of ballots to the back lounge area, which had been designated the official counting room.

'Well, that's fifteen minutes of my life I won't get back,' Emma muttered as they walked outside.

'Great turnout,' Bel said as she viewed the crowd in the park. The population was swollen with people from smaller townships and farming families from remote stations making the trip to Wessex for an outing. Bel loved seeing people greeting each other after long spells of isolation, bumping into familiar faces and catching up on gossip and news. The phone and the internet could only do so much, and face-to-face contact was a luxury when you lived so far out of town.

'Bel!'

Bel and Emma turned to find Larkin waving madly from the middle of the street.

The group walking towards them stood out like a sore thumb; they could have been filming an advert for RM Williams or Thomas Cook. It wasn't that they were dressed inappropriately; it was that everything looked brand-new and so . . . well, stiff. Bel had to stop herself looking for any price tags that may still be attached.

'Oh look, it's Country Chic Barbie and her friends,' Emma said in a saccharine tone.

'Stop it,' Bel said, biting back a grin. There was no real love lost between her cousin and her best friend. It wasn't usually a problem, since the two hardly ever occupied the same space, but growing up, it had occasionally been difficult during school holidays when Bel wanted to spend time with them both.

Emma couldn't deal with how spoiled and entitled Larkin had always been. While everyone else around here made do, the Buckleys from Glentoberon loved to come to town, show off and flaunt their wealth. Bel did think Emma was remembering things with a slightly jaded edge, though. Or maybe it was that Bel was used to the way her relatives were and ignored it. Either way, Emma couldn't stand Larkin and Larkin simply didn't have anything in common with Emma, which always put Bel in an awkward spot.

'There you are! I've been looking for you everywhere,' Larkin called. 'Oh. Hello, Emma,' she added in a noticeably less enthusiastic tone.

'Larkin,' Emma responded, equally unimpressed.

Bel's gaze was drawn to Tate, who was walking towards her, the smoulder on his face already tripping her heart rate and drawing out an embarrassingly sappy smile.

'Oh, geez,' she heard Emma whisper, and she sent back a harshly whispered, 'Behave!'

'Tate, this is my friend, Emma. Emma, Tate.'

'Hi *Tate*,' Emma said, using her secretary-of-the-progress-committee voice. 'I've heard *all* about you.'

'All good things, I hope?' he said, sending her a grin. Bel took secret delight that his smile seemed to catch Emma a little off guard, judging by the quick clearing of her throat she needed to do all of a sudden.

'Absolutely,' Emma assured him.

'I was hoping I could borrow Bel for a little while, so she could show me around town?'

'Sure, no problem.'

Bel sent her friend a quick look, silently asking if she was sure, and was relieved not to find any hidden irritation. There was no such thing with Emma, anyway—you never had to guess if you were in trouble.

'I'm going to buy popcorn and head over to the jumping castle to watch my husband try to wrangle our wayward children.'

'I'm going to find the others,' Larkin announced. 'Bel, you take care of Tate for me,' she said with a wave and, behind his back, a wink.

Eight

'So,' Bel said once they were alone. 'Here we are.'

'Here we are.'

'You've come on a great day for exploring Wessex. It's normally not this busy,' she said.

'I know. I remember from when I drove through here the other day. This is a vast improvement.'

Bel felt a moment of discomfort as she recalled that first day. It was a blessing, really, that he didn't remember her.

'This is the pub,' she said, deciding she may as well jump into tour-guide mode. 'We have the Chinese restaurant across the road and, just outside of town, we have the truck stop, which actually does a decent burger.'

'Ah, yes. The Big Burger.' Tate nodded wisely.

'Yes. That's the one. The grocery store,' Bel continued as they strolled down the street. 'The bakery and chemist.

That used to be the newsagent, but it closed down, which is why we now sell lottery and scratchies at the general store.'

'We?' he asked.

'Uh . . . as a collective, I mean.' It wasn't that she didn't want him to know they'd already met; it was just that since it hadn't come up before, it coming up now would be awkward.

'Why do you still live here, Bel?' he asked after a few beats of silence.

The question took her by surprise. 'I don't know. It's home, I suppose. The only one I remember.'

'Don't you want to go out and explore the world?'

Bel moved her shoulders slightly. 'Well, yes. I guess. I keep meaning to do it, and it just hasn't happened. I mean, I was all set to leave town when I was younger, but then Gran got sick. I guess it kind of stretched out longer than I originally thought it would.'

'But there's nothing stopping you leaving now?' he asked, glancing across at her.

'I guess not,' she said.

'So why don't you?'

She considered the question before answering. 'I don't really have anywhere to go.'

'Go anywhere.'

'Oh sure,' she said with a chuckle, then looked at his face and sobered. 'I'm not like Larkin. My side of the family doesn't come from money. I don't have rich parents to pay for a holiday.'

'I wasn't talking about a holiday. Study or get a job somewhere in a field you've always been interested in. Go out and experience another city.'

She shook her head quickly, wondering why, when Dean had questioned her the other day about the same thing, it had annoyed her. Yet now, when Tate asked, she found she wasn't irritated at all. 'It's not as easy as just deciding to leave.'

'It's exactly as easy as that. You have to make the decision and then the rest will all fall into place.'

Inwardly, she scoffed at his oversimplified advice. He came from money. They all did. They had no idea how most people lived when there was no trust fund to draw from. Like she could click her fingers and get a job and find a house.

'You should think about it.'

Bel sent him a noncommittal smile and they walked on. A group of boys rode past on skateboards, artfully dodging a few pedestrians ahead of them, but Tate instantly pulled her towards him, holding her firmly against his side as the boys went past in a blur of colour. After they'd gone, he kept his arm around her and Bel thought that if her heart continued to beat so erratically, it might actually burst from her chest.

'You said you worked for a mining company. Is the company itself based in Perth?' she asked as a way to distract herself from the warmth of his arm against her waist.

'It's actually up in the Pilbara, a couple hundred kilometres from Port Hedland.'

'Do you spend much time onsite?'

'I do have to go out there fairly often. But my apartment is in the centre of Perth, right on the river.'

'That sounds nice.'

'It is, although I don't get as much time there as I'd like.'

'That's a shame.'

They walked on in silence, listening to the country music blasting from a set of loudspeakers and the chatter of the people strolling around them.

'You should plan a trip over sometime. I can show you around.'

Bel looked across at him, surprised by the offer, but even more surprised at the fact she didn't automatically dismiss the idea. *That's . . . odd.* 'Everything seems remarkably on track for the wedding day,' she said, changing the conversation to avoid further analysis.

'It should be,' he said. 'They've hired one of the best wedding planners in the business.'

Ah yes. Gisele, a name spoken in hushed, reverent tones for months.

'Hungry?' he asked as they passed by a caravan that was producing a mouthwatering aroma of barbecued onions and meat.

'Starving.'

Tate ordered their food, then they found a spot to sit on a bench beneath one of the many trees planted in the centre of the main street, which was now closed to traffic and made the perfect impromptu picnic spot.

'Tell me about Bel Buckley,' Tate said as they ate, sitting side by side.

'Not much to tell. I'm pretty dull.'

'I doubt that.' He grinned. 'Larkin told me bits and pieces.'

'Oh? Like what?'

'That your parents died when you were young, and you were raised by your grandparents. That you live in your gran's house and that she's tried to get you to move to the city but you seem stuck out here.'

'I wouldn't say I was stuck,' Bel said, and again wondered why she didn't feel the same outrage at Tate's comments that she'd felt at Dean's. Maybe Dean bringing it up had hit a little too close to home. When he'd known her, her dreams for the future had been very different to what she'd chosen.

'You must get bored, though? I mean, what do you do all day? Surely if you like to shop and go out, it would be easier closer to the city?'

'I don't really need to go shopping and spend all day lunching with friends. I'm not like Larkin and the others.'

'No, I can see that. I like that about you. The whole socialite thing gets old after a while. I prefer someone with a bit of substance.' He paused. 'You're different to anyone else I've ever met, and I can't pinpoint the reason.'

That would be because you've never associated with the working class? That snarky little voice inside Bel's head was certainly vocal today. She squashed it back down. It wasn't his fault he came from the same kind of wealth and private school background as her cousin. Although she wondered at his open dismissal of the women he would most likely normally associate with.

At some point, they'd moved closer together and she could feel the solid length of his thigh against her own, which was very distracting—as was whatever cologne he was wearing. She resisted the urge to lean in and sniff his neck.

'The movie should be starting soon,' Bel said, searching for something to take her mind off the fact she could almost feel her skin burning from the contact.

'Actually, I was thinking it would be nice to find some place a little quieter . . . maybe you could invite me back to your place?'

Bel swallowed. Her place? Alone, with Tate? A roar of desire rushed through her, almost drowning out the noise around them. Her heart rate kicked up a notch as she pictured them sitting together on the lounge, just the two of them, with no distractions. Her gaze dropped to his hands and she imagined them holding her face as he leaned in and kissed her deeply. Her lips and skin tingled at the thought.

'Ladies and gentlemen!' the loudspeaker suddenly announced, making Bel jump. 'Vote counting has now concluded and the winning sculpture will be announced in front of the pub. Please make your way over.'

'Wow, that was fast,' Bel murmured. 'Come on, I don't want to miss it.'

'Okay,' Tate said with good-humoured resignation.

The crowd that gathered filled both sides of the main road and there was a palpable hum of curiosity in the air. Bel spotted Bob Baxter standing close to the front of the pub, wearing a jovial grin as he shook hands with people around him. Bel had never liked the man. There had been rumours circulating for years about some of his dodgier dealings and there had always been something insincere about the way he smiled, something she'd never really trusted.

He was a self-made man, having built his truck stop up into a very successful business, and he'd grown his empire with purchases of fuel stations across the Central West as well as his own transport business. In the early years, he'd tried to bully the Dwyers into selling him their business too. When that hadn't worked, he'd tried to lure their customers away by lowering his fuel to ridiculous prices the small business hadn't a hope of matching. But the people of Wessex had not abandoned Dwyers'. It was part of the local fabric, an icon of the town, and it suited locals to buy fuel in the centre of town instead of driving the kilometre or so out to Baxter's. So Dwyers' had survived. Bel suspected it was something that still irked Bob to this day.

Betty Miller made her way through the pub doorway and out to the microphone that had been set up on the footpath, tapping it and setting off a high-pitched squeal that had everyone wincing.

'It has been my great pleasure to oversee this historic event. Putting Wessex on the tourism map has been a dream myself and the progress committee have shared for many decades. With the commencement of this latest project, not only will we provide some local jobs but we will also open up our little town to the rest of the country and beyond, bringing greater prosperity to us all. Without further ado, I am happy to announce the statue with the most votes, which will become our town's mascot, is . . . Elvis Peckley!'

The gathered crowd cheered, and Bel joined in. Now the festival really had something to really celebrate. For all Betty's dramatic flair, she was right about one thing—Wessex needed a tourism boost before it turned into a ghost town. If they had to pin all their hopes on a statue, Bel was glad it was something like a historical rooster instead of a commercialised giant burger that would only benefit one person; the person who was storming towards the microphone looking anything but jovial.

'This is ridiculous!' Bob announced. 'I demand a recount—and an impartial overseer.'

'Impartial?' Betty exclaimed indignantly. 'Are you insinuating, Robert Baxter, that I was somehow biased?'

'Everyone knows which way the progress committee wanted this vote to go.'

'How dare you!' Betty gasped, reminding Bel of an angry chook as she seemed to puff up to double her size.

'Wow . . . this is kind of intense,' Tate said quietly.

'We should have grabbed some of that popcorn on our way over,' Bel whispered back.

'I'm officially calling for a recount,' Bob repeated, leaning closer to grab the microphone.

Emma appeared at Bel's elbow and they swapped incredulous looks. 'Can he even do that?' Bel asked.

'I don't know. I'm fairly sure there was a "voting decision is final" clause, but I'm not sure about asking for a recount.'

Pandemonium broke out as Betty attempted to wrestle the microphone from Bob's grip, causing it to squeal loudly again and eliciting a group moan as the audience covered their ears.

Somewhere along the line, the Rotary president, Sid Buchanan, had situated himself in between the warring parties and was now attempting to broker a truce, taking control of the microphone and turning it off, thus ending the background commentary, and choosing instead to raise his voice to announce that they would take a short break to sort things out.

'The movie's about to start, we'd better get over there,' Emma said, turning to walk towards the park across the street.

Bel felt Tate's hand slip into hers and she looked down at their joined fingers, feeling that previous rush return.

'You coming, Bel?' Emma asked, turning around.

'Uh . . . actually,' Bel said, reluctantly dragging her gaze from Tate's to look at her friend. 'I think we're going to head off.'

Emma blinked. 'Oh. Okay. Are you sure? You always loved movie night. The kids are looking forward to it.'

'Yeah, I know, but I . . .' She glanced over at Tate briefly. 'Tell the kids I'm sorry. I'll come out and bring them doughnuts after school.'

'Okay. If you're sure . . .'

What was Emma's problem? She should be happy that Bel was going to be hanging out with a man. It's what she'd been trying to push her into for years. And why would she use her children as a guilt measure? That was plain unnecessary.

'Everything okay?' Tate asked as Bel watched Emma go.

'Yeah. Everything's fine. My car's over this way.'

Tate slid his arm around her waist and Bel's previous annoyance was forgotten as butterflies flared to life inside her. A giddy sensation filled her head.

When they pulled up in her driveway a few minutes later, the silence in the car was heavy. She turned off the ignition and they sat together in the growing darkness.

'Here we are,' she said, turning towards Tate and trying for a cheerful tone to cover the nervousness that was rapidly trying to overtake her.

A loud rumble of thunder echoed outside. Then the heavens opened and rain began pelting the roof of the car. Before Bel could even register this sudden turn of events, Tate leaned across, his lips touched hers, and she forgot all about the storm outside. She was filled with a heady mix of surprise, lust and the urgent need to move closer.

She wasn't sure how long they kissed for—it could have been a second or an eternity—but as soon as he eased away, she fought the urge to whimper.

'I don't remember making out in a car being this uncomfortable, do you?' he asked.

Bel resisted the urge to snort. As though she had any experience making out in a car . . . or anywhere else, for that matter. Her teenage years had clearly not been as exciting as his. She'd lost her virginity to Tubby Smithfield at his brother's twenty-first birthday party behind his family's old shearing shed. The only notable thing about it was that Tubby was so drunk, he barely remembered it. She, on the other hand, had spent years trying to forget.

'You okay to risk making a run for it?' he asked.

'Sure,' she said. She could do with a splash of cold water to help quelch the fire-like sensation that was burning her from the inside out. Launching out of the car, she yelped, racing for the protection of the front porch. Brushing her dripping hair out of her face, she unlocked the front door, frantically trying to recall how tidy the house was. Thankfully, as she shook off droplets of water and scanned the vicinity, she discovered it was in reasonably good order.

'I'll get us some towels,' she said, heading for the bathroom where she quickly patted her face dry and assessed the damage to her hair and make-up before returning to hand him a clean towel.

'This isn't how I imagined your house,' he said as he roughly ran the towel over his face and head.

Really? You imagined my house?

'It's a lot more homely than I was picturing.'

'Is that a bad thing?' she asked nervously.

'Not at all. It just surprised me. You journal?' he asked, bending down to pick up the glossy hardback book in shades of pink and sparkly gold foil.

'I . . . uh, yeah. A little bit.'

'I didn't imagine you doing that either,' he said, turning the book over in his hand. She watched nervously, remembering she'd slipped her soulmate list inside for safekeeping.

'Can I get you a drink? Or a coffee?' she asked, feeling a rush of relief as he replaced the book on the table. Tate straightened then closed the gap between them, kissing her.

I can't believe this is really happening. How many nights had she sat curled up on the lounge, reading a scene from a book and longing for it to be happening to her . . . and now it finally was.

'God, that day we walked in on the dress fittings, and I saw you—'

Bel pulled back and looked at him. 'You *saw* me?'

His soft chuckle distracted her enough to let him continue. 'I saw . . . *most* of you,' he corrected. 'I couldn't stop thinking about you.'

Bel groaned. 'I feel like such an idiot.'

'You shouldn't. That was one of the hottest things I've seen in a long time.'

'What?'

'Your legs,' he said, closing his eyes as though to bring forth the image, 'in those heels, with that sexy backside wiggling about. That was something.' He opened his eyes again and found hers with a lethal intensity that made her stomach tumble. 'You're like no one I've ever met.'

She could only imagine. He was used to dating sophisticated, classy women. But the way his voice had gone all rough and gravelly was doing the most amazing things to her body. The books were right. Who knew? She'd always suspected the descriptions of love scenes were pure fantasy, but here she was, swooning and preening like a simpering heroine.

He leaned in and kissed her more deeply, and all humiliation ebbed away on a rush of hungry need.

Surely this was all part of some amazing dream and she was going to wake up on the lounge with her book across her face. And yet, the sensations she was experiencing were all so very . . . real. *Oh God, if this is a dream, please, please, please don't let me wake up.* A long, low moan escaped her as he moved his lips down the column of her throat and lower, sending a quiver of wanton abandonment throughout her body.

Who even *was* she right now?

Nine

The next morning, Bel frowned at the persistent ringing that had woken her from a deep sleep. She fumbled on the bedside table, trying to locate the phone, and mumbled a groggy, 'Hello?'

'Are you still in bed?' Emma asked.

'Yes. Why? What time is it?' Bel rolled over and sat up, peering at the phone screen.

'It's nine o'clock!'

Bel scrambled further up in the bed. It couldn't be. She never slept in. She started work at six and could never manage to get her body clock to sleep longer on days she wasn't working which, in fairness, was only every second Sunday.

Then again, it wasn't every night that she had unbelievable sex with a drop-dead gorgeous specimen of manhood like Tate

McBride. She glanced regretfully at the empty side of the bed. He'd reluctantly left a few hours ago because the groomsmen had an early start, spending the day in Toormanlee.

'I'll be there in five. I've got coffee.'

Bel only had time to pull on some clothes and run a brush through her hair before Emma was knocking on the front door.

'Are you coming down with something?' Emma asked, heading to the lounge room.

Bel almost ran into Emma as she abruptly stopped, and it took a moment for Bel to work out what her friend was staring at.

Crap. She hadn't had time to clean up. Bel's gaze fell to the wet towels along with the pile of discarded clothing—or, more to the point, her discarded clothing, left where it'd been flung as Tate had peeled it off.

Bel hastily began gathering it up, snatching her bra from where it had landed on the table lamp, and dumped everything in the laundry. As she re-entered the room, she found Emma watching her with a strange expression.

'So, I take it you had a good night?'

Bel straightened her shoulders and reminded herself she was a fully grown adult and not under interrogation from a parent. 'I did, actually.'

Emma put her hands on her hips and tilted her head slightly. 'It's not that I'm not thrilled you've found this guy. I'm just . . . a little bit concerned that maybe you're jumping into something you may not be ready for. I mean, he's only here for a few days. Are you sure this is such a great idea?'

'I thought you'd be happy, not all judgy.'

'I'm not judging you,' Emma said, sounding a little hurt. 'I'm worried that you're setting yourself up for heartache.'

'You're the one who's always trying to get me to go out with someone.'

'I was thinking more in terms of someone local, someone who isn't going to leave in a few days and you'll never see again.'

Emma's words hit a little too close to home. Bel didn't want to think about that part.

'I'm glad you're having fun, really I am,' Emma said gently, 'but . . . be careful. These people aren't like us. They think coming to a place like Wessex is *quaint* and *interesting*,' she said, rolling her eyes, 'but they don't look back when they leave. They're all eager to get back to civilisation and wash off the country stink. A guy like that won't stay in a place like this.'

'Maybe I don't want him to stay,' Bel snapped. The truth hurt, more than she was ready or willing to admit. She didn't want to lose this brief tingle of happiness.

'Then enjoy the fling,' Emma said. 'But don't start feeling things for him that aren't real.'

Bel reached out for the coffee cup and sat down, eager to push away the uncomfortable feeling of reality beginning to settle in the pit of her stomach. 'The rain put a bit of a damper on the movie night, I'd imagine,' she said to change the topic.

'Quite literally,' Emma agreed, taking a seat opposite. 'We had to make a run for the car. Ended up drenched. The kids thought it was great. Which reminds me, Dean has your chair. He said he'd drop it around. I think he was pretty disappointed that you didn't come back.'

'Why?'

'Because he was obviously there to see you.'

'No, he wasn't.'

'Bel, seriously? A good-looking, single guy would choose to sit in a park with a bunch of kids instead of hanging out at the pub, where every other male in town preferred to be?'

'Craig wasn't at the pub,' Bel pointed out.

'Craig is a married man who didn't have a choice,' Emma corrected.

'Dean was probably feeling sorry for his mate who has a terrifying wife who doesn't let him go to the pub,' Bel joked.

'Craig can go to the pub whenever he likes, so long as he doesn't expect sex any time afterwards. If I'm at home taking care of children all day, we both go out or we both stay home.'

'Fair enough,' Bel said easily. She didn't disagree, and she knew Craig valued his time with his family when he came home. He was not one of those men who felt he needed to escape the wife and kids to drink with his mates. He genuinely missed them when he was away.

'In all seriousness, Bel, I do think Dean was disappointed.'

'Well, it wasn't like I was there with him. I didn't know he was going to be sitting with us.'

'He said he thought you guys agreed to meet up when he dropped by your place yesterday.'

'He asked if I was going and I said I was. It wasn't a date.'

'Maybe he figured it could be?'

'Well, it wasn't and I'm free to choose whoever the hell I want to choose to spend my time with.'

'Okay, don't shoot the messenger,' Emma said, holding up a hand. 'I'm just saying, he obviously thought he'd be seeing you.'

Great, so now she felt bad about a stupid miscommunication. 'I don't know how many times I have to tell you. I'm not interested in Dean Preston.'

Emma cocked her head to the side. 'I don't get it. He's perfect for you.'

'I have my list of perfect-for-me and it brought Tate here.'

'Okay, fine. You do you. Maybe after Mr Perfect goes home, you'll be able to think more clearly.'

Bel didn't want to think about when this thing would be over between her and Tate. She didn't want to lose the giddy, bubbly excitement that filled her whenever she thought about him.

'So,' Emma said, sitting her cup down. 'I'm sorry I brought up all the other stuff and rained on your parade. I should have led with this: tell me everything. I want all the details.'

The earlier weirdness between them dissolved and they were back to normal, with Emma being her most outrageous, no-boundaries self, and Bel found herself giving a somewhat censored version of her night. They ended up giggling and chatting for the rest of the morning.

After Emma left, Bel couldn't help thinking about her friend's warning as she cleaned the house. What would happen when Tate left? Sure, it was easy enough to say she was happy with whatever this thing was. People had holiday flings and one-night stands all the time. But she never had. She had no idea how she was going to feel after this ended.

The thought dampened her earlier excitement.

Over the next few days, Bel successfully managed to block Emma's warning from her mind. Things were even better than she'd ever imagined. She and Tate couldn't keep their hands off each other. It was madness. They snuck away at any opportunity. While part of her felt extremely naughty, another part kept reminding her that this thing was only temporary and it was going to come to an end all too soon. That thought always sobered her, but not enough to stop. Tate was like a drug she couldn't get enough of.

Not for the first time since the official countdown had begun, Bel was impressed by the military precision of the whole event. Everything had been meticulously marked off from what Bel could only imagine was a daunting-looking spreadsheet. Gisele's assistant had arrived, and if Bel had thought the wedding planner was already in action, it was nothing compared with the level of intensity of the final few days. Maya, the almost identical clone of Gisele, spent the day following her boss around with her eyes glued to a tablet and her ear attached to a phone.

The logistics of the whole thing were quite mind-blowing. Wessex had only the one motel and the pub for accommodation, and that had all been booked out by the groom's family. The majority of the remaining guest list was being brought in from Toormanlee by a small fleet of buses. They were double-checking with the bus company responsible for delivering the two hundred-odd guests. Bel could only wonder at the additional cost that would be. It was practical, though, considering the distance, plus the road conditions were not exactly ideal for the luxury vehicles she imagined that crowd would be using. The local roadside assistance company would have a field day pulling Ferraris out of potholes left, right and centre.

The rather fancy-schmancy new brick-and-stone building with huge glass windows her aunt and uncle had commissioned for the reception, known as the Orangery, as Bel was primly corrected when she'd accidentally called it a conservatory, was the current hive of activity. There'd been myriad delays with the project, so much so that her uncle had often referred to the whole project as cursed. It hadn't helped that Larkin had only informed him of the need to have the replica seventeenth-century building built for her reception a mere four months out from the wedding, after she'd been inspired by multiple episodes of *Escape to the Chateau*.

Builders had been working at warp-speed to have it finished and, despite Bel's misgivings, they'd managed to do it, with just a few minor finishing touches to go inside. Which was lucky because the rain hadn't really stopped and would have been a hindrance if they were still working on the outside.

The manicured lawn between the house and the Orangery was looking slightly waterlogged but her uncle had assured everyone only the evening before that the groundskeepers had designed the garden with ample drainage. It would be good as gold for the wedding day.

Bel could get used to being on holidays. No early starts, no long, boring days and plenty of free time to be with Tate. The continuing rain had messed with the wedding festivities, with planned outings like mini golf and tennis cancelled, which gave Bel and Tate more time alone. She'd even taken up her cousin's offer of staying at Glentoberon, since it made it easier to see more of him.

Everything was working out perfectly.

Ten

Bel was walking past the kitchen when the door to a cupboard under the back stairs opened and she was grabbed, one hand around her waist, the other across her mouth. She didn't have time to scream, and when she did, it only came out as a muffled noise as she struggled against being dragged into the small, dark storage area. It took only a fraction of a second to realise who her abductor was—even in the dark, there was no mistaking that scent—and the fight left her, replaced by a far more powerful emotion: lust.

'I couldn't resist. I saw you coming and I found this little hidey-hole the other day. Ever since, I've been thinking about you and me in here.'

'But the kitchen is just there,' she protested weakly as he began kissing the side of her neck.

'So we'll have to be quiet,' he said in a low voice that did dangerous things to her pulse.

His fingers were already deftly unbuttoning her shirt and moving to her jeans. Within moments, he was skilfully caressing her and driving her to the brink of insanity. Never in her wildest imagination—and she had a pretty wild imagination—had she ever thought she would be having mind-blowing sex in her aunt's storage room with someone like Tate McBride. This didn't happen in real life . . . only it *was* happening. She couldn't believe her world had taken such a huge turn.

As she collapsed against his chest, both of them breathing heavily, she heard voices closing in and instantly jerked upright in his embrace.

'Honestly, Stanley, do you have to wear those dirty pants inside? You're supposed to be hosting your daughter's wedding and you come in here dressed like some . . . hobo!'

'I've been out moving sheep. What do you want me to wear, a tuxedo?'

'You have employees for that.'

'Well, not enough, when I discover most of them have been roped into unloading supplies for this bloody wedding instead of the job they're actually paid to do,' Bel's uncle grumbled.

Bel clutched Tate's forearms tightly. What if one of them opened the door? Oh, dear God, she would die of absolute humiliation.

She felt Tate chuckle silently and would have hit him if she could risk moving. Finally, the voices began to fade as her uncle, clearly having had enough of his wife's chastising, decided to take himself off. But Aunt Lois was apparently not done and was close on his heels.

'You can let go now,' Tate murmured. Bel released her grip on his arm, blindly searching for her clothes and quickly pulling them on. 'Bel, calm down. It's fine.'

'We could have been caught.' Now that he wasn't kissing her and she was able to think straight, the implications of what could have happened began to sink in.

'But we weren't,' he threw back calmly. 'Come on, admit it. Risky sex is hot.'

'It's nerve-racking,' she said. But, to her astonishment, she realised he was right. She'd been completely into it. This man was bringing out all kinds of strange revelations in her, and she liked it. 'Larkin will come looking for me if I don't get back.'

'Okay. I'll see you later,' he said, kissing her once more.

Bel slipped into the downstairs washroom and reviewed herself in the mirror. Her eyes were bright and her cheeks were pink, and she looked exactly like someone who'd just done something naughty—guilty and a little bit smug. She quickly splashed her face with water and smoothed down her hair before shaking her head. This was . . . well, she wasn't sure *what* this was, but whatever it was, she'd never been happier.

Bel tried to search for something to distract herself in order to endure another hour of pre-wedding beauty. The assembled bridesmaids were in the home gym, which had been converted into a day spa for the occasion, reclining in chairs and currently sporting god-awful black charcoal facial masks. It looked like they were wearing a weird diving suit hood, with holes cut out for their eyes and nostrils. Bel would much rather be spending the time with Tate. She brought up an image of him standing by the window, naked, to take her mind off the boredom.

'You're very quiet, Bel,' Gigi said, startling her. Being spoken directly to by any of the other bridesmaids was unusual enough, but having them notice something like that instantly put her on guard.

'I'm just enjoying the spa . . . thingy,' she said, hoping she sounded relaxed and appreciative.

'I guess you're probably in need of a rest.'

'What do you mean?' Bel tried to act casual, hoping the mask would help.

'I couldn't help but notice that you've been disappearing at odd times, sneaking in and out of your room at night. You seem . . . *happy*,' she said.

'I'm usually happy,' Bel replied weakly. Sweat prickled along her hairline and she was starting to feel claustrophobic. *How long do these stupid masks have to stay on for?*

'Not *happy*, happy. This is . . .' the woman sent her a sly grin, '. . . like *good sex* happy. Bel, have you met someone?'

Oh Lord. Here we go. It wasn't like it was a big deal. She knew for a fact Niki and Oliver had a thing. She'd been telling them all about it for the last two days.

Larkin tilted her head slightly and looked mildly annoyed.

'Oh, spill the beans already,' Kelly moaned. Bel glanced over in surprise at the woman lying on her back with her eyes closed. Kelly gave a long-suffering sigh. 'Larkin, your innocent little cousin has been getting jiggy with Tate.'

Getting jiggy? Is that seriously still a thing?

'Oh, that?' Larkin said, waving a hand like she was shooing away a bothersome fly. 'Isn't it great?'

Bel's gaze snapped across to her cousin's. She'd known? Not that they'd been keeping it a secret, but they'd tried not to interrupt the wedding-related program or risk stressing the bride.

Niki swapped grins with the other women. 'You think small towns are bad for gossip? You've clearly underestimated the ability of this group to sniff out a juicy scandal. Besides, we knew something was up when Gigi's charms failed to bag Tate. That was a dead giveaway.'

'Like I was really trying,' Gigi sniffed, taking a sudden interest in inspecting her nails.

'Meow,' Niki said.

'At least I'm not taking someone else's sloppy seconds.'

'What's that supposed to mean?' Niki shot upright in her chair.

Bel's gaze switched from one side of the room to the other like she was a spectator at a tennis match. She had no idea what was going on but she had a sneaky suspicion this was about to get more than a little interesting.

Lisa discreetly leaned over and turned up the volume on the stereo, and the sounds of pan flutes and windchimes grew louder. 'How about I lead a meditation session?' she suggested cheerfully.

'I want to know what you're implying, Gigi,' Niki said, ignoring Lisa's attempt to defuse the situation.

'Oh, come on. Like you don't suspect already,' Gigi said, rolling her eyes.

'Suspect what?' Niki demanded, sounding on the verge of hysteria.

'I've saved a heap of motivational quotes that I wanted to share,' Lisa tried again, frantically scrolling through her phone's images.

'Oliver is a manwhore.'

Niki's mouth dropped open and the room went silent.

'Everyone, let's take a deep breath in—'

'Shut up, Lisa!' Niki, Gigi and Kelly yelled in unison.

'Okay, that's enough. You're all ruining my vibe,' Larkin said, standing up. But even the queen bee couldn't douse this scrub fire.

'He's playing you,' Gigi said, leaning forward, 'and you're so desperate to keep his attention that you're ignoring what you know.'

'I am *not* desperate.'

'No, you aren't. You're above that crap, but for some reason, when it comes to Oliver, you've forgotten who you *are*.'

'We have something special. He said so.'

'Isn't that the same thing he told you, Kelly?' Gigi asked the woman who was now turning pale under her expensive salon tan.

A confused look replaced Niki's earlier indignation. 'What?' She swapped her glance from Gigi to Kelly. 'What's she talking about?'

Kelly simply shook her head, gaping like a fish out of water.

'God, the *drama*,' Gigi groaned. 'Oliver slept with Kelly two days before we got here. And the day before that, he slept with some Greek tycoon's daughter at the yacht club. He tried to get *me* into bed on the first day here and he even boasted to the other guys that he was going to bag Little Miss Wessex here, only now it's pretty obvious that Tate decided to stake a claim. Well played, by the way, Bel. That wide-eyed innocent look gets 'em every time.'

Bel was too shocked by the barrage of revelations to immediately register the backhanded compliment Gigi had thrown at her. And clearly Niki had stopped listening at some earlier point, focusing only on what had affected her.

'You're lying. You're just jealous that he chose me. Kelly's not even his type.'

Kelly snapped out of her stupor. 'What's *that* supposed to mean?'

'It's not your fault, Kelly. He only goes for old family wealth. Your father's too new money.'

'Are you serious right now?' Kelly blustered.

'Are you saying Gigi's telling the truth?' Niki asked, kinking an eyebrow.

'As a matter of fact, yes. It's true. So there. He doesn't care about old money.'

Bel felt like she'd been sucked into some reality show nightmare. *How the hell do you stop this ride?*

'I can't believe you would try and steal my boyfriend!' Niki yelled.

'He was my boyfriend before he was yours!'

'Just stop!' Lisa yelled over the top of the ruckus. 'This is hurting my chakra.'

Bel glanced towards her cousin, who was standing with her eyes shut and seemingly trying to remain calm. 'Enough!'

This time, everyone stopped. 'I am not having my wedding day ruined by backstabbing and name-calling. Gigi, stop being a bitch. I know that's going to be difficult, but *try*, okay? Niki, I'm sorry you found out about Oliver and Kelly this way, but Gigi was right, you are lowering your worth by being with that creep. The only reason he's in the wedding party is because he's Tristan's cousin. You can both do better than him, so just stop it. As for Bel and Tate, I was the one who set them up, so if anyone has anything snarky to say, you'd better be okay saying it in front of me. Am I clear?'

A murmured sea of 'Yes, Larkin's followed.

'Right. Now, I want you all to make up. No one and nothing is going to ruin my wedding day.'

'I'm sorry, Niki,' Gigi said. 'I just want you to be the powerhouse boss-woman you were destined to be, babe. You can do some much better than Oliver. You both can,' she added, turning to include Kelly.

The women stared silently at one another, then all three embraced in a group hug, so artfully mindful of their wet nail polish and face masks that it was more like an almost-hug.

With all parties somewhat mollified and order restored, Lisa got to lead them in a guided meditation. Bel was grateful for this, if only to be able to close her eyes and wish herself far, far away from all this insanity.

'So we don't have to sneak around anymore?' Tate asked as they lay in her bed later that night.

'Nope. Apparently, we were the worst kept secret this side of the Blue Mountains.'

For a moment he was silent and Bel turned her head to look up at him. 'What's wrong?'

'Nothing,' he dismissed, but the continued silence warned her it was definitely something.

'Is it a problem that people now know?'

'Not a problem as such,' he said. 'I just prefer my privacy.'

Well, she hadn't exactly wanted to take out an announcement in the local paper either, but they were all grown-ups and clearly the others had no qualms about sleeping around, so there was hardly going to be any scandal.

Bel was distracted when he ran his fingers along her arm, sending a shiver of delight across her skin, and decided to let his unusual response go.

'There was something else I found kind of interesting. I heard that Oliver told you he was interested in me. Is that true?' She felt awkward for asking, but Gigi's announcement had stirred her curiosity.

His touch paused. 'Oliver has a tendency to shoot off his mouth.'

'So he did?'

'Until he didn't,' Tate said.

'What does that mean?'

'I took him aside and I told him you were off limits.'

'This was before the movie night?'

'Yep.'

'But we weren't even together at that point.'

'But I knew we were going to be,' he said, then looked down at her. 'Are you saying you wanted Oliver to hit on you?'

'Of course not.' She frowned. 'I was surprised, that's all. I've never had anyone be . . . territorial over me.'

'Is that what I was being?' he chuckled.

'That's how it seems.'

'I know what I want, and I don't let anyone else take what's mine.'

Bel wasn't sure what to say to that. A small part of her questioned if this could possibly be something she should protest against. She wasn't property, and she didn't belong to anyone. Yet, lying here with him, feeling the warm heat of his skin against her own, the part of her that had conjured up this protective, confident man to slay dragons and take care of her was purring in delight.

Eleven

Bel woke the morning of the wedding wondering what had roused her. *It couldn't be.* Her eyes shot open. *Oh no . . .* The rain was more torrential than ever.

She considered pulling the covers back over her head, but there was really no point. Sooner or later, she was going to have to deal with Larkin, who was not going to handle this meteorological road bump at all well. Deciding she was *not* going to deal with this uncaffeinated, Bel gave a fatalistic sigh, pulled on a pair of jeans and a T-shirt then headed downstairs in search of a coffee.

It was still early and there were no signs of anyone else being up, which was a small relief. She didn't feel up to morning small talk. Not that that was going to be on anyone's agenda today. Already she could picture the entire household walking on eggshells around Larkin and Lois. Gisele would be earning her exorbitant salary today.

A movement outside the large kitchen window caught Bel's eye and she spotted a figure across the yard, walking over from the shearers' quarters the men had been staying in. Tate. Her stomach did a curious little flutter as she thought back to the previous night and an almost shy smile crossed her face. She still found it hard to believe this man was somehow attracted to her . . . her! She felt a flutter of panic as he jogged across the yard to the back door, her anxiety laced with a dash of terror at being found out. She wasn't part of this life, no matter how Larkin dressed her up, and, sooner or later, Tate would work that out. A small wave of sadness washed over her as reality hit: time was running out. Tomorrow, everyone would start leaving and Cinderella would have to return to Dwyers' and life would go back to the way it had been B.T.—Before Tate.

'Good morning,' Bel said, forcing away the sadness that threatened to overshadow her mood.

'It is now,' he said. He took off his coat, shook it out then slipped his arms around her waist. They shared a long, unhurried kiss. How was she supposed to give this up?

The sound of another heavy downpour interrupted the moment.

'Oh no,' she whispered as her gaze turned to the windows. A white curtain of rain blocked the view of the cottage outside. There was no deluding themselves that this was going to miraculously clear up in time for the wedding. Even if it did, the manicured lawn was already under ankle-deep water.

'Oh crap,' Tate said softly.

'Larkin is going to—' Bel started before she was interrupted by a loud scream from inside the house, '—freak out.'

'Oh, well,' Tate mused. 'Lucky they finished the Orangery with a day to spare. Without that, it'd be a disaster.'

'This is a *fucking* disaster!' Larkin screamed a mere hour later when Stan came in to announce that the roof of the new Orangery had begun leaking and part of it had collapsed, throwing the back-up plans into chaos.

'What are we going to do?' Lois gasped, turning to the wedding planner with a distraught look.

For the first time since Bel had met her, Gisele looked oddly panicked, not the kind of thing you would hope to see in your wedding planner during a crisis. 'I just need a moment,' she said, touching her fingertips to her temple.

'We don't have a moment!' Larkin shrieked as she threw her hands in the air. 'We're expecting two hundred and fifty guests to start arriving within a few hours! You said the rain would stop!' she cried, turning on her father.

'We may have to consider postpon—' Stan started before being drowned out by both his wife and his daughter with their emphatic 'No!'

'We have to be practical about this,' he said, trying for a gentler tone. 'Where are we going to fit that many people at such short notice?'

'Uh, sorry to interrupt,' Henry said from the lounge, looking up from his phone, 'but about that. They've just announced road closures.' He winced. 'The road to here is one of them.'

'What? No! No, no, no,' Gisele uttered as she snatched the phone from Henry's hand and stared at the screen. 'Maya!'

'I'm here,' the assistant announced from two steps behind her boss. It was barely seven o'clock and the woman was already dressed in a pencil skirt and button-up blouse, tablet in hand and ready for action.

'Get me the bus company. There has to be another way.'

Bel chewed on the inside of her lip as she sat quietly on the other side of the room, next to Tate.

'Is there?' he asked.

'Not that a bus would be able to use. And even then, if the main roads are closed, any dirt track would most likely be under as well, or too boggy to use.'

'So we won't have any guests?' Larkin asked, frantically searching the faces around her. She burst into noisy tears.

There was a knock on the door and Tristan's muffled voice sounded on the other side. 'Can I come in?'

'No!' Gisele and Lois both yelled back, eyeing the door in alarm.

'It's bad luck!' Lois added.

'Oh, seriously, Mother!' Larkin said, wiping her eyes as she marched to the door. 'How much more bad luck can we have? I want to see my fiancé.'

'Oh, God,' Aunt Lois said in a tone that suggested her daughter had just opened the gates to hell.

'Is it just me or does this entire thing feel like it should be a reality show on prime-time TV?' Tate murmured close to Bel's ear, sending a trail of goosebumps down her arm.

'Right?' She shouldn't be wishing they could sneak back to her warm bed while her cousin was having a complete meltdown, but with Tate seated so close, her body was not listening to her brain.

Gigi and Niki appeared at the open door, model-gorgeous even as they were blinking and blurry-eyed, asking what had happened.

'It's raining,' Larkin wailed.

The two women turned their gazes to the windows before looking back at each other. 'My hair will never stay straightened in this!' Niki bleated.

Bel bit back a retort.

'All right. Listen up, people,' Gisele announced, clapping her hands to get everyone's attention. 'It does seem that all roads leading in and out of Glentoberon are currently closed and guests will be stranded in Toormanlee. However,' she said, raising her voice over the sudden outrage, 'we can get the groom's family here from Wessex, and there will be a number of local guests who should be able to make it. So while numbers are down significantly, we will at least be able to relocate the reception venue to the house, which makes everything achievable, given the limited time. But we will need all hands on deck.'

It was decided they would set up at the rear of the house, where the dining room opened up through large French doors. They would position the bridal table to take centre stage inside, and more tables and chairs could spill out onto the wide back verandah.

With a solid plan now in place and not a moment to lose, the whole house sprang into action.

The inside of the Orangery was a disaster zone, but thankfully most of the table decorations hadn't yet been set up. It was now a case of moving the tables and chairs out and redistributing the decorations with a little creative genius.

Throughout the morning, the rain continued to fall. Bel knew everyone was keeping an eye on the water levels, which were steadily on the rise.

She was walking past a gathered group of men when she heard her uncle delegating a number of jobs, which included taking the four-wheel drive to meet the guests who were being brought out from town by boat.

'I'll do that,' Tristan volunteered, opening the door of the vehicle. 'Uh . . .' he said, turning back to face Bel's uncle. 'Is there another car?'

'Not big enough to carry that many passengers or to handle the wet roads out there. Why?'

'I . . . uh . . . it's not automatic.'

'Well, of course it's not automatic,' Uncle Stan said impatiently. 'What? You can't drive a manual?'

Bel saw Tristan shuffle uncomfortably before giving a small shrug.

'Do *any* of you know how to drive?' Uncle Stan asked, incredulous.

Uncle Stan was being a tad harsh, Bel thought, feeling sorry for Tristan. He seemed genuinely deflated that he'd fallen short in his soon-to-be father-in-law's eyes.

'Well, we know how to *drive*,' Leo declared, sounding somewhat insulted by the question. 'But I haven't heard of anyone driving a manual lately. They're almost an extinct species.'

'Not around here, sonny,' Stan growled.

Why isn't Tate stepping forward? Bel frowned. Surely he could . . . her stomach dropped. This wasn't how it was supposed to play out. Jax would have instantly stepped forward. He drove Jeeps through the jungle and armoured vehicles through war zones. He'd even taken control of a helicopter when the pilot was shot!

Stop it. Tate isn't Jax. Jax isn't real.

'I don't have flamin' time to play courier as well as check on the livestock,' Uncle Stan muttered.

'I'll go, Uncle Stan,' Bel said.

She crossed to the big four-wheel drive and hoisted herself into the driver's seat.

'Well thank God someone around here is useful,' Stan muttered, turning away.

She avoided looking at any of the other men, not wanting to embarrass anyone and uncomfortably aware of Tate's gaze. But when she did risk a quick glance as she started the engine, he simply gave her a cheerful wave before heading back inside.

The rain was relentless, and by Bel's second trip, it was evident that the flood situation was worsening by the hour. The first trip, she'd made it almost to the edge of town. By the second run, she could barely make it fifteen minutes up the road.

She grabbed two umbrellas and climbed out of the cabin as she spotted the silver tinny moving towards her. As far as the eye could see was an ocean of water where paddocks had been only the day before. Her uncle and his workers had been out moving livestock and, seeing how fast the water was rising, it was lucky they'd done so. Animals would stand no chance out there alone.

The rain fell heavily and was loud on the umbrella she held over her head as she leaned down to help steady the boat for the bedraggled passengers who clambered to their feet, clutching plastic garment bags and suitcases, looking like refugees instead of the well-off socialites Bel knew they were. Tristan's parents had arrived in the first load and had been given a room at Glentoberon. This lot were his brothers and their wives. They were expecting two more boats with the celebrant, photographer and caterers any minute. How Gisele was making all this happen, God only knew, but Bel suspected the woman's talent for organisation would rival the most operationally experienced military quartermaster's.

'They're getting their money's worth out of you,' a familiar voice called. Bel looked up to find Dean, dressed in a bright orange rain jacket with 'SES' printed on the front, climbing out of the boat.

'Sorry?' she asked, tilting her head slightly.

'Bridesmaid *and* chauffeur? I would have thought you'd be busy getting your hair done or something. Where are all the men?'

'You think only men can come out in the rain and pick up passengers?' she quipped.

'Nope, just thought maybe there'd be enough of them hanging round and they might make themselves useful.'

'It's all hands on deck. Everyone else has been enlisted into relocating the reception.'

'I see. Well, I guess that's pretty important,' he said lightly, turning away to steady the boat.

'How's it in town?'

'Town's okay, only a few houses on the outskirts have minor flooding so far, but we're cut off. The roads in and out are going to be closed for a few days, depending on how much more rain we get.' He lifted a suitcase out and placed it on the bitumen. 'Oi!' he called as the last man got out of the boat and started hurrying towards the four-wheel drive. Dean nodded at the suitcase. 'No baggage porters here, mate.'

The man trudged back, mumbling an apology before picking up the case and jogging towards the vehicle again.

'They're a different breed, all right,' Dean muttered.

'Well, I better get them back to dry land,' Bel said, lifting her hand in farewell as he got back into the boat. She watched him wipe a hand across his face beneath the hood of the raincoat. It always humbled her how SES members volunteered their time and lives to help people, going out in the kind of weather most others took refuge from. It was heroic.

She tried not to think about Tate and the others back at Glentoberon, sitting around drinking hot chocolate. *That's not fair.* They were visitors. It wasn't as though they could put their hands up to do SES work. That involved training. She felt a twinge of something like disappointment then chastised herself. *Not everyone can be a hero.*

'Be careful out there,' she said. Something shifted on his face, a fleeting expression that she wasn't even sure how to describe. He looked . . . almost serious? Or taken aback? And then it was gone.

'Hope the wedding goes well. Stay dry.'

Back at the house, it was surprisingly calm, considering all the upheaval. Aunt Lois was in her element as Lady of the Manor, fussing about and making sure everyone was comfortable. There was plenty of food and drink flowing, and spirits seemed to be holding up remarkably well . . . although that could have something to do with the fact there was *a lot* of drink flowing.

When Gisele was satisfied she had everything mostly under control, Larkin and the bridesmaids were sent inside to get ready. Bel reluctantly traipsed up the staircase to endure make-up and hair.

Finally it was time to put on her gown. The soft fabric slid over her body and flowed like a dusty pink waterfall. Her long hair had been braided to one side and pinned in a messy low bun, with a few loosened tendrils to help soften the look. As Bel stared at her reflection, she found herself wondering. She was no longer the plain-Jane girl-next-door who worked at Dwyers'. She wasn't sure she ever would be again, even when she had to give up the glam squad and the Adonis-like lover. Who was this glamorous woman staring back at her, really?

With one final glance in the mirror, Bel took a deep breath and mentally prepared herself to head back into the fray.

On a normal wedding day, bridesmaid duties would involve the odd pep talk and bucketloads of reassurance. This bridesmaid gig, however, demanded a whole new level of dedication. The fact that it involved a natural disaster, a last-minute change of venue and around seventy-five per cent of the guest list being unable to attend made it well and truly above Bel's pay grade. This kind of thing should have come with a handbook, but it didn't, so everyone was fumbling their way through it as best they could.

After a few glasses of champagne, they'd finally managed to calm Larkin down enough to get her dressed and ready for photos. Larkin wasn't the first bride to have her wedding day sabotaged by rain and she certainly wouldn't be the last. At least she had a team of people working nonstop to ensure it would still be a dream wedding day.

As she and the other bridesmaids walked down the grand staircase and through a gorgeous archway of fresh flowers, Bel couldn't help but catch her breath at how beautifully everything had been transformed. Fairy lights were draped along the wrought-iron lacework of the front verandah posts, while bunches of freshly picked gum leaves and greenery hung from the roof beams above the foyer, interspersed with delicate glass tea light globes. The rustic French provincial theme looked just as stunning set against the timber and ironwork of the homestead building as it would have in the purpose-built Orangery.

Her gaze moved towards the men lined up in their black tuxedos at the side of the archway, pausing on the tallest, most handsome one as she neared them, before she veered to the opposite side of the arch. She'd always thought he was drop-dead handsome, but in a tux, Tate was downright lethal, like a real-life Jax Lexington. She felt his eyes on her and lifted her gaze. For a moment, her heart seemed to stop. Smitten was a word that she'd always heard her gran use, and for some reason it came to her then. She was smitten. Completely and utterly smitten.

The 'Bridal March' struck up and Bel reluctantly dragged her eyes from Tate's face to watch Larkin make her way down the staircase on the arm of her father. Bel's heart hitched a little at the sight of father and daughter. That was something she would never experience, walking down the aisle with her dad. Her mother would never be sitting at the front of the congregation, wiping a tear from the corner of her eye, and Gran wouldn't be sitting beside her, wearing that proud, beaming smile she always wore. But Bel could imagine them all here now, still connected and part of the family even though they'd been gone for so long.

She cleared her throat and blinked hard to fight the tears that were threatening. She met her cousin's gaze and smiled reassuringly. Larkin looked like a princess. Her ivory satin gown glowed like moonlight as she moved gracefully towards her soon-to-be husband and took his hand.

The celebrant's soothing tone rose above the falling rain. 'Welcome, friends and family. We are gathered here today to celebrate the love between Larkin and Tristan.'

Twelve

'That went surprisingly well,' Tate said as they moved slowly around the dancefloor a few hours later. After the wedding service, there'd been photos, not with the backdrops the bride had been hoping for, but Gisele and the photographer had managed to come up with some clever workarounds that would be just as stunning.

'All things considered,' Bel said. She had been in a dreamlike state since they'd started dancing. Pressed so close to him, her head fitted perfectly against his neck and each time she breathed in she caught the scent of his aftershave, warm and a little spicy. She could feel the heat of his hand on the small of her back through the thin material of her dress, and if she closed her eyes and tried really hard, she could almost imagine they were completely alone, just the two of them moving to the music.

'You took my breath away when you walked down that staircase earlier,' Tate said, moving his lips closer to her ear.

A row of goosebumps ran down her arm and a giddy sensation of longing filled her. She felt like Cinderella at the ball—happy and excited and desperately ignoring the fact she was a complete intruder. When everyone else went back to their usual lives, so would she, and all that would be left was a beautiful, sad memory.

'Hey? What's wrong?' he asked, easing back so he could see her face.

'Nothing. Sorry.'

'It's not nothing. Tell me?'

'This is going to end tomorrow. I knew it would,' she added quickly, 'but I just didn't expect it to come around this fast. I'm not ready for it to be over.'

'It doesn't have to be.'

'It kind of does,' she said. 'You live on the other side of the country.'

'Come with me.'

'What?' Bel chuckled nervously.

'Fly back with me. You said you've never been to Western Australia. Now's your chance.'

'I can't just . . . leave,' she said, battling to not let a surge of excitement derail her logical train of thought.

'I've never wanted anyone as much as I want you. Come with me. Be spontaneous. Live a little.'

As her brain began listing the million sensible reasons why she *couldn't*, her heart began replaying all the lonely nights she'd spent lying in bed, dreaming up scenarios to escape, not one of them anywhere near as tempting as the man who held her in his arms.

She wanted to have new experiences and adventures. She wanted to *live*. She wanted to go out into the world and just . . . *do something*. But could she? Dare she?

In true Larkin style, a helicopter arrived to whisk her and her groom away. She made a grand departure with all the fanfare of a celebrity, albeit a Wessex celebrity. Before long, the groom's family had also enlisted the help of Gisele and her extensive resources to, quote, 'Get us outta here!'

Tate and Bel made their escape to her room, eager to be alone.

'You are so beautiful,' Tate murmured against the side of her neck as he trailed kisses along her skin.

Bel still had trouble handling his flattery. She wasn't used to someone telling her she was beautiful, and it didn't feel real. She felt like an imposter and his compliments made her uncomfortable, even though this was what she'd wanted—a man's undying attention.

He unwrapped her like a present, allowing the dress to cascade to the floor so she could step out of it, leaving her clad only in two strips of delicate lace. He feasted his eyes on her hungrily before making short work of removing them.

Bel found herself observing the scene as though it came straight from a book—there was a finesse about his movements—so confident and sure. She almost didn't have to contribute; each time she went to help take something off or move in a certain way to assist him, he gently lay her back and shook his head. He liked to take the lead . . . like any hero would, she reminded herself. Like Jax did.

His earlier offer replayed in her mind. Why would she give something like this up? He was her dream, quite literally, come true. As his mouth continued to do the most delectable things to her body, Bel let go of her remaining inhibitions. There would be plenty of time later to overthink every minute detail. Right now, she only needed to live in the moment and feel. And it was feeling freaking amazing.

It had been two days since the wedding, and the rain had finally stopped. The water had receded enough to reopen the roads and Bel was pretty sure there had never been a more relieved exodus of people in the history of Wessex.

Back at Bel's place, Emma was staring at her, open-mouthed, her spoon poised halfway above the sugar bowl as she made their coffee. 'You're what?'

Bel bit back the rush of nervous excitement. 'I'm going with Tate, for a week.'

'To Western Australia?' Emma said. 'On the other side of the country?'

'Yes. That one,' Bel said dryly. Some of her excitement faded at the look on her friend's face. 'I really like him, Em.'

'You don't even know this guy,' Emma said. 'It's only been a week.'

'I admit it's been pretty fast, but I . . .' Bel let out a frustrated groan as she searched for words that wouldn't sound ridiculous to Emma. 'I think he's my soulmate.'

'But you've only. Known him. A week!'

'I get how it sounds. When I say it out loud, I hear the crazy too, okay? But what I feel is completely different. He was sent to me, Em. I know you don't believe in all that stuff, but I do, and I'm telling you, sometimes the universe puts things in our path for a reason. This is the push I need to actually do something. And weren't you the one who was always telling me I should leave? Find a man?'

'Yes, but I didn't necessarily mean a complete stranger who lives on the other side of the bloody continent!'

'You can't choose where love lives.'

'I thought that was the whole point of you conjuring up your dream man? So you *could* choose?' Emma shot back.

'Yeah, well, I forgot to add his location in there, so I guess that's on me,' Bel said snarkily. With some effort, she softened her tone. 'I know it's a bit of a shock, but this feels right, Em. I don't want to sit here and wonder what if I'd gone when he asked me. You know? There's been too many what-ifs in my life. I'm only going for a week. Who knows, I might get there and hate it, but at least I'll have something exciting to remember.'

'It's all happened rather fast,' Emma said, frowning.

'I know. And I know you're only looking out for me, but I need you to be happy for me right now. I'm going,' Bel said in a quiet voice, holding Emma's gaze firmly.

'Okay,' Emma said with a resigned shake of her head. 'But you'd better keep your phone location app on. I'll be keeping a close eye on it.'

'Stalkerish much?'

'You'll thank me if he turns out to be a serial killer,' she muttered.

'Thank you,' Bel said, hugging her.

'For what?'

'Always looking out for me. I do appreciate it, you know.'

'I know. And I do want you to go and have fun. I guess I'm just worried that it'll be too much fun and you won't come back.'

'If it is, isn't that a good thing too?'

'Yeah. It is. Okay,' Emma said, rolling her eyes. 'Fine. Go on a holiday with your drop-dead gorgeous book-cover model and have lots of wild, hot sex. Don't worry about me over here, doing the dishes and washing clothes all day. I'll be *fine*.'

'Oh, you love it. Stop complaining. I'll be back before you know it.'

'You'd better be.'

Two days later, after clearing out the fridge and switching everything off, Bel pulled the front door shut behind her and let out a deep breath.

She took one step off the front verandah, then another and another until she reached Tate's smiling face as he held open the car door. She braced her shoulders and resisted the urge to turn around and take one last look. *It's only a week.*

Thirteen

Bel soaked in the scenery, excited to be in a new city. The sky was a gorgeous shade of blue with only a few fluffy white clouds to break up its vastness. A winding, pristine river was skirted by lush green parkland and in the distance was a sprinkling of high-rises. When the taxi finally reached Tate's apartment building, Bel climbed out, shooed away by Tate and the driver unloading their bags. The gleaming building overlooked the river in what looked like a very upmarket part of the city and Bel itched to explore her surrounds—although possibly after a long hot shower and a sleep. It had been a big day: getting up early, driving to the airport and then lots of waiting. But they'd made it and her adventure was well and truly under way.

Bel followed Tate inside the impressive lobby, and she tried not to gawk like the tourist she was at the sparkling chrome and glistening tiles as they walked across to the elevators.

'Doing okay?' Tate asked as the doors slid closed.

Bel nodded and smiled up at him. 'I can't believe I'm here.'

'Better believe it. Tomorrow, we'll play tourist and you'll get a proper look at the place.'

Tate held the door open for her to walk into the apartment and Bel let out an audible gasp as she took it all in. It was like something out of a movie. Wide glass windows and sliding doors opened out to views of the river, bridges and wharfs below. Bel stepped outside onto a large balcony entertainment area. A cluster of outdoor lounge chairs sat up one end with a fire pit in the middle then a dining table at the other end. A built-in stainless-steel barbeque gleamed in a modest outdoor kitchen area. Huge pots with lush green palms were scattered around, a row of them stretching off to one side along the glass-panelled balustrade. Four high bar stools were tucked under a timber bar top, the perfect place to take advantage of the stunning, uninterrupted view.

'What do you think?' Tate asked, coming up beside her.

'This place is . . . Oh my God, I can't even . . .' she stammered, lost for words. 'I don't know how you tear yourself away from it to go to work.'

'It's not easy. Come on, there's more to see,' he said, taking her hand; she followed him reluctantly away from the view.

She couldn't wait to come back out here in a few hours and watch the sunset.

'Hang on,' she said, releasing his hand to take out her phone. 'I'm texting Emma to let her know I got here.'

'Bel, she's not your mother.'

Bel glanced up after hitting send. 'She's my best friend.'

'She's a little overprotective, and seems to have a lot of say in your life.'

'Emma?' Bel said with a chuckle. She was surprised to see he was serious. 'She's just looking out for me.'

'Don't you think it's time you lived your own life and stopped worrying about what other people think?'

'I'm here, aren't I?'

'Yes, you are, and I plan on showing you how great it is over here.'

He planted a gentle kiss on her mouth that melted into a tender, lingering moment, wiping away her confusion about his comments. 'Come on.'

Inside, the apartment was tastefully decorated in oatmeal and creams with lots of Tasmanian oak-like timber, giving the interior a light, airy feel. It was beautiful but it wasn't what she'd call cosy. It was too sophisticated for that. Bel felt a small pang for her little house back in Wessex, but firmly pushed it aside. *You're here now. On an adventure.*

The kitchen was open-plan, sleek and modern, and Bel imagined herself cooking dinner as she looked out over the magnificent view.

A hallway behind the living area was lined with doors, and Tate opened one on the right to reveal a huge suite, including a small balcony overlooking the city with a glimpse of the river. A walk-in wardrobe was next to a substantial bathroom with a double shower and a giant sunken bathtub that took pride of place in front of a massive window. Bel eyed it warily, noting the absence of anything as unsightly as curtains or blinds, and wondered if many people in the building not so far across the way had telescopes.

'Across the hall is the spare room and another bathroom,' Tate said, cutting into her thoughts.

This place was sophisticated and expensive—exactly the kind of place Jax Lexington would live in. *Stop it*. She knew she had stop thinking about Jax and making these kinds of comparisons. It didn't seem like a healthy thing to do to compare your real-life boyfriend with your fictional one. In fact, it was rather delusional, if she were being honest. And yet... at times, she couldn't help making the comparisons. Both were charming and handsome and had a smile that could melt hearts. It had seemed like Jax had stepped out of a book and turned into Tate. She'd spent so long fantasising about Jax, it wasn't an easy thing to turn off overnight. She knew Tate wasn't a storybook hero; he wasn't an ex-special forces operative who could survive almost impossible odds and walk away from exploding buildings. He was just a man. And so what if Tate hadn't really done anything outrageously heroic? It wasn't as if they were living a danger-filled world like the one in the Lexington Millionaires series. This was real life, and these comparisons simply weren't practical—and were possibly a little bit crazy.

Whether he was the real-life Jax Lexington or not, meeting Tate was the most exciting thing that had ever happened to her. Taking a chance meant taking risks and trusting that everything would be okay. For way too long, she'd taken the safe road, too scared to let go of what she was comfortable with. Where had that gotten her? She was almost thirty and she hadn't even lived.

Tate had been sent to her for a reason, and she wasn't going to throw away her chance at finding her happily-ever-after just because this had happened fast and without much warning. People did wild things for love all the time. Why couldn't she?

Had she fallen in love? She wasn't exactly sure. It *felt* how every single romance she'd ever read said that it was supposed to feel. She had the butterflies in her stomach, and that breathy feeling when he kissed her. Was *he* in love? He'd asked her to come back here with him. Surely men didn't randomly ask that of complete strangers? She knew these feelings had caught him by surprise too—he'd said so—but . . . was it love? What else could it be?

Bel opened her eyes and for a fleeting second was confused. Then all the sensations came crashing down around her. She smelled the clean, fresh smell of new furniture and barely walked on carpet and saw the early morning sunlight filtering in through huge glass windows. She felt the feathery light touch of expensive sheets and the heavier weight of an arm across her torso. She rolled her head sideways and soaked in the image of the man beside her. He was perfection. Seriously, how did he manage to look so damn perfect even when he was asleep? Something no mere mortal could achieve, especially her. When she woke up, she mostly resembled a cockatoo, and she didn't want her first morning on her new adventure to start out with bed hair.

She slowly slid out from under Tate's arm, dug out her toiletry bag and tiptoed her way to the bathroom across the hall so as not to disturb him.

She'd intended to climb back into bed and wait for him to get up, but after brushing her teeth and splashing her face with water, she found herself too wide awake to go back to sleep. Instead, she went out to the kitchen, greeted by a view through the ceiling-to-floor windows that was nothing short of breathtaking. The pale pinks and purples in the sky suddenly gave way to a glowing ball of golden light that bled across the horizon and filled the room with a warm yellow glow. She'd never seen anything quite like it before. Sure, she'd seen her share of sunrises—she did have to open the store early every morning—but the view in Wessex was nothing like the view from a high-rise building overlooking a magnificent river.

Bel eyed the coffee maker on the kitchen bench and felt her mouth start to water. She wanted a coffee so bad, but she had the feeling that even if she could figure out how to work this monstrosity of an appliance, it would be loud enough to wake the dead—or, in this case, the hunk of spunk up the hallway.

There was nothing else for it; she'd have to go out. It was still early. She could nip out, buy a coffee and then duck back before Tate even knew she was gone. She looked at the clock. He'd told her once that he liked to sleep in when he wasn't working. With a final frustrated glance at the coffee machine, she left the kitchen.

She tiptoed back into the bedroom and quietly rifled through her suitcase until she found what she needed, then stealthily withdrew once more. As she dressed, she considered that if she got desperate for a job, she could maybe try her hand at becoming a cat burglar. Or a secret agent. She found the key in the beautiful handblown glass dish on the hall table where Tate had dropped it last night and slid it into the pocket of her jeans, along with her phone, then softly eased the front door shut behind her.

Armed with directions for a cafe from the young man at the front desk, Bel headed outside. There were more people around than she'd expected for the hour, plenty of dog walkers and joggers, and she paused to tilt her head back and breathe in the crisp morning air. The city felt alive.

She located the cafe, noting it was, like most things in this part of town, very fancy. The display cabinet had obscenely decadent pastries and other delicious offerings and it would have taken a will of steel to resist. Bel added a croissant to her order and enjoyed the heady smell of calories that floated around her while she waited.

She had planned to take her coffee straight back up to the apartment, but she decided to take a quick walk first. She walked to Barrack Square and then across to the jetty, leaning against the railing as she listened to the gentle slap of the water against the luxurious yachts. *You certainly don't get this in Wessex.* This was like a whole other world.

Tipping her cup up, she was surprised to find she'd finished her coffee. She pulled out her phone, starting at the time. She'd been away longer than she'd intended.

When she opened the door to the apartment, she found Tate standing at the kitchen bench, waiting.

'Where have you been?' he asked. His tone was off; not angry, but definitely short.

'Sorry, I ducked out to grab a coffee and lost track of time. It's so beautiful out there.'

'I thought we planned to go sightseeing together?'

'We did. We are. I only went down to the wharf. I didn't want to disturb you while you were sleeping.'

'I thought you'd take advantage of the fact you didn't have to get up and go to work to sleep in too.'

Bel gave a wry smile. 'My body clock didn't get the memo.'

'I got up to cook you breakfast.'

'Oh. Great. I can help,' she said brightly, until she saw him shrug and straighten.

'Let's just go out for breakfast,' he said with a huff.

'Okay,' Bel said. 'If that's what you want to do.'

'I don't feel like cooking now. I'm going to jump in the shower. Will you be ready to leave after that?'

'Of course,' Bel said, sending him a smile that he barely saw as he headed for the bedroom. It faded slowly. What had happened to change his mood?

By the time they were both ready to leave the apartment, things seemed to have righted themselves and he was back to his usual, charming self. He took her to a cafe not far from his apartment and they sat outside where they could see the water and watch the growing crowds. 'Two of the big breakfasts, thanks,' Tate said, smiling at the waitress after they'd been seated and she'd returned to take their orders.

'Oh, I don't usually have too much for breakfast,' Bel said, startled that he'd ordered for her.

'It's the best thing on the menu. Besides, you'll need it, I've got a big day planned.' He nodded firmly at the waitress, and she scurried off to place their order.

She wasn't sure how she felt about him taking charge like that—but a take-charge guy was kind of sexy. After all, Jax was that kind of man—confident and decisive. *But not once had he ever decided what his date should be eating*, a little voice pointed out. Which was also true. She let it go though, he was probably just excited about showing her all the things he enjoyed about where he lived.

Bel was glad for her big breakfast once they started their day. They walked for miles, taking in the parks and the art on the Promenade, then wandering across the Elizabeth Quay Bridge before taking a sunset river cruise and eating dinner down near the jetty.

'So, what do you think?' Tate said as they sat on his balcony afterwards and looked out over the river and the lights of the city beyond.

'Of what in particular?'

'Of this place. Is it as great as I told you it would be?'

'It's amazing,' she said, absolutely meaning it.

'Are you glad you decided to come?'

'I am.'

'Could you see yourself staying?' he asked quietly.

Bel moved slightly so as to see his face. 'Staying?'

'Yeah. Moving over here. Permanently.'

Move here. She'd been soaking in the atmosphere of the place, taking in everything around her, and envying the people who were lucky enough to call it their home. She hadn't been imagining herself becoming one of them . . . until now. A million thoughts began racing through her head. Was it all happening too fast? But then, how could it be too fast when she'd manifested him? She'd been ready to meet her soulmate, to be swept off her feet—and she had been. She was living the Jax Lexington life, minus the espionage and near-death experiences. *This is what you've been waiting for.* But there were other questions, practical ones like what would she do? How would she support herself? Where would she live?

'I can see the wheels spinning in that head of yours,' Tate chuckled.

'There's a lot to think about. I'm not sure how it would work. I don't know if I could move in with you.' It was one thing to do something like a short stay. That was out of character enough, but to move in together, like a couple? She could hear Emma's voice in her head, demanding to know what the hell she was thinking

'I'd have to find a job.' *Leave my old one.* 'Leave Wessex.' *Leave home.* She was almost stunned by the idea.

'Would that be the end of the world? I mean, it's not like you were going anywhere there,' he pointed out.

Bel felt a tiny ripple of irritation at his words. Jax would never irritate her. He always knew the right thing to say. She tried to think exactly what he *would* say in this situation and honestly couldn't. *Jax would never be having this conversation.*

But Tate was right. Wessex was not going to change any time soon, and her job was not going to get any more stimulating either. But what else could she do? *Anything. You could literally do anything else.* Which was also true.

'I don't know . . . I guess I could think about it.'

'I think you should,' he said, and she looked up into his serious gaze. 'Because I don't want to say goodbye to you in a few days' time.'

'But . . . why?' she asked, genuinely confused by his request. 'Why me?'

'You're stunning,' he said, shaking his head, 'and different to anyone I've ever met. You've got this innocence about you that I know I won't find with anyone else.'

'I think it's probably because I don't come from your world. I'm not like Larkin and the others.'

'And that's exactly what I like.'

'But you don't really know me. What if you get sick of whatever it is you seem to like about me? What if you want . . .' she trailed off, searching for the right words to voice her concerns, the courage to say them. *What happens if the novelty does wear off? What will you do then?*

'All I know is I've never been this captivated with anyone. I want to see where it goes.'

His words dripped down her spine like warm honey, melting her uncertainty. She was utterly enchanted by him and when he looked at her with that brooding, almost hypnotic gaze, the heady emotion was impossible to resist. And she refused to let any little niggly concerns that were floating in the back of her mind spoil the moment.

They spent the next three days exploring further afield, places like Fremantle and Rottnest Island, Margaret River and its wineries. Tate spared no expense as they dined and wined their evenings away, spoiling her with amazing experiences.

Bel took extra care dressing for dinner when Tate informed her they were going to a well-known restaurant. She came out only to stop short at the frown on his face. 'What's wrong?'

'Where's the white dress I gave you the other day?'

'It's pretty revealing,' she said, confused by his abrupt question.

'It's probably more appropriate for where we're going.'

'What's wrong with this?' she asked, looking down at the new black satin wide-leg pants and gold halter-neck top she'd brought with her. She felt incredibly chic in the outfit.

'I prefer you in dresses.' He shrugged. 'Go try the white one on for me.'

Bel stared at him for a moment, unsure exactly how to take his request. His frown vanished and that sexy smile of his was back in place.

'Sorry, babe. No, you're right. What you're in is fine. It's just that, when I booked the restaurant, I was picturing you in that dress.'

Now she felt weird. Maybe pants weren't a good idea. Her previous excitement over getting ready was replaced with the same nervous anxiety she'd had during the wedding, unsure that what she was doing was good enough compared to the other women, who seemed so confident and graceful. They knew what to wear and how to put on make-up, the kinds of things Bel really hadn't cared about before meeting Tate. They would have known the white dress was the thing for this occasion without needing to be told. 'No, it's okay. I'll go try it on.'

As she stepped into the slinky gown, Bel tried to push away the disappointment that had gathered in her stomach. What did she know about any of this anyway? The last thing she wanted to do was to be an embarrassment. She tugged at the dress's neckline, which exposed a lot more cleavage than she would normally be comfortable with, but gave up when it refused to budge. She changed her heels and headed back out.

'Beautiful,' he breathed.

She smiled then melted as he slid a hand behind her neck, pulling her towards him for a deep kiss. Maybe she'd been overly sensitive before. Was it really such a big deal to feel annoyed that he'd asked her to change outfits? How could she be upset when he was helping her and when this was his reaction? *Jax would never ask any of his women to change their clothes.* The thought came from out of the blue, and she quickly pushed it away with another: *The women Jax dated would have known what to wear.* Tate was wonderful—the perfect boyfriend. He'd been showering her with gifts since she'd arrived. He was attentive and affectionate. He lived in the perfect place with a perfect view. Everything was . . . perfect, so much so that she often wondered if her alarm was about to go off for work and she would wake to discover it was all just a magical dream.

However, even dreams did eventually have to end. Early one morning, Tate's phone went off and he was summoned back to work.

'I'm really sorry, Bel. If I could hand this over to someone else, I would, but there's been an emergency and I need to go out there and sort it out. It should only be for a night. I'll call you later,' he said, kissing Bel and leaving her standing in the kitchen.

She only had three days left until she had to go back, and it looked like she'd be spending almost half of it by herself. But it wasn't Tate's fault, so she tried not to mope about. It did give her some much-needed breathing room to sort through the multitude of emotions that had been swirling inside her over the last few days. She couldn't think straight when Tate was near her. He made everything seem so . . . possible. It was only now he wasn't here that she could start to unpack everything and try to make sense of what she was feeling.

Tate made it clear he wanted this relationship, or whatever it was between them, to continue. That just wouldn't be practical if she was in Wessex.

Only, reality was trying to point out a few details. She'd have to give up her job . . . her house . . . her friends. Was a relationship worth all that sacrifice? Emma had her husband

and her own family. The Dwyers would train someone else to do her job—it wasn't exactly brain surgery. Wessex wasn't going to collapse without her; life would continue whether she was there or not. It was her happiness and future that she should be putting first for once. After all this time, she finally had a chance to do something new.

Around mid-morning, Bel decided she couldn't stand being alone with the thoughts running around on an endless loop inside her head. She grabbed her handbag, slid on her sunglasses and headed out.

The hustle and bustle of the city was a welcome relief. The energy was contagious—it wasn't the same busy, impersonal, city-rush of Sydney. Perth had a more laid-back feel which appealed to Bel immensely.

She noticed a number of cafes had 'Positions Wanted' signs in the windows and she took down their names. It wouldn't hurt to maybe do a little reconnaissance, perhaps do up a new résumé to hand in to a few places. After stopping in for a coffee and some lunch at one such place, Bel looked across the street and noticed a bookshop. It stood out among the more modern buildings around it, with its little cottage-type front and brightly coloured flowerpots hanging on either side of its doorway. After finishing her meal, Bel decided to investigate. She never could resist a bookstore—that new book smell wrapped around her shoulders like a familiar friend hugging her and she breathed it in deeply.

She took out her phone and recorded a video showing the cute little store, knowing her followers would be as excited as she was to have a look inside.

The interior was much larger than she'd expected from the street. Shelves lined the walls with new titles, and tables of every size and shape were artistically scattered around the centre of the store. A huge, whitewashed timber table housed a stack of books in shades of lilac and purple, which surrounded a large milk jug overflowing with lavender. Another nearby table, this one lower and round, had a display of vibrant yellow and orange books, while a bookshelf to her left had been filled with books of different-coloured spines, arranged in a rainbow effect. A small room to the rear of the store had a red arched door with red and white spotted mushrooms painted on either side of it. FAIRYTALE LAND, read the timber signpost pointing inside.

Bel could only sigh as she continued to explore.

In the romance section, two women in their mid-twenties were talking quietly as they picked up books and put them back down again.

'I don't know which one to buy. I've found myself in a real reading slump lately. I want something amazing to reignite me again, you know?'

'I'm in the same boat. There is literally nothing to read.'

Bel tried to bite back the urge to correct her. There *literally* was . . . they were standing in the middle of a bookshop! 'Excuse me, sorry,' Bel butted in apologetically. 'I couldn't help but overhear and I was wondering, have either of you read Alison Gatsby? She has a series called Lexington Millionaires. I've read them cover-to-cover so many times, I've lost count.' She reached to the shelf behind the women and pulled out book one. 'It's a great book, if you're getting a bit tired of the same old tropes and need to shake things up a bit. I think you'll like it.'

'Thanks,' the first woman smiled as she began eagerly reading the back cover. 'This does sound good. I think I'll try it.'

Bel found herself smiling. It was always satisfying when one of her posts or reviews about a book or an author struck a chord with other readers—even more so when they came back later to say how much they'd loved her suggestions—and it was even better when she was face-to-face with someone. She could *see* their expressions and *hear* the anticipation and excitement in their voices as they discovered a book that had given her so much joy herself—and the fact it had happened so spontaneously made it even more special.

Another woman, about sixty-odd, walked up behind Bel as she turned away from the first two. 'Excuse me, but do you know where the thriller section is?'

'Oh, I'm sorry, I don't work here,' she said, but recalled walking past it on her way to the romance section. 'Although I think I saw it, two aisles over.'

'Oh. Thanks so much,' the older lady said as she wandered off.

'Would you like to?' a voice asked, making Bel glance to her right.

'Sorry?' Bel asked the short-haired, middle-aged man who was leaning against the shelf.

'Would you like to work here?'

Bel blinked, unsure what he was playing at.

'I'm Terry Collingwood, owner of Bookish Delights. I overheard your sales pitch.'

'It wasn't really a pitch. I'm just an avid reader helping out some other readers.'

'Seriously, I'm in desperate need of someone who knows their stuff. The last kid I hired stood at the front counter and stared at their phone all day. Do you have any idea how difficult Christmas lunch was after I had to fire my own nephew?'

'Oh dear,' Bel murmured sympathetically. 'Well, I might be looking for a job . . . if I decide to stay on over here. I only came for a visit, but . . .'

'Sounds like fate, doesn't it?' He smiled, and Bel's breath caught slightly at his choice of words.

Yes. Yes, it does.

'Let me get you a cuppa and we'll have a chat,' Terry said, leaving her to stare after him mutely. 'Come on, we have a coffee station.'

Of course they did. This place was heaven.

Fourteen

Bel waited until Tate was due home before she told him that she was going to stay. The heart-melting smile that broke out across his face pushed aside any lingering doubts she may have had about jumping into this whole thing, feet first. They decided to cook dinner together to celebrate.

'Here's to us and a new beginning,' he toasted as they sat down to eat.

'There's even more good news,' Bel said after taking a sip from her glass. 'I got a job.'

'Doing what?'

'Working in a bookshop.'

'It could be worse,' he said. 'You could have been working in a supermarket or something.'

The insult took her momentarily by surprise. She pretty much *had* been working in a supermarket. 'I'm really looking forward to it,' she said quietly.

'You don't have to work right now if you want to take your time and find something better.'

'I'll need a job to afford rent when I find my own place,' she reminded him, trying to shift the disappointment his offhand remarks had caused.

'Why would you find your own place?' he asked. 'There's no point if you're going to be spending most of your time here.'

Bel blinked. He was asking her to move in? 'I can't just leech off you,' she protested weakly.

'You're not. I won't be here all the time, so you'll have the place to yourself a lot and I'll have someone to keep an eye on things while I'm away.'

She took another sip of the red wine and savoured its smoothness, feeling its warmth deep within her as she paused to consider this. His logic sounded, well, reasonable, but still . . .

Tate reached out and slowly slid his hand up her thigh beneath the table, and Bel felt a different warmth spread through her. Suddenly their topic of conversation didn't seem very important. She was probably overthinking this. Bel traced her fingers up Tate's arm, returning his provocative smile, and dinner was left to go cold on the table as they continued their celebrations in bed.

Later, Bel sighed happily against Tate's chest. Only a few weeks earlier, if someone had said she'd have a charming, gorgeous man wanting her to relocate across the country and move into his luxe apartment, she'd never have believed them. What was there to think about? She'd manifested her dream man and the universe had delivered him. This was what she'd wanted.

'Are you crazy?' Emma almost shouted down the line.

'I really like it here, Em,' Bel said. 'I'm not ready to come back.'

'But you have a job, remember?' Emma reminded her.

'I've handed in my notice at Dwyers'.'

'Handed in your notice? Can't you ask for longer leave? Do you have any idea how hard it'll be to get a job when you come back?'

'I have to jump in completely or I won't jump at all. I'll deal with that problem if it arises.'

Emma let out a short huff. 'What if you're wrong about this?'

'What if I'm not?' Bel shot back, smiling to herself.

'Okay,' Emma said, and Bel could picture her friend throwing her hands in the air dramatically. 'You're a grown woman and you can make your own decisions. I am happy for you, Bel. I've been waiting for so long to see you this happy.' She let out a long sigh of defeat. 'I'm being selfish. I'm not sure what I'll do around here without you.'

The two women went silent as Bel felt a rush of gratitude for this friend who'd been beside her since childhood. She was like a sister, and Bel knew she was going to miss her terribly. But the excitement of doing something so spontaneous and adventurous tempered the sadness.

'Well, what are you doing with your house?'

'I'll probably rent it out.'

'Don't sell it,' Emma said flatly. 'Just in case.'

Bel hadn't planned to sell it. It had been her gran's house and had far too much sentimental value to sell off without a great deal of thought. Despite what her friend might be thinking, she wasn't a complete idiot. She understood how impetuous this all seemed, but she wasn't jumping into it without a safety net. At the same time, she didn't really want to entertain the thought of what if it all went wrong; that felt like it was dooming any possibility of a happy future.

'I'll drop by every now and again and water the garden and keep an eye on things,' Emma said, breaking into Bel's thoughts. She more than anyone else knew what a huge step this was going to be, and what it took for Bel to even consider doing something like this. She might not be completely sold on the whole idea, but Bel knew her friend wouldn't hold her back.

The only person who'd been immediately excited by her decision to stay in WA with Tate had been Larkin, who of course, claimed complete responsibility for the match in the first place.

It was nice to have at least one ally. She knew Emma was happy if she was happy, but her support had been heavily shrouded in concern—unlike Larkin who'd been planning a couple's get-together as well as regularly updating the group chats, which had gone from wedding texts to honeymoon photos and updates.

It had been three months since Bel had started her new job and she couldn't have been happier. Terry was the best boss she'd ever worked for, though she only had one other to compare him to. Still, in a contest between him and the Dwyers, he came out miles ahead.

Bel had started placing reviews under books on the shelf to assist customers in choosing their next read. As she had done with her BookTok, she tried to make them stand out and offer something different to the same old boring book reviews she'd come across herself over the years.

> *Little Women*: Please note the misleading title, these women are all normal size, but don't let that deter you. This story has been loved through the generations and is well deserving of the title 'classic'. If you haven't read this book, I urge that you do so (I really must insist!) immediately . . . like, *right now* . . . why are you still standing there reading this review card? Pick up the book and head to the front counter!

Terry gave her strict instructions to continue her reviews and, as customers shared photos of them online, they began to draw a lot of attention to her BookTok page.

'My kids showed me your tok-tik thing last night. Apparently, you're famous,' Terry said one day, poking his head around the corner of the office at the rear of the shop where Bel had been working.

Bel shook her head with a smile. How on earth had this man kept his business alive without having any clue about social media marketing? 'TikTok is my guilty secret. It started out as a bit of fun, but it's grown into almost a second full-time job, keeping up the content.'

'It seems to be making a difference to the store. I'd forgotten Bree had set up an account for the shop a while ago, trying to drag her old dad into the future. So you maybe want to handle the social media side of things, you know, get it up and running?'

'I've been thinking a bit about that,' Bel said, eager to share her ideas. 'Maybe I could do some author interviews for content across the shop's social media pages? And do more events. Have book launches and author appearances, host some night events and have special out-of-hours access for readers who come along? That kind of thing.'

'I've been wanting to do more along those lines. I haven't had the time to dedicate to it. If you're up for it, I'd love to delegate all that to you,' he said.

'Absolutely.' Bel beamed. The ideas had been flooding her mind ever since she'd started working in the bookshop. There was so much potential to grow it into something even more amazing.

She was glad she had her job. She'd have gone mad sitting about at home all day without Tate. She still had to pinch herself, though, whenever she looked out at the view from the windows; she really was living a life of luxury, even if there were times when she felt it was all a little . . . cold. Tate didn't have much in the way of personal items, and no photos of family decorated the apartment. She knew he had a much older sister—he being the later-in-life baby of older parents—and that his mother and father were both still alive. But he wasn't really close to them. Instead of photos, he had art. Bel had tried to appreciate the expensive pieces hanging on his walls, but she just didn't understand how something that looked like a painting one of Emma's kids brought home from daycare could be worth that much money. The apartment was luxurious to a fault, but it lacked a soul.

And it didn't feel like home. When her phone charger had refused to work one day, Bel had gone in search of a spare, certain that she'd seen one around. She'd opened drawers in the bedroom and found his incredibly organised socks, undies and clothing meticulously stored in his wardrobe, but no charger. She'd gone into the office and gingerly peered into his desk drawers. She rarely went in there. If he was working, she left him alone, and the door was always shut when he wasn't there. It felt like she was trespassing, even though she lived there.

Opening a drawer beneath the desk very carefully so as not to disturb anything, she'd found a charger, but also spotted something gold and shiny underneath and picked it up, curious. The slim lighter was elegant and screamed money, probably real gold. Certainly it was nothing like the plain old plastic ones they sold at Dwyers'. Turning it over, she'd discovered the letter L engraved on the other side and wondered who it belonged to. Clearly not Tate, since he didn't smoke and it wasn't his initial. Besides, it had looked far too feminine. Bel had placed it back where she'd found it and closed the drawer. She hadn't stepped foot in the office since.

Tate's work took him out of town a lot and he worried about her, always calling her mobile to check in. Sometimes he called through the day while she was at work, and she couldn't always answer. Then he'd call the shop.

She'd apologised to Terry more than once about it, and tried to always catch his calls on her mobile, but Terry was understanding. 'He's clearly worried about his girl when he's out of town. Nothing wrong with that.'

And there really wasn't, she often told herself. He was being protective when he called, like he was when he asked her to promise not to go out alone.

'Tate, I have lived on my own for a number of years now,' she'd frowned when he'd first brought it up.

'Yes, but not in a city,' he'd countered.

'It doesn't seem like a terrifying place.'

'I don't want you going out when I'm not here.'

And it wasn't like she was a big nightlife person. At night, she'd cook her dinner and then settle down to read. It passed the time and kind of felt familiar—almost like her old life, before Tate had blown in and turned it upside down.

When Tate was home, they would always eat out and dress up, which was still fun, but Bel craved some normal time, just the two of them pottering about the apartment, spending lazy days watching movies or doing couple stuff, like cooking together. Tate wasn't exactly into lounging around—he was always full of energy and wanting to go out and do something. She didn't get much reading time when he was home either.

'Do you have to read all evening?' he'd said one night when they'd been lying in bed.

'I haven't picked up a book in days,' she'd said with a laugh, before it became clear he wasn't joking.

'Every time I want to talk to you, you've got your face stuck in a book.'

'I'm sorry. I didn't realise.'

'Well, you wouldn't, would you, when you're too busy reading your smutty girl books. If you're going to read, at least pick something a little more classy,' he'd said, nodding down at the Jax Lexington book she held.

'It's not smut,' she'd protested. It was one thing to complain about her reading, but it was another thing entirely to bring Jax into it.

'Yeah, right. That half-naked Neanderthal on the cover suggests otherwise.'

She'd resisted the urge to point out he looked almost identical to said Neanderthal.

So she'd stopped reading when he was home. In all fairness, it probably had felt as though she were excluding him. It wasn't a huge deal; there was plenty of time to read when he wasn't there.

But lately, she'd also begun to notice he was finding fault in a lot of other things too. Maybe it was the normal transition between the honeymoon stage and a couple adjusting to living together, but there was definitely some kind of change taking place.

One morning after he'd gotten back from a trip away, Bel stretched and got up to take a shower.

'What are you doing?' he asked, reaching out a hand to lure her back to bed.

'I have to get ready for work,' she said, dodging his attempts to waylay her.

'It's Saturday.'

'We've got a big author talk today. I have to be there.'

'But I just got home,' he pointed out, sounding oddly confused.

'I know, and I've missed you, but I have to go in today.'

'I don't even know why you want to work in that place.'

'What do you mean?'

'I mean, it's hardly a big career move, is it? What happened to you wanting to go to university? I thought that was the whole plan, that you'd be *doing* something?'

'I *am* doing something. I really love working with books, recommending them to people. You know how much I love doing all that on my TikTok page. It's a dream come true.'

'Yeah, but it's hardly a proper career.'

They rarely talked about her online presence. Right from the start, he'd dismissed it. 'I don't do social media,' he'd said when they'd first been getting to know each other.

'What? Not at all?'

'Nope.'

'How come?'

'Why would I want everyone knowing my business?'

'Well, you don't have to post about that. You can keep up with what everyone else is doing.'

'Why would I want to? If I wanted to know something, I'd call them.'

So social media was not something they'd discussed much.

'I'm happy working there,' she said now, trying not to let his attitude dampen her enthusiasm.

'You have so much potential, and you're wasting it working as a shop assistant.'

In truth, she had been looking at university when she first arrived, but nothing had really caught her attention. She was more confused than ever, with the huge selection of courses on offer. It was a big decision to make, choosing a degree. What if she didn't like it once she started? She wanted to take her time to figure out what she wanted to do, not rush into it.

'We can go somewhere nice tonight,' she said, changing the subject as she pulled on her skirt.

'I'm going out to a work function tonight.'

'Oh. Well, I could come with you to that,' she said. She was keen to meet some of the other people in his life.

'No one's taking partners.'

'Oh.' She couldn't help feeling deflated. 'Well, maybe one weekend we can have a few of your work friends over for a barbecue or something?'

'I don't think so.'

'But . . . why?'

'I told you, I don't like to socialise with colleagues in my private time.'

'But I don't know anyone here, other than the people I work with. I just thought it might be nice to meet some new people.'

'They aren't your kind of people.'

Bel frowned. *What on earth does that mean?*

'I think I'll go back to sleep for a bit,' he said. 'Since you've got better things to do.'

'It's not better things to do. It's work.'

'I'll see you tonight. Don't wait up.'

He turned away and thumped his pillow into form before lying back down. She tried not to feel as though she'd been dismissed like some naughty child. She hated when they disagreed. It wasn't often, but ever since she'd gotten her job, he'd been rather dismissive of it, showing no interest whatsoever when she tried to tell him about her day. She couldn't lie—it hurt.

But . . . maybe he had a point? Maybe she should be using this opportunity to do something more. Only she wasn't sure what that might be.

The author event went smoothly and they had a great turnout. Afterwards, when Alissa, who also worked at the bookshop, and Terry suggested going out for a late dinner with the author, Bel hesitated.

'Well, Tate doesn't really like me going out without him,' she said, then winced. When she spoke the words out loud, they sounded strange.

'Didn't you say he was going to a work function?' Alissa asked.

'Yeah, he was,' Bel said, then she decided. *Why not?* 'You're right, he probably isn't even going to be home until late. Sure, let's go.'

They headed down to a small bar attached to a swanky hotel in one of the tourist hotspots and celebrated the night's success. Fiona, the author, was a delight. Her books always flew off the shelves and it was exciting to listen to the conversation flowing about bookselling and writing and everything in between. Bel felt like she was really one of the team, and she loved every minute. At one point, Fiona mentioned the writers' group she belonged to and their need for more editing services. 'In my spare time, I freelance edit, but I'm turning people away every day. There's just not enough quality services out there.'

'Didn't you say you did some proofreading, Bel?' Alissa asked.

'I've done a bit over the years with some of the romance writers I've met online,' she said, but quickly added, 'I haven't done it professionally or anything. Mainly as a favour, here and there.'

'Well, if you're ever after any work, let me know. There's plenty out there.'

Like she could add *another* thing onto her plate.

When she got home, Tate was still out and the apartment was silent. Her earlier high from an enjoyable day and fun night with new friends fizzled out.

She had everything she'd ever dreamed of—she lived in a beautiful city, in an apartment to die for, with a man who was everything she could ever hope for—yet it all felt kind of . . . unreal, and not in a good way. She couldn't even put her finger on what it was that felt wrong. She'd tried a number of times to talk with Tate about her unease, but he kept brushing off her concerns, saying there was nothing wrong with the way they were. Only that could be part of the problem; she wasn't sure exactly *what* they were.

The attraction was still there, as strong as it had been in the beginning, but it was like they were running on the spot, not really going anywhere. She was no closer to understanding him or knowing him on any deeper level than when they first met.

She kicked off her shoes and headed for the shower.

The next day, they took a drive to a winery and had lunch in a trendy restaurant. Bel caught herself wishing that maybe for once they could have found a takeaway and had hamburgers. She'd been craving them for the last few days—an old-fashioned, cafe-style burger and chips. But Tate liked the finer things in life. Just like Jax did, she reminded herself. Maybe she hadn't quite thought this whole thing through. A lifestyle you had no experience with was all well and good for a while, but Bel was beginning to suspect that, deep down, she wasn't cut out for fancy food and getting dressed up all the time. It took her ages to do her hair and make-up whenever they went out. Not that she didn't enjoy all the new experiences Tate was insisting she have, but there were times she really just wanted to pull on some comfy tracksuit pants and a big, loose shirt and eat a greasy hamburger.

Tate left for the mine site early Monday morning and Bel almost found herself breathing a sigh of relief. The acknowledgement literally made her stop in her tracks as she was walking to work. She shouldn't be feeling this way. This was what she wanted. This was what she'd manifested.

Her mood lifted once she got to work. It was simply impossible to be sad when you were surrounded by books.

Later that day, she looked up as a tall, well-dressed woman came to the front counter. Her long blonde hair gleamed like a satin waterfall and her manicured hand gracefully slid her oversized designer sunglasses to the top of her head, revealing thick dark lashes and model-high cheekbones.

'Hello. Can I help you with something?' Bel asked, trying not to feel completely inadequate. For the first time in ages, she felt like the old Bel.

'I'm Lucile.'

'Hello,' Bel said, still wondering if she was supposed to know the woman.

'I wasn't sure if I should come in here or not.'

Bel tried to keep her face open and friendly but was beginning to suspect this was not going to be a request about finding a book.

'I saw you the other day . . . with Tate . . . and something about the way you looked reminded me of another place and time.' Lucile stopped, looking almost embarrassed. Then she cleared her throat quickly and continued. 'You reminded me of myself, not so long ago.'

'I'm sorry,' Bel said when the woman paused and continued looking at her. 'I don't understand. Do you know Tate?'

'Yes, I knew him. I was his fiancée.'

Bel felt her mouth open then abruptly closed it. 'Did you say fiancée?'

'He didn't mention me, I take it,' Lucile said with a wry smile.

What the actual . . . 'Uh, no.'

'I'm not surprised. Look, I didn't come in here to cause trouble,' Lucile said. 'It's just . . . I saw you the other day in a restaurant, in a white dress, looking utterly miserable. The same white dress he'd bought for me,' she said, then lowered her tone and added pointedly, 'and made me wear. Among others.'

Bel felt her head begin to spin.

'I left him, Bel. He was a controlling and sometimes violent man. I know it's none of my business, and you don't have to listen to me, but I couldn't live with myself if I didn't try to warn you.' The woman gripped the edge of the counter before continuing in a rush. 'He isn't who you think he is. He finds women he can control. He sweeps them off their feet and charms them with his good looks and his money and then grooms them into a certain image. It doesn't seem that bad at first, but trust me, if you start to rebel, you'll soon see a side of him that is dangerous.'

Bel could only stare at the woman. Surely this was a joke? *She must be mistaking Tate for someone else. There's no way . . .*

Lucile smiled wanly. 'I guess I probably wouldn't have believed someone telling me this stuff out of the blue either, back then,' she said, turning away.

'Wait,' Bel said. Lucile stopped. 'Are you sure we're talking about the same man?'

'I wish we weren't, for your sake. You seem like a nice person. I guess that's why I wanted to try. Sometimes he dates socialite women, but he gets bored with them. He can't manipulate them in the same way. I knew you weren't one of those. Neither was I.'

Bel's heart sank as Lucile walked to the exit. She desperately wanted to believe this woman was some jealous ex-lover out to cause trouble, but there was something sad and real in the depths of her eyes that made Bel wonder.

Lucile reached the door and, pausing before exiting, called back, 'Be careful, Bel.'

That night, after a late closing, Bel, Terry and Alissa were at the nearby Chinese restaurant having dinner when Tate called.

'Where are you?' he demanded. 'You're not at home.'

His brusque question caught her off guard. *But maybe he's had a stressful day.* 'I'm having dinner.'

'With your boss? Alone?'

'No. Alissa is here too.'

She'd taken the call away from the table, and she noticed the other two were now looking at her quietly. She smiled to reassure them.

'It's late,' Tate said.

Bel glanced at her watch. 'It's barely even nine-thirty.'

'I don't like you out alone at night.'

'I'm perfectly safe, Tate. Like I said, Alissa's here. And Terry.'

'I don't like you out with other men either,' he snapped.

'It's not other men,' she said, lowering her voice and turning away from her colleagues. 'How do you even know I'm not at home?'

'I've got the cameras at home linked to my phone. How else do you think I keep an eye on the place while I'm away?'

She knew about the security camera but he'd never told her there was more than the one, or that they could be streamed to his phone. The knowledge irritated her. She tried to remind herself they were just there for safety, that it was only a coincidence he'd noticed she wasn't home . . . only, it didn't feel like he was simply checking in. It felt like he was checking up on her.

'Okay, well, we were going to wrap it up soon anyway. I'll be heading home shortly. Don't worry about me. I'm fine. Goodnight.'

'Was that your boyfriend?' Alissa asked when she rejoined them.

'Yeah, he was making sure everything was okay. He's away with work.'

'He certainly checks up on you a lot,' Alissa continued.

Bel was torn between feeling ill at ease about Tate's dominating attitude just now and Alissa's slightly judgy tone. 'He's a little protective,' she said. 'I moved here from somewhere a lot smaller. He worries about me.'

Alissa sent her a small smile and thankfully dropped the subject, but her concerned expression rattled Bel more than she cared to admit. That hadn't been a normal phone call, and coming straight after the strange encounter with Lucile, Bel was feeling odd. She tried to dismiss her unease, but she suddenly realised she was doing that a lot these days. That first morning when she'd gone out for coffee he'd had a strange reaction too, and she'd put it down to his being tired and out of sorts. But as she thought back to some of the other things she'd brushed off as bad moods or being overprotective, Bel felt something inside of her drop. *Oh God. How did I miss so many red flags?*

Later, as Bel let herself into the apartment, she resisted the urge to look around for the cameras. After she'd showered and climbed into bed, her phone buzzed. A message from Tate: 'Now get some sleep.'

Bel lay in bed, staring into the darkness as a cold, uncomfortable sensation coursed through her body. He was watching her right now, she realised. Lucile's words ran through her head. *He isn't who you think he is.*

'You look terrible,' Terry said to Bel two days later. Tate was still away and she hadn't been able to sleep ever since finding out about the cameras and receiving Tate's rather creepy text. Maybe she was being oversensitive and the lack of sleep was probably making her a little paranoid, but she couldn't help feeling that every move she made was being watched. She hated being in that beautiful, sterile apartment now. Even reading couldn't take her mind off it.

'Gee, thanks,' Bel said to her boss without bothering to lift her gaze from the computer as she organised an order for a customer who'd called earlier.

'Bel . . . I was wondering. Are you still looking for a place to rent? I remember you asking when you first started here.'

'Oh. Well, kind of. Only I can't find anything I can afford.'

'I was thinking, there's a space upstairs. We used to use it for storage before we fixed up the basement. It hasn't been cleaned out in a while but there's a kitchenette and a bathroom and you'd fit a bed and lounge with no problem. It's yours if you want it.'

Bel stared at her boss blankly as she tried to digest what she'd just heard. 'Uh . . . how much rent would you want?' she asked.

'We can sort out something,' Terry said reassuringly. 'Maybe you can do my weekend shift every second week or something? It's going to need a good clean, and most people would think it was too small and dated, which is why I haven't ever bothered trying to rent it out.'

Tears welled up and began to overflow from Bel's eyes. Maybe it was the lack of sleep, or maybe it was because she was so relieved she had a way to extract herself from the situation. Lucile's visit had been replaying over and over in her mind. Even if it turned out Lucile had been lying, the truth was, Bel wasn't comfortable being so dependent on someone else's provision—someone she really didn't know at all. She stared at her boss, realising suddenly that she knew Terry and his community far better than she knew Tate and his.

She quickly swiped at her eyes and lowered her gaze, feeling ridiculous. 'I don't know why I'm crying. Thank you,' she managed, clearing her throat.

Terry thankfully didn't make a big deal of it. 'Go up and have a look and see what you think,' he said, gesturing towards the front door and holding up a key. 'The stairs are around the side.'

Bel accepted the key with a watery smile. She hadn't even been aware there *was* an upstairs until five minutes ago. She'd noticed the staircase when she took out the rubbish, but always thought it belonged to another shop.

At the top of the staircase, she turned the key in the unassuming timber door and went inside. It opened into an open-plan area with a small kitchen on one side and a doorway that she assumed led to a bathroom on the other. Shafts of sunlight streamed into the room from three dusty windows looking onto the main street, filling the space with a warm, cheerful glow. The place could certainly use a bit of a scrub, but already she could imagine a comfy second-hand lounge and a tall lamp making the perfect reading spot in the corner, with a small kitchen table and bed on the other side.

She needed her own space, now more than ever, after the camera incident. Maybe it was nothing. Maybe she was making more out of it than it really was. However, if she was going to really step into her new life, she needed to do it on her own, without the comfort of a luxury apartment and a boyfriend to pay all the bills.

It had started to feel like she was being kept . . . owned, like a weird kind of doll or something—as if Tate was dressing her up and playing with her as it suited him. Was she overthinking it? She'd wondered more than once. When she tried to view her situation from an outside perspective, it sounded like every woman's dream—a gorgeous man who seemed happy to have her with him and share his ridiculously expensive life. But if everything was fine, why did that little niggle of concern keep getting louder with each passing day?

She found Terry in his office and held out the key. 'I'd like to take it.'

'Then you better hang on to that,' he said, nodding his head at the key. 'Do you need a hand getting your belongings from your current place?' His tone remained calm and easy, but there was a firmness in his expression that spoke volumes.

'I don't have much. I'll be okay,' she assured him. She only had one suitcase. 'Thank you, Terry,' she said, feeling a little embarrassed that her boss had figured out she was in some kind of trouble, yet so grateful that, despite not knowing the details, he had stepped in and offered her this lifeline without asking any questions. She felt her throat tighten once more.

Now she had a plan, all she had to do was tell Tate.

'Why would you want to rent when you can stay here for free?' Tate asked when she told him the news later that afternoon.

'That was the original plan,' she said, shrugging. 'I'm not comfortable having you pay for everything.'

'I like having you here.'

'I love being here,' she said. And she had. When he wasn't in a mood, everything about their relationship was amazing. He was thoughtful and generous to a fault. But then there were the other times, when he was overprotective and demanding, when he wanted to dictate what she wore. That was just . . . weird. 'Everything we did was so fast. And I don't regret any of it, but maybe we need to take things a little bit slower, to enjoy things a bit more.'

'That doesn't make any sense,' he said, a small frown etching onto his forehead. 'We're crazy about each other. Why slow down?'

'Who is Lucile?' she asked quietly.

'What?' he asked, his eyebrows snapping together.

'A woman named Lucile came into the shop the other day and introduced herself,' she said. When he didn't reply, she added, 'You didn't tell me you'd been engaged.'

'It's ancient history.'

'It's also important.'

'So, what did she say?' His intense expression sent a prickle of unease through the pit of her stomach.

'Not a lot. I was just surprised when she introduced herself as your ex-fiancée.'

'There's a good reason she's my ex—she's crazy. Clearly she said something else if you're moving out.'

'You know I've been looking for an apartment, and one came up today out of the blue. It's not because of Lucile. I feel like we've been moving so fast. Nothing has to change between us, we can just move at a bit of a slower pace,' she added.

'When you know it's right, why waste time?' he countered stubbornly. 'You said it yourself, we instantly clicked.'

Well that wasn't entirely true. 'When did we first meet?' Bel asked him, deciding to bring up the one thing that had been bugging her from the very start.

'What?'

'Do you recall the first time we met?' she asked.

'The night of the cocktail party at Glentoberon,' he said, clearly humouring her.

'That wasn't our first meeting.'

'Yes, it was.'

'No. It wasn't,' she said, shaking her head and standing up from the sofa to take a few steps away. 'I met you for the first time the day you arrived in Wessex.'

'I think I would have remembered that,' he said in a condescending tone.

'I gave you directions to Glentoberon.'

He gave a small dismissive chuckle. 'No, you didn't. I asked someone at the petrol station for directions,' he said then stopped. His frown grew deeper as he stared at her. 'No way.'

'Way,' Bel said. 'So we didn't click instantly. It was only after I'd had my makeover for the wedding. Before that, you didn't even give me a second glance.'

'I . . .' He seemed to be struggling to make sense of the whole thing. 'That's why you're moving out? You're punishing me for not recognising you?'

'No,' Bel said. 'Tate, I used to be too scared to change my life. I was happy for everything to stay the way it was because it was easier. Then you walked into that store and everything was different. For the first time ever, I wanted to change everything. I wanted to make you see me—*really* see me. You were the reason I finally wanted to do something with my life, try new things and see new places. I wouldn't have done that if it hadn't been for you. And here I am,' she said, throwing out her arm and smiling, 'in a brand-new city, in a brand-new job. I've loved and appreciated everything you've done for me, but I want to be able to know I did some if it myself. Just because I have my own flat, it doesn't have to change things. I mean, you go away so often, it won't be that different.'

'It changes everything. You know I don't have much time when I'm back. I don't want to waste any of it commuting between wherever you are and here.'

'It's not that far—' she started to protest.

'Were you and Larkin having a good old laugh about this?' he said, cutting Bel off aburptly and throwing her with the sudden change in direction.

'What are you talking about?'

'Was it some kind of dare? Your makeover? The old ugly-duckling-to-swan thing?'

His words genuinely shocked her. 'Of course not.'

'Funny you never mentioned that it was you at the petrol station. I guess you didn't want to risk it.'

'I wasn't hiding anything. All it took was contact lenses, a few new clothes and a new hair colour and you were completely brainwashed.' She'd always thought the Clark Kent and Superman thing was too far-fetched to be believable but, after this, she wondered if maybe there was something to it. 'It's not my fault you're so shallow that you didn't recognise me.'

He looked away from her and folded his arms across his chest. 'I won't stop you leaving,' he said. His face could have been carved from stone. 'But if you walk out that door, don't bother coming back.'

The finality of his statement stole her breath. How could he switch his emotions off so quickly? Did he even have emotions to switch off? Was what they'd had really so meaningless? That emptiness in the pit of her stomach she'd felt after Lucile's visit returned, and she could no longer ignore what she'd been trying to rationalise ever since that day.

Bel took some time to muster her composure then turned to go and pack her belongings. She fought the urge to cry; she wasn't going to give him the satisfaction.

This Tate was not the same charming man she'd first met. There was certainly nothing about him now that reflected any of Jax Lexington's qualities. Seeing that coldness . . . it was like she'd been in the dark and someone had just switched on the lights. This man was nothing like Jax.

He'd gone from someone she'd blindly decided to throw away her old life for to the cold-hearted bastard sitting out there on the sofa, waiting for her to leave. She'd clearly been fooled. Suddenly, Lucile's warning didn't seem so hard to credit.

With the last of her things collected from the bathroom and her clothes squeezed into her suitcase, she did a final check, like she was leaving a motel room. Who had she been kidding? This place had never been a home—and it was never going to be *her* home. Maybe she had been just as guilty of burying her head in the sand and only seeing what she'd wanted to see as he had.

She didn't look at Tate as she walked to the front door and placed her key on the hall table. She simply opened the door and listened for the last time as it hissed closed behind her.

There was no going back. She could only go forward.

Fifteen

TWELVE MONTHS LATER

Bel's little flat above the bookshop had become both her sanctuary and her workplace. A few times she'd thought to find a bigger place, but there really wasn't any need. She could set up with her laptop comfortably at her kitchen table and the location was convenient to everything she needed.

The bookshop, although it paid well for retail, wasn't the highest earning job in the world and it had made her more than a little uncomfortable that she didn't have spare cash or an emergency fund.

The cost of living was a lot higher here than in Wessex, so she'd turned her attention to researching ways to make extra income. Then she'd remembered Fiona, the author whose event they'd held, and what she'd said about freelance work.

She'd taken the plunge and enrolled in a course for copyediting and proofreading, then put out a call to her wider romance writers contacts and registered herself for content writing and editing on an outsourcing site. Within weeks, the work started trickling in. She felt a huge sense of achievement when she received heartfelt praise from her clients, and as their reviews came in, so too did the bookings. Some of the work wasn't exactly stimulating, since it was more business-related, writing articles and social media content, but she also picked up the odd fiction-editing project and that was where her heart truly lay. It gave her an incredible sense of fulfilment.

The night she'd left Tate, she'd made a tearful call to Emma. She'd felt bad for worrying her friend, waking her up in the very early hours due to the time difference and sobbing incoherently. But, in true best friend spirit, Emma had let her cry before stepping in to get to the bottom of it. Then she'd instantly switched to lioness mode. 'What a creep. No, that was definitely not overreacting. The camera stuff was without a doubt red flag material. Thank God you got out of there.'

Bel had gone on to break the news to Emma that she still wasn't planning on returning to Wessex.

'Staying? But . . . why? There's nothing to keep you there anymore.'

'I know it sounds a bit strange, but I don't want to come back like a dog with its tail between its legs. I feel like a complete idiot.'

'You're not an idiot. You certainly aren't the first one to have fallen for a handsome face and run off into the sunset,' Emma had said.

'Yeah, well . . . it's too soon. And as much as I hate to admit it, you were right to try and push me to leave town all those times. I should have done this sooner, without the possibly narcissistic control freak of a boyfriend,' Bel had added wryly. 'I like it over here. I really love my job. I get to talk about books all day to people whose eyes don't glaze over.'

'If you come home, I promise I'll hang on every word you say,' Emma had said, and Bel had imagined the playful pout on her friend's face.

Emma had shown her support by finding an elderly tenant for her house, Bert, who had been searching for somewhere to live. Even little Wessex hadn't escaped the rental crisis, and accommodation was scarce.

Bel still missed her best friend terribly and had the odd bout of homesickness, but she honestly believed she'd made the right decision.

Within four months, she'd cut back to only a few days a week in the bookshop, and by eight months she was working in her own business full-time. She rarely thought of Wessex as home anymore. She was a different person to the one who'd left town, lovestruck and stupid.

She tried not to think too much about that either. 'Tate wasn't the guy I thought he was.' The minute she had said the words out loud on the phone to Emma that night, the truth had dawned on her. He wasn't the guy he'd presented himself as, but he wasn't the man she'd made herself believe he was either. He wasn't Jax Lexington. She'd been so caught up in trying to escape reality that, at the first glimpse of something remotely out of the ordinary, she'd blindly convinced herself he was *the one*.

Terry had encouraged her to go out and meet new people, but after trying the dating scene a few times, she really couldn't find anything exciting in the nervous first dates and men who were never quite right for her. There'd been the odd weirdo—including one guy who'd had a strange obsession with her feet—but the majority of the men appeared to be perfectly normal. Nevertheless, her heart wasn't in it. Maybe it was still too soon. None of them gave her the same tingles as Tate had. Certainly none of them had possessed his fiction-hero good looks and confidence, although she could freely admit now that this was not necessarily a bad thing. Looks were certainly unimportant when they hid a controlling personality. No, she'd learned her lesson—romance was for books, not real life. Never would she allow herself to be swept away like that again.

Taking her cup of hot chocolate to bed after a late night editing, Bel switched on the soothing music she listened to in the evenings to wind down and finished her drink before snuggling into her comfy bed. She was content, living a new life in an exciting place with unlimited possibilities. She wasn't limited to town gossip or a job with nowhere to go. Her business had been steadily growing and she couldn't be prouder of everything she'd achieved. Who would have thought? A small-town girl from Wessex was doing okay in the big city.

Bel blinked uncertainly in the dark room, disoriented. Then the ringing of her phone registered.

She scrambled across the bed to answer it, a tightness in the pit of her stomach. *No good news ever comes at this hour.*

'Bel?' Emma's voice shook. 'Craig's had an accident. They don't think he's going to make it.'

It felt strange watching the scenery begin to transform as they got closer to Wessex. Nothing had really changed in the last fifteen or so months. It was the same paddocks, an endless patchwork of greens and browns and yellows stretching out forever, crops in some and flocks of cloud-like sheep grazing in others. Yet everything felt different. The place hadn't changed, but she had.

Bel glanced as inconspicuously as she could at the man driving, pondering the changes she saw there too. Something about him seemed different, but she couldn't quite put her finger on what.

Dean Preston wouldn't have been her first choice for a lift from the airport, but she wasn't about to add to Emma's problems by being picky. Her friend had more than her share of worries right now. She'd been a mess during that panicked call. Craig had somehow fallen from his tractor and hit his head, and that split-second, Bel knew, had changed life for everyone. He'd been flown to Sydney in a vegetative state, which often came with traumatic brain injuries, and they'd been unable to assess what degree of cognitive or physical damage he had sustained.

Bel had wanted to book a ticket home immediately, but once Emma had calmed down, she'd told her to hold off until they knew more.

Bel hadn't been able to go back to sleep and had spent the night worried for her friends. Early the next morning, Emma had called; Craig had made it through surgery, but he was a long way from being out of the woods.

Emma would be shouldering the burden of not only the property, which was their business, but also four young children and a household that would still need her undivided attention. This wouldn't be over in a week or two, either. They were potentially looking at a year—probably more—*if* he even recovered. They simply had no way of knowing the extent of the brain injury yet.

Bel had made her decision then and there—she was going home.

She'd spent a frantic few days packing and organising. The size of her flat had stopped her buying much, so apart from a few things that she'd get shipped to follow her, she only had two more suitcases than when she'd first arrived. She left the flat furnished—the furniture had all been second-hand anyway—and hoped that Terry could make some use of it.

By the time Terry had dropped her at the airport, she'd managed to completely clear away twelve months of her life, barely leaving a sign that she'd ever been there. It was a strange feeling.

'It was good that you could come back. How long are you staying for?' Dean asked as they drove, breaking into her thoughts.

'As long as I'm needed.'

'I heard you were working in a bookstore. They must be okay if they're giving you so much time off work.'

She glanced across at him. 'I've been working for myself for a while now. Luckily I can do it from pretty much anywhere.'

He looked different. He'd trimmed back his beard to a dark stubble and she found herself intrigued by his newly visible jawline. It had always amazed her how facial hair—either the removal or the growth—could make such a huge difference to a man's appearance.

'What kind of business are you in?' he asked.

'I do a bit of copyediting and content writing. I have a lot of corporate and business clients as well as creatives.'

'Yeah? Wow. That sounds impressive.'

'I kind of fell into it, but I really love it.'

'That's great.'

'Yeah. What about you? Still farming?'

'Yep. Can't see that changing any time soon.'

'I heard you've been helping out on Craig and Emma's property. That's really nice of you.'

'It's what we do,' he said simply. 'There'll be more neighbours and mates lending a hand whenever they can. Everyone's a bit snowed under with the harvest, but we'll get it done. Em's been amazing. Can't imagine how hard it's been to keep it together for the kids the way she has. She'll be glad you're here, that's for sure.'

'Em told me you were the one who found him,' Bel said.

He glanced across at her briefly. 'Yeah. Not that I could do much. I noticed the harvester hadn't moved in a while and thought he might need a hand. But when I got there, I found him on the ground. He must have climbed up top to clear a blockage or something and slipped. He was in a bad way. Em and the kids arrived a few minutes later.'

'I can't imagine how terrifying it would have been for her, and with them there . . .' she said. *God, poor Em.* She quickly turned to look out the window, blinking hard.

'Everyone's been doing what they can. I heard there's a fundraising page being set up to help with some of the expenses,' he said, lifting a finger from the steering wheel in acknowledgement of a passing ute driver. 'People chip in however they can when someone's going through a rough patch.'

That was the thing Bel loved the most about her community. They'd always band together to take care of one of their own. Something she'd noticed wasn't always the case in a big city—she'd been lucky to have met Terry, who had been her saving grace.

'It's still strange seeing you like this,' Dean said after a short silence.

'Like what?'

'Like that,' he said, giving her a brief look up and down. 'You look like a whole different person.'

Bel let out a small huff. 'I swapped glasses for contacts and cut my hair. I don't look that different.'

'It's not so much the look,' he said slowly. 'It's everything. You seem more . . . I don't know . . . confident or something. Like one of those models.'

'A model?'

'I don't know,' he said, sounding flustered. 'It's your attitude. Everything seems to have changed. The way you walk and even how you talk. It's like the old Bel disappeared and you're someone else now.'

She wasn't sure how to respond. She tried to work out if he thought this was a good or a bad thing, but she really couldn't tell.

As they came into Wessex, Bel caught sight of the latest addition to town and her eyes widened. 'Whoa.' The huge object grew even bigger the closer they got.

'You like the Big Cock?' Dean asked with a smirk.

'I imagine every man in Wessex has been enjoying saying that each time they go past.'

'Well, it *is* impressive.'

It was something, that's for sure. With Elvis being the clear winner of the community vote for Wessex's mascot, even after a recount, the committee had wasted no time in getting things under way. Emma had been keeping Bel updated on the statue's progress, but seeing it in person was a whole different experience. It was *enormous*, well over seventeen metres tall. Visitors could climb a staircase right up to the top to look out, getting a panoramic view of the main street, which had been given a facelift since Bel had left. Brightly coloured pots of petunias and geraniums sat outside most of the stores, and the street's facades and verandah posts had been given a fresh coat of paint. It lifted her spirits to see the place looking so much more vibrant.

As they passed by Dwyers', Bel felt a little tug of affection. It felt like a lifetime since she'd seen the old place.

It had been a little over a year since the wedding and the big flood. Larkin had invited Bel to the one-year anniversary celebration, a reunion of the wedding party for a week-long trip to Vanuatu, where Larkin and Tristan had gone on their honeymoon. She'd politely refused, and the current status of the cousins' relationship was non-speaking.

Bel was okay with that. She'd rather repeatedly kick her little toe on the corner of the table than attend a week-long reunion with Tate. Larkin had told her he was planning to bring a date, as if that would somehow make it better.

The drive out to Emma's passed by in a blur of landmarks—the O'Donnal's rusty old milk can letterbox, and further along, the Simpsons' home-made, brightly painted metal mailbox, which was shaped somewhat like a horse, or donkey—its true identity was an ongoing debate around town, and was made even more confusing by the fact that neither animal was kept on the property. They passed by the faded Flowers for Sale sign on the old readside stall that hadn't been used for years, and the little white wooden cross beneath a huge old gumtree, a memorial to Bobby Robinson, who'd died decades earlier in a car accident. All the things that she'd driven by a thousand times and never taken that much notice of. Suddenly they meant something; they were all little markers of home.

The cattle grid at the entrance to Emma and Craig's driveway rattled beneath Dean's ute and the house appeared ahead. The brightly coloured play equipment and the massive trampoline, surrounded by neatly kept shrubs and flowerbeds, was still there in the front yard. Everything looked the same, only Bel felt a sadness lingering. No laughing children played on the equipment, no one rode the bikes that lay on their sides, abandoned, and it was unusually quiet.

Bel went to help unload her suitcases, but Dean waved her away. 'You go up and say hello. I can bring these in.'

The front door opened with its familiar squeak and Bel looked up to see Ayla, Emma and Craig's eldest, standing in the doorway. Her heart lurched at the child's hesitant expression. Once Ayla would have run down the stairs to greet her with a huge hug. She was now eight, and taller than when Bel had last seen her. Jack the cattle dog stood protectively by the child's side until he recognised Bel. His thick tail thumped on the floor and she smiled slightly at the dopey grin on his blue-grey face.

'Hello,' Bel said, stepping closer to Ayla. 'Look how tall you've got.'

'Hello,' Ayla said, almost shyly. 'Are you here to look after us?'

'I am. I came back to give Mum a hand. Where are the others?'

'In their rooms. Mrs Sheppard said we all needed to give her a break.'

Bel remembered Mrs Sheppard from her gran's CWA days. She could understand the woman maybe needing a little rest. She'd seemed old when Bel was a kid, so she had no idea what age she was now, but she probably wasn't up to running after four active children.

She made her way inside and found Mrs Sheppard in the kitchen. She greeted the older woman, who somehow managed to look exactly as Bel remembered her as a kid, and Bel barely had time to ask how she was before Mrs Sheppard was grabbing her handbag and bustling out the door. 'Thank you,' Bel called, and Mrs Sheppard gave her a wave without turning around.

Bel turned back to Ayla with narrowed eyes. 'Did you guys give Mrs Sheppard a hard time?'

'No,' Ayla said with a beguiling innocence that may have fooled some people but not Bel, who'd know the child since she'd been in the womb.

'Ayla Louise Prichard,' Bel said, planting her hands on her hips.

'We didn't do nothing. She said we were being too noisy and sent us to our rooms.'

Bel decided to give Ayla the benefit of the doubt, seeing as Mrs Sheppard's days of being able to handle loud children were probably long gone. Emma had been stressed enough trying to sort out the kids' situation from Sydney, being unable to take care of them herself and with her parents travelling overseas. The ladies of Wessex had been doing shifts in the Prichard house so as not to disrupt the children's routine even more.

'Okay. Well, let's go and tell the others they can come out. We've got a lot of stuff to do.'

'Like what?' Ayla asked curiously.

'Like having fun,' Bel said.

'So we don't have to go to school?' the little girl asked hopefully.

'Fun *after* school,' Bel amended as she walked down the hallway to the bedrooms.

She opened the door to Ben's room. 'Hey, kiddo.'

The little boy looked up from a picture book and Bel felt her heart break a little. Where was the lively little ratbag she used to know? 'Hello, Aunty Bel. Are you here to take care of us?'

'I sure am,' she said, crossing to the bed and sitting down. 'Is that okay?'

He shrugged and turned back to his book.

It was understandable that the kids would be feeling confused. They'd had a revolving door of people taking them to school and bringing them home, coming and going. It was no wonder they weren't sure what to expect. But she was here now, and determined to restore some kind of normality for them.

'Aunty Bel!' Lucy and Ivy came running through the door and jumped on her lap. Bel hugged them tightly. *At least not everything's changed around here.*

'When's Mummy and Daddy coming home?' Ben asked.

'I'm not sure. It might be a little while yet.'

'My daddy got taken away in an ambulance,' Ivy said with wide eyes.

'That must have been a bit scary,' Bel said.

'There was blood,' Ayla said solemnly.

Bel wasn't sure what the protocol for dealing with childhood trauma was—did you let them talk about it? Did you try and explain it or did you ignore it? She had no idea. 'Daddy's got a lot of doctors and nurses taking really good care of him. I know you miss him a lot and you're probably really worried about him,' she said gently. 'But at the moment, he needs to be away in hospital so he can get better. Mummy needs to stay there with him for a little while too, until the doctors can give her some more news. But I'm here to take care of you guys until Mummy can come home. And I was thinking, maybe we can do something to surprise them when they come home?'

'Like what?' Ivy asked.

'I don't know. Can you guys think of anything?'

'What about the chook pen?' Ayla suggested. 'Mummy's always asking Daddy to fix it, but he never has time.'

'That sounds like a good idea. What do you think, Ben?' Bel asked.

'Yeah,' he said. He was still staring at the book, but Bel noticed he hadn't turned a page in a while and suspected he was listening more closely than he appeared to be. 'But you don't know how to fix things.'

Okay, well, the kid has a point. She couldn't be too offended though, at least he'd given her a glimpse of the ratbag she remembered.

'But *I* do,' Dean said from the doorway he was leaning against, having silently appeared God only knew how long ago. Bel found herself slightly distracted by the way his folded arms pulled his T-shirt a little tighter across his chest. Her eyes lifted to his face and she quickly looked away when they met his.

Crap. Bel cleared her throat quickly. 'There you go. Uncle Dean knows how to fix a chook pen. Yay, Uncle Dean,' she added weakly, without looking at him.

'How about we go out and take a look at what needs to be done? You wanna show me what you're thinking?' Dean asked Ben. Bel saw the young boy's chest puff out a little.

'Can we come too?' Ivy and Lucy asked, bouncing on the bed.

'Sure. Why don't we all go out? Coming, Aunty Bel?' Dean asked as the kids all flew past him and headed out the back door.

Bel gave him a quick smile. 'Thanks for that.'

'No worries. I think it's a good idea, give them something to take their minds off stuff.'

'Will you have time though? You're in the middle of harvest.'

'I'll make time,' he said simply as Bel drew level with him in the doorway. Was it her imagination or did his eyes suddenly get a whole lot more sultry? And why was she suddenly feeling like she'd just experienced a hot flush?

What is happening here?

'Come onnnnnnn,' Lucy bellowed from the back door.

'The natives are getting restless,' Dean murmured as Bel moved past him, almost brushing against his torso in the process.

Bel squashed down all the weird, wayward feelings that had suddenly sprung to life and hurried outside. Did you get jet lag from flying across the country? That had to be it. A hot shower and a good night's sleep and everything would be back to normal—whatever the hell that was nowadays.

Later that evening, after Dean had left and Bel had gotten through the whole dinner and bath routine, she read down the list on the fridge. 'Bedtime book,' she said out loud. Now this was more like it. Finally, something she could handle. 'What book are we reading?' she asked.

'I'll get it!' Ivy said, running down the hallway.

'No! I will!' Ben shouted after his twin.

'Ben, let Ivy get the book,' Bel started to call out, but already a fight had erupted in the enclosed verandah that was a playroom for the children. With a long-suffering sigh, Bel followed the yelling and took control of the book the siblings had been wrestling over. 'Any more fighting and I'm not reading tonight. Now, let's go out to the lounge room and find a place to sit.'

'Mummy always reads us our bedtime stories in her bed,' Ivy said, leading the way towards Emma and Craig's bedroom. 'So we all fit.'

'Fine, but no more fighting,' Bel warned in her best don't-mess-with-me tone, although she was fairly sure none of the kids were feeling the least bit intimidated. They all settled onto the bed. Bel had to admit, this was a pretty lovely way to wind down at the end of a long day. With two little bodies curled up on either side of her, Bel looked down at the book and a surge of childhood memories came flooding back. 'The Magic Faraway Tree,' she read. She'd been obsessed with this story and had read all the Enid Blyton classics when she was little. Which was most likely where her love of reading had come from.

She recalled her grandparents always teasing her that she was like a cat—they'd never know where she was until they called her for food. Then she'd uncurl herself from a sunny spot in the corner of the room or come in from where she'd been sitting under a tree in the back yard, reading. These stories of faraway lands and magical creatures had been her escape from grief and loneliness when she'd first moved to Wessex. Much like her later escape from everyday life with the Jax Lexington books.

'Joe, Silky and Moon-Face were very pleased that Joe was the right way up again,' Bel began reading, and soon she was as engrossed as the four children snuggled beside her, all of them lost in the magical world of make-believe.

Sixteen

'Any news?' Bel asked the next evening when Emma rang to say goodnight to the kids.

'They took out his feeding tube and he's awake a lot more often now. He's not able to speak yet, but he can squeeze the doctor's hand in response to stimulus, which they've said is a big thing.' Bel knew Emma was trying to stay positive, but there was a hint of hopelessness underlying her friend's voice.

Bel felt a heaviness in her stomach. None of this seemed real. 'Well, that sounds positive.' She tried for an optimistic tone, but how on earth did you deal with the fact that your once fully functional husband was in an almost vegetative state, unable to do the most basic of things?

'It's . . . it's so hard, seeing him so . . .' Emma let out a small, tortured sound. 'He can't talk, Bel. He can't eat on his own. He cries,' she said, and stopped abruptly to gather herself. Bel heard her take some shaky breaths. 'The nurses say it's all normal for his condition, but it's so damn hard to watch. Everything is just so . . . shit,' she finished.

'I wish I could be down there for you,' Bel said, feeling helpless.

'No, I'm fine. Honestly. Craig's family have been amazing. I have someone with me all the time. It's just . . . I'm so tired. I want this to all be over so we can come home. But even then, they keep saying it's going to take a really long time before—*if,* she corrected and gave a sniff, 'he ever gets back to normal again.'

'And when that time comes, you know that you'll have all the support you'll need. I'll stay for however long it takes.'

'But you have your own life to get back to.'

'I don't have to be anywhere except where I'm needed. I'm not going anywhere.'

'Thanks, Bel. I can't thank you enough, for being there for the kids.'

'You don't need to thank me. God, Em, you've got enough to worry about without having to stress over the kids as well.'

'They sounded a lot happier tonight. The poor things have been passed around from one person to the next since it happened. I barely had time to explain anything before I had to leave. I feel so bad, abandoning them like that.'

'You didn't abandon them. It's a horrible position for you to be in. They are worried about Craig, which is completely understandable, but we think we've managed to come up with a distraction of sorts, so hopefully it'll take their minds off things for a bit.'

'Oh yes, they told me they had a big surprise for when we come home. Something to do with building. Should I be worried?' Emma sounded a little more like her old self and Bel breathed a silent sigh of relief.

'Absolutely not,' Bel reassured her blithely.

'They also told me Dean was involved, so at least there's adult supervision.'

'Gee, thanks a lot for the vote of confidence. I can YouTube as well as the next home handyman, you know,' Bel said with an exaggerated sniff.

'But seriously, it's great the two of you can help each other out. I think the kids will be thrilled. So, how's things going with Dean?'

'What do you mean?' Bel asked, a little too quickly. Rookie mistake. Emma's curiosity radar would pick up on that instantly.

The slight pause on the other end of the line confirmed it. 'You two had a weird vibe going on once. Is it still there?'

'There's no vibe. He's great with the kids and he's helping out because he's your good friend. End of story.'

'Uh-huh.'

'Would you stop trying to play matchmaker?'

'I always said you two would be perfect together,' Emma reminded her.

'Not happening.'

'Why? He's a perfectly nice guy.'

'Because I'm not looking for a boyfriend right now. I don't even know where I want to live. The last thing I need is to add a complication.'

'Would it be so bad to move back to Wessex?'

'I don't know if I can. I mean . . . I'm sure everyone knows I left here like some lovesick puppy with a guy I barely knew and it didn't work out. When I see people now, I know that's what they're thinking.'

'I think you give your love life way too much credit. There have been bigger scandals in town since yours, you know.'

'Like what?' Bel asked, curious despite herself.

'Like Susan McDonald cheating on Alfie with Bruce Allsop, then Alfie going off and having an affair with Bruce's wife, Cheryl.'

'Really?' Bel remembered Cheryl Allsop being a quiet, church-going woman in her late fifties, not at all like someone who would have an affair in retaliation.

'Then there was the whole Danny Limburg thing.'

'Who's Danny Limburg?

'He was the stepfather of Josie Cunningham. You remember her, she went to school with us for a few years, left in like Year Nine or something.'

'Oh. Yeah.'

'Well, Danny left her mother . . . and married Josie.'

'Get. Out. Of. Town,' Bel gasped. 'That's *so* wrong.'

'Apparently, it's true love.' Emma said with a doubtful sigh. 'Anyway,' she continued, snapping Bel from her abject horror, 'you aren't returning with a broken heart and your tail between your legs. You have a successful business. You're self-employed. You have nothing to be ashamed of.'

She supposed that much was true.

'You don't have to decide straight away. Stop thinking about it for a while. You'll know what you want to do when the time's right.'

They said goodnight and Bel felt a little better. Em was right—as usual. Just like the kids, perhaps she could use a bit of a distraction, and *maybe* Dean was just the distraction she needed to take her mind off her uncertain future.

'Lucy! Ivy! Do you have your socks on?' Bel called from the kitchen bench on Monday morning, as she fumbled with the plastic film she was using to wrap the sandwiches.

'My sock feels funny! I can't wear it,' Lucy yelled back.

'Ben? Are you dressed?'

'I can't find my green tractor.'

'We don't have time to play with your tractor, mate. We need to get to school.'

'It's for show and tell! I need it!'

Bel sent another frantic glance at the clock on the wall and swore.

'You have to put a dollar in the swear jar,' Ayla said in a sing-song voice as she sat on a stool, swinging her legs.

'Sorry. I shouldn't have said that.'

'Can I say that word?' Ivy asked, coming into the kitchen.

'No. It's a grown-up word.'

'How come grown-ups can say bad words?'

'They shouldn't,' Bel conceded, biting back another bad word as the cling wrap stuck to everything except what she wanted it to. 'How the hell does your mother do this every day?'

'Another dollar!' Ayla chortled.

'Hell isn't a swear word,' Bel argued.

'What the hell?' Ivy said, staring at the lunch Bel had packed.

'Okay, you're right. I'll put in another dollar,' Bel said. 'Just put the lid on the lunch box and pack it in your bag,' she told Ivy, who was still examining its contents doubtfully. 'Ben! We have to go!'

'I can't find my tractor!' he yelled back angrily.

Bel let out a long sigh. They hadn't even left the house and she was exhausted. People actually did this motherhood thing on purpose?

'Got everything under control, I see,' Dean said as he opened the back door.

'I thought I did,' she mumbled, heading into the lounge room only to find Lucy playing with her kitchen set, barefoot. 'Lucy! Where are your shoes and socks? We're running late.'

'I don't like those socks. They're scratchy.'

'Can you please go and see what Ben's doing?' she asked Dean. 'I need to find some different socks.'

Fifteen minutes later, she had all four kids strapped in their car seats and was standing by the driver-side door. 'Thanks for your help,' she said to Dean. 'Oh,' she added, swivelling back to face him, 'what was it you came over for?'

'I stopped by to see if you needed a hand, but you had it mostly under control,' he said.

'Yeah. Mostly,' she said, grimacing.

'I'm going to take some measurements for the pen while I'm here.'

'Okay. Well . . . thanks again.' She waved and closed the door, starting the engine of Emma's four-wheel drive. They were only ten minutes late, which wasn't too bad, all things considered.

But she was going to need to get everyone out the door a lot faster if she was ever to match Emma's standard.

After school and daycare drop-off, Bel returned to something that she'd been wondering about ever since coming back to Wessex. There didn't seem to be any noticeable influx of tourists. There weren't any motorhomes or caravans in the specially designated carpark the committee had located within easy walking distance of the main street, just dusty utes and dirty four-wheel drives like the one she was in—farm vehicles and locals. The Big Rooster had been officially open for a few months now, but there was no sign that it was the drawcard the committee had been hoping it would be. A shame, considering all their hard work.

Bel pulled up at the bowser outside Dwyers', unable to help the fond smile that found its way to her lips as she thought back over the years she'd spent working here. The familiar jingle of the bell and the smell of the old shop triggered another avalanche of memories.

Doreen glanced up from her crossword puzzle and looked at Bel over the top of a pair of smudged glasses. 'Well, well, well. Look what the cat dragged in,' she said in her raspy, pack-a-day voice. 'I heard you were back.'

'Hello, Doreen. Yeah, I came back to help out while Emma is in Sydney with Craig.'

'Sorry business. Sounds like he was a lucky boy. Not too many would have survived an accident like that.'

Their district had lost too many people through farm accidents over the years. It could be a hazardous job, working with big machinery in remote locations, and often alone.

'He's putting up a good fight.' Bel tapped the card on the reader and waited for the payment to process.

'How's Emma doing?'

'She seems to be holding it together, but I can't imagine it's easy for her. All she can do is wait and see what the extent of the damage is. She said they'd have a better idea in a day or two.'

'So, you gonna be looking for your old job back?' Doreen asked. Clearly, compassionate Doreen had left the building, replaced once more by blunt, to-the-point Doreen.

'Uh . . . no. I haven't decided if I'll be staying.'

Doreen gave a low grunt. 'Apparently, no one wants to work anymore. Looks like I'll be stuck here until the day I drop off the perch.'

'Oh. Well,' Bel said awkwardly, unsure how to respond to that. 'I'd better get going. It was nice to see you again, Doreen.'

The woman muttered something unintelligible before going back to her crossword and Bel headed out to the vehicle. It was strange to think that once, that job had been her life. Doreen could have been her, years from now, if she hadn't left Wessex. A shiver ran up her spine.

Bel moved the four-wheel drive to the carpark beside the Big Rooster and got out, staring up at the huge rooster with quiet admiration. They really had done a great job. She took a photo, feeling like a tourist, and then felt sad because that was what they'd been fighting so hard to achieve, yet there *weren't* any tourists coming out to see their little town.

Well, I'll be one—and proud of it. She climbed the windy staircase inside the statue and emerged at the top of Elvis's comb, taking photos of the main street and the vista of farmland beyond. The views were amazing.

After a few more close-ups of Elvis, she wandered down the main street and snapped some more photos. Pride began to seep through her veins. She'd always loved her hometown, but she had a new appreciation for it after being away. It was as though she were seeing it through brand-new eyes. She supposed to an extent that was true. She felt like a different person to the one who'd left in lots of ways, some good and some not so good, but her experiences had given her a new perspective on life. Craig's accident had also given her something to think about—life was precious and it could be over in a moment.

She waited to cross the road as an old ute rumbled its way past, giving a smile and nod as she recognised Bill Matheson. She was glad he was still around.

The bell above the cafe door jingled when she walked in and Larrisa glanced up and beamed. 'Bel! I heard you were back in town. How are you?'

'Hi, Larrisa. I'm great. The cafe looks fantastic,' she said, taking in the new furniture and décor.

'Yeah,' Larrisa agreed, but her voice had lost its enthusiasm.

'You don't like it?' Bel asked, confused.

'Oh, no, I love it. Once the committee started work on Elvis, the whole place got caught up in our big town makeover,' Larrisa said. 'Lots of businesses invested in shopfront renovations and sprucing everything up for the big invasion of tourists, only that never really eventuated. Now, most of us are left paying out of pocket, spending money we're hard pressed to earn back with no tourist trade coming in.'

'Oh Larrisa, that's such a shame. But I don't understand,' she said. 'What happened? I mean, last time I heard, the committee had plans to advertise and get things happening.'

'After the Bob Baxter thing at the market night, the committee went off track. It became a personal war between Betty and Bob. Once he took his support and money away, we lost a big part of our tourism campaign, and I think the committee was tired.'

It was hard to believe such passion and drive had simply fizzled. Bel knew Emma had stepped down as secretary, but she had been so wrapped up in her own problems at the time, she hadn't really asked what was going on. Now she wished she'd been paying better attention. Not that she would have been able to do anything, but still . . .

Bel chatted to Larrisa for a little while longer and ordered a coffee. She caught up with a few more familiar faces, all seemingly happy to see her. No one mentioned Tate or the fact she'd run away with a stranger and left her life behind. She gave a small, dry chuckle at how worried she'd been that everyone would be talking about it. Em had been right; people had more important things to think about than Bel's moment of madness over twelve months ago.

She sat in the car and pulled out her phone, going through the images she'd taken earlier and posting a few on her Instagram with the caption, 'I found Elvis! #Elvislives #Wessex #localtourism #smalltownfeels #cocksofinstagram'.

Dropping her phone into her bag, she started the car and headed back to Fernvale.

The next day, Bel was feeling a little chuffed. The time from getting up to getting out the front door was improving, and she was even making some new drop-off and pick-up *mum* friends. Well, people that she knew enough to smile hello and goodbye to, at least. Sparked by the positive response to her Elvis post, Bel decided to do a follow-up post and record a video at the museum to explain the origin of the Big Rooster, which a few of her followers had asked about. To be honest, it was nice to have an activity to take her mind off things at Fernvale. Distracting the kids from worrying about their dad and missing their mum was a full-time job, so anything to break the strain was welcome.

She hadn't been inside the Wessex Museum since . . . she had to stop and think about it. Probably since primary school? It was inside an old church that had been closed for years, on a block of land sitting back from the main street. The large weeping willow that had been there forever brought back fond memories, and well-tended flower gardens had been planted along the gravel path leading to the two large arched doors at the entrance. As she walked inside, a familiar smell of musty old books and timber polish hit her in the face, instantly taking her back in time.

'Mabel Buckley, is that you?' a gentle, almost whispery voice asked from nearby, making Bel jump slightly as she waited for her eyes to adjust from the bright sunshine to the dimly lit museum. 'I thought it was. I heard you were back home.'

'Oh, Mrs Simpson. How nice to see you.' The woman was a local legend, involved in every committee and worthwhile cause in town. She'd been working in the museum even back when Bel was a kid.

'You too, dear. Are you back for good?'

'Oh, no. I mean, I don't think so. I came back to help Emma for a while.'

'How is she? How's Craig?' Mrs Simpson asked, frowning and shaking her head in concern.

'Still a long way to go before they'll know what's happening. But Emma's her usual optimistic self.'

'She's a good girl,' the older woman nodded sagely. 'Give them my love when you speak with them, won't you?'

'I sure will.'

'What brings you in here then? Doing a bit of family history research?'

'No, I was just posting about the Elvis statue, and it seems to have gathered a bit of interest. So I thought I might do a post about the origins of it and give my followers some background on the story. You know, for a bit of fun.'

'Your followers?' Mrs Simpson asked, eyeing her oddly. 'Have you started a cult, dear?'

'No, social media followers. You know, like Instagram and Facebook? TikTok,' she added, fading off as the woman continued to stare at her doubtfully.

'Oh, I see. Well, unfortunately, that may prove somewhat difficult.'

'What do you mean?' Bel asked. The old woman turned away, beckoning her to follow. They wound their way through a maze of old machinery until they came to a stop in front of a glass display case with a golden nameplate that was engraved: 'Elvis Peckley. *Guinness Book of World Records*, largest rooster. May 1952.'

Bel frowned as she looked from Mrs Simpson to the empty display case.

'Elvis is missing.'

Seventeen

'How does a one-metre-tall stuffed rooster go missing?' Bel asked Mrs Simpson.

'It was a few weeks ago. I came in and found his case empty. He'd vanished into thin air.'

'Did you report it to the police?'

'Yes, but they didn't really have much to work with. I don't think it was very high on their list of priorities, to be honest.'

'But he's our town mascot.'

'Yes, I know,' Mrs Simpson sighed. 'Unfortunately, no one really seems to care.'

'I care,' Bel said firmly. *And who the hell would steal an old moth-eaten taxidermied bird?*

'Yes, well, apparently it was someone's idea of a joke. Whoever took him left a note. They obviously thought they were being terribly funny. I didn't even bother mentioning it to the police. I could see they thought the whole thing was a complete waste of their time.'

'A note?' Bel repeated slowly.

'A ransom note, dear,' Mrs Simpson said. 'It's in the office.' She bustled away before Bel could stop her, coming back a few moments later with a sheet of paper in a clear plastic sleeve. 'I put it in this to preserve any DNA, in case the police ever came back and decided to take it seriously.'

Clearly, Mrs Simpson watched a lot of crime TV.

'We have your rooster. Don't call the cops or the bird gets it,' Bel read the hastily scrawled, almost unintelligible writing, and bit back a mirthful snort. Okay, so it did seem that Elvis's disappearance was some kind of practical joke. Still, he had heritage value, especially since there was now a monument erected in the middle of the main street for him. 'You probably *should* hand this into the police,' Bel said, giving back the note.

'There's no point, it will only confirm what they already think: that it's just a silly prank. They assured me Elvis would most likely turn up again soon. Probably a bunch of bored kids with nothing better to do.' Mrs Simpson sighed. 'I'm sure they're right. He'll eventually be returned. Anyway, have a good look around and call out if you need any help,' she said, already moving off.

Bel took a photo of the empty case, feeling oddly disappointed. She'd been looking forward to doing the follow-up post about her little town. Now she had *literally* nothing to show for it.

> Sorry folks, Elvis has left the building... The king of roosters has been caught up in fowl play.
>
> Earlier today I dropped into the Wessex Museum to visit the original Elvis, the cock who was the inspiration for the Big Rooster I posted about the other day. Elvis belonged to a local farmer and won the *Guinness Book of World Records* title of biggest rooster, bringing much fanfare and notoriety to our town as shown here in the local gazette.
>
> Sadly, I have just heard the disturbing news that Elvis has in fact been kidnapped. That's right. Vanished without a trace, only a short and rather simple ransom note left in his place. I, for one, am outraged and demand a proper investigation! Come on #Police_NSW... we want #justiceforElvis. #bringbacktheking #WhereIsElvis

Bel added a photo of the empty case and one of an old newspaper clipping that was on the wall behind the display, then hit send. Okay, so she may also be guilty of making fun of the whole thing, but she felt like she owed it to Elvis to at least mention it. Clearly no one else had, which seemed strange. Though, she conceded, no stranger than the fact someone had actually broken in to a museum and stolen a dead rooster in the first place.

As she arrived back at Emma's house, she noticed the four-wheel drive parked at the front.

Why is Dean here?

She walked around the back to find him dropping large timber posts onto the ground next to recently dug holes. He was wearing jeans and a blue work shirt with the sleeves rolled up to his mid-forearms.

'Hi,' she said as she approached him, and he glanced up to see her. 'I didn't know you were coming over to do this today.'

'I had an unexpected breakdown that meant I had a few hours to kill while I wait for parts to arrive. I figured I'd get a start on the chook pen.'

'You don't waste any time,' she said, observing how much he'd done already.

'It won't do itself,' he said with a shrug.

'Can I give you a hand?' It was the least she could do when he was giving up his own time to make the kids' surprise for their parents a reality.

'Sure. Can you hold this upright for me?' He positioned one of the posts for the pen in the ground and waited for her to take hold of it. He picked up a long, heavy-looking tubular metal tool and lifted it effortlessly. 'So, what happened between you and the bloke from the wedding?' Dean asked as he drove the post into the ground.

Bel used the loud banging to cover her surprise at his question. 'It didn't work out.'

'I gathered that much. But what happened?' he said, taking a break to lean his arm on the top of the post and look at her.

She found herself straightening her shoulders a little under his scrutiny, feeling a tad defensive at his blunt curiosity. 'He didn't turn out to be who I thought he was.'

'That's a shame,' he said, moving to the next post.

'Doesn't matter. I don't regret it. If it hadn't happened, none of what I have now would have eventuated.'

'It might have,' he said, grunting with effort as he lifted and dropped the post into its hole.

'I doubt it. I think I had to be out of my comfort zone and forced to find a solution to my predicament, or it wouldn't have happened. I was too comfortable here.'

'Are you going to move back into your gran's place?' he asked.

'I'm not sure. I don't particularly want to tell Bert he has to find somewhere else.'

'It's your place. You can do whatever you want.'

'I feel bad. Emma told me when he moved in that Bob Baxter had kicked him out of his rental to sell it and Bert had nowhere else to live.'

'I thought you were supposed to be a businesswoman?'

'Businesswomen can have compassion and ethics, you know,' she countered.

'Good to hear,' he said. 'But that doesn't solve your problem. If you stay, you'll want your house back.'

'I haven't made up my mind yet. It's not a pressing issue.'

'Craig's recovery is going to take a long time. Emma's probably going to need someone around to help out with the kids for a while.'

'I'll stay here as long as she needs me,' she said calmly. 'I'm in no hurry to leave. I can work from anywhere.' She grasped the post and watched as Dean applied himself to driving it deeper and backfilling soil around the base.

'You know, since you've been back, I haven't seen you reading. You used to always have your nose stuck in a book.' His observation surprised her. No one in town except Emma and Bel's grandparents had ever commented about her reading before. She thought no one had ever really noticed. She'd always felt like she was rather unmemorable . . . and yet, clearly, he'd *seen* her.

'I don't have time to read anymore,' she said. It *had* been a long time since she'd read anything. Since her business had taken off, she'd been too busy to do much of anything else. She had tried to pick up one of her Jax Lexington books, but they'd lost their magic somehow and she'd felt too sad to try again. Jax was forever going to be linked to Tate. That may have been the saddest part of the whole relationship, the fact that it had crushed something that had once been such an important part of her world.

'That's a shame. You should make time for the things you like doing.'

Dean's words caught her off guard. When was the last time someone had encouraged her to have interests? Tate certainly hadn't—unless they were also *his* interests. 'Says the man who seems to be working around the clock.'

'It's harvest time, that doesn't count,' he said, lifting his eyes from the post and sending her a small off-centre grin that provoked a warm sensation in the pit of her stomach.

Bel cleared her throat quickly. 'So, what *do* you like doing? What's your thing?'

Dean moved to the next hole and lifted another post from the grass, taking his time to answer. 'It's been a while, but I like fishing. Dad had an old fishing boat we used to take out to the dam once in a while. I've been meaning to do it ever since I came back, but I haven't found the time. He let the place go over the last few years, so it's taken a lot to get it back up and running.'

Bel grabbed the timber and held it steady in the centre of the hole. 'You must be making progress if you've got something to harvest. So that's good,' she remarked.

'Yeah, it's getting there. But what I hope to do is head down the regen path.'

'What's that?'

'Regenerative farming. It's been around for a while, but for a long time it was viewed as something the greenie, hobby-farmer types did. But it's backed up with a fair bit of scientific evidence that's making a lot of farmers, particularly the big corporate holdings, take note.'

'What is it, though?'

'It's all about soil health. Giving paddocks a rest by planting them with things that can grow and decay back into the ground and add in important nutrients between crops. They're called 'cover crops' and they also help retain water in the topsoil and make it more resistant to run-off and erosion. Basically, you end up with more fertile land that's a lot more drought- and flood-tolerant.'

'Sounds promising.'

'Yeah,' he said. 'It's a long-term thing, something that takes time to implement. But I'm keen to give it a go.'

She was distracted by the movement of his arms. Despite the fact he was wearing a shirt, she could imagine the limbs underneath, biceps bulging, muscles contracting and extending as the metal sheath lifted and pounded down hard, driving each post deeper into the—

'Bel?'

'Sorry? What?'

'You can let go of the post now.'

'Oh. Right.'

'You okay? Maybe it's too hot for you. I'm nearly done anyway, why don't you go inside and get a drink? I'll be in after I pack all this up.'

'Are you sure?'

'Yeah. All good.'

Bel didn't bother trying to argue. She was glad of an excuse to escape and get a grip on whatever the hell that was. Maybe he was right—she probably had heatstroke or something. A nice cold drink would do the trick to unscatter her brain.

This was so inappropriate, she chided herself as she set things out in the kitchen. What kind of shallow best friend was she? She was supposed to be taking care of Emma's children during a really stressful time, not having stupid X-rated thoughts about a guy who shouldn't even be on her radar when it came to sex . . .

As soon as she thought the word, images of sweat rolling across a muscular torso flashed before her eyes. 'Stop it!'

'Sorry?' Dean's confused voice came from behind her.

Shit. 'Pardon?'

'Stop what?'

'Oh. No, not you. I was . . . never mind. I made some drinks and an early lunch. I thought it might be cooler out on the verandah.'

'I'll clean up,' he said, squeezing by her as she piled some sandwiches onto a plate. Bel raised her eyes and caught his gaze. They simply looked at each other for a moment before Bel swallowed nervously and eased back to allow him past.

This is getting ridiculous.

A few minutes later, Jack the dog scrambled up from where he'd been lying under the table and jumped up and down excitedly, alerting her to Dean's return.

She couldn't be imagining this weird attraction thing, could she? *Oh God . . . what if I am? What if it's all me?*

Knock it off already! You are a mature, intelligent woman of the world—

'Jack. Off!' Dean ordered.

A chuckle escaped Bel before she clamped her lips shut. *So mature.* 'I made sandwiches,' she announced, pushing the plate towards him. He thanked her and took one.

'Did you know that Elvis was stolen from the museum?' she asked as a way to break the silence that had fallen as they began to eat.

'Elvis?'

'The rooster. The *real* rooster.'

'Really?'

'I don't get it. Why hasn't there been a huge fuss made of it?'

'Because it's a dusty old stuffed rooster?'

'It's the centrepiece to the town's tourism campaign,' she corrected.

'Then the town needs a better centrepiece.'

'I bet Bob Baxter had something to do with it,' she mused as she took a bite of her sandwich.

'I'm pretty sure Bob has more important things to do with his time.'

'Yeah, like hold a grudge against the progress committee who didn't vote for his stupid Big Burger,' Bel said.

'He's building his own burger, so I don't think he's holding a grudge.'

'He's what?'

'Apparently, he's hired an architect to renovate the truck stop into a huge burger. At least, that's what I heard. I have no idea if it's true.'

'Such a team player,' Bel said sardonically. 'Two big things in the same town. Way to divide the community.'

'Well, when you think about it, there's probably not that many places that have more than the one big thing. Maybe it'll be a better drawcard to have two?'

Bel gave a small shrug. 'One certainly hasn't seemed to work so far.'

Dean finished eating, thanked her for lunch and left to go back to work. As she listened to the sound of his engine fade into the distance, Bel found herself pondering the strange attraction that had been popping up whenever they were around each other lately. Why was it happening now, when it hadn't before? What was suddenly so different?

Her phone pinged and she grabbed it. She opened her Instagram account and gave a small, surprised chuckle. Her post was attracting a bit of attention.

Well, good. Poor old Elvis. And bloody Bob! If he did have something to do with it, she hoped that raising a little awareness might make him squirm. After all, it would make him look a bit stupid—a big-name businessman stealing a rooster from the museum. Seriously. How petty.

Two days later, Bel selected a trolley and began tossing in items from her list. The kids were like a swarm of hungry locusts, devouring the contents of the pantry within a few days of a shop. Emma had sent her a list of things to help with the whole lunch box conundrum and suggested she bake a big batch of biscuits. Clearly the woman was under a great deal of stress if she was suggesting that Bel bake. However, after seeing how fast the kids had gone through the last pack of biscuits, she decided she might have to give cooking a go, if she didn't want to go broke supplying bought ones.

'Hi, Bel,' the cashier said, greeting her cheerfully. Margret had been working here for as long as Bel could remember. 'I loved the post about Elvis!'

'Oh. Thanks,' Bel said with a quick smile. She hadn't even been aware Margret followed her on social media.

'Gotta love a good mystery. And fancy little old Wessex trending like that!'

Bel was slightly distracted by the fact Margret sounded so comfortable using the word 'trending', so it took a moment for the whole sentence to register. She gathered her purchases with a confused frown. Once in the car, she located her phone and began scrolling.

'Holy hell,' she whispered. Twenty-one thousand views and six hundred and thirty-four shares? She'd tagged the state police, and their social media team had set the internet ablaze with their reply. They had shared her post, and a large photo of Elvis, pre-kidnapping, now filled her screen.

Have you seen Elvis? Approximately one metre tall, shaggy appearance, somewhat stuffy personality? If so, we want to hear about it. Believed to have gone missing from the Wessex Museum three weeks ago.

This was insane. She opened her messages and found two requests for comment, one from a local newspaper, the other from a radio station. She shook her head in disbelief before sending off quick replies to both and putting her phone away. First things first—she needed to get some biscuits baked.

Eighteen

Bel lifted her head from her arms where she'd been resting it, feeling defeated. She'd just taken her second batch of biscuits from the oven and they were as terrible as the first. She didn't know what she was doing wrong. How hard could it be? It was basic science. You measured out a bunch of ingredients and followed the instructions. It should have worked.

The sound of heavy footsteps coming up the steps outside made her give an irritated sigh. The kitchen was a mess and she hadn't gotten a single other thing done all morning.

'Hey,' Dean said. 'Whoa.' His cheerful tone nosedived rapidly as he surveyed the chaos. 'What happened here?'

'Me. I happened,' she snapped. 'I've been trying to cook these bloody biscuits for the kids' lunches and it's not working.'

'They don't look that bad,' he said, eyeing the biscuits cooling on the wire rack beside her. He picked one up and bit into it. 'Oh fu—' His muffled exclamation was lost as he put a hand to his mouth to feel for broken teeth.

'They're a little hard.'

'Just a tad,' he agreed, and dropped the half-eaten biscuit in the bin. 'We'll give these to the dog,' he said, taking the tray outside. He returned seconds later wearing a lopsided grin. 'Apparently he's had enough.'

'Great. Even the dog won't eat my cooking.'

'It takes a bit of practice,' Dean said. 'Is there more flour?'

'In the pantry,' she said a little grudgingly. She'd really wanted to discover a new talent for cooking. 'I should have known you can also bake,' Bel said as he carried out a new packet of flour and placed it on the bench.

'Not really. But I figure, between the two of us, we can work it out. It can't be that hard, right?'

Bel sent him a narrowed glare. 'That's what I thought two batches ago.'

'Well, third time lucky?'

He really was annoyingly cheery. It kinda made her want to stab him with a fork.

'Where's the recipe book?'

'It's from a website, Emma sent it to me.'

'Well, there's your problem. You have to use the old-fashioned paper method. Emma must have a cookbook around here somewhere . . . here we go,' he said, triumphantly holding up a pretty hardcover book with *The Country Women's Association Cookbook* emblazoned across the front.

'Seventy years in the kitchen,' Bel read aloud. 'Surely there's a foolproof recipe in there we can use.' She was almost certain Gran had had an older edition of the same book. Not that Bel had ever read through it. She'd missed out on the cooking gene.

Dean looked around for a place to put the book, then gave a small grunt. 'Maybe we should clean up a bit first?'

They worked side by side until the dishwasher had been stacked and the bench wiped down, restoring the kitchen to its original condition. 'Are you sure you don't have something more important you need to be doing?' Bel asked him.

'Nothing that can't wait. Besides, you're going to need something to feed the kids when they come bounding through that door in a few hours' time. I'd say this is pretty important.'

It's not like they're going to starve. She decided to keep that thought to herself. If he thought he could do better, who was she to stop him?

'Do we have a sifter?'

'I have no idea.'

'It says we need to sift the flour.'

'But do we really?' she asked doubtfully. 'I mean, surely it can't make that much difference?'

'Did you sift it before?'

'No. Who has time for that?'

'And how did that work out?' he asked.

Fair point, she conceded. *Unnecessary to point out, but fair.*

'I need a coffee—want one?' she asked, already taking two cups from the cupboard and switching on the jug. 'I think I'll buy a coffee machine for Em next time I go into Toormanlee. Instant isn't doing it for me.'

'You've become a coffee snob, I see.'

'I wouldn't call myself a snob. I have . . . acquired an appreciation for good coffee.'

'Hmm.'

'What's that supposed to mean?' she asked, looking at him over her shoulder.

'Nothing.' He continued tapping the side of the sifter before putting it aside and returning to the book. 'Beat butter, sugar and vanilla until pale and creamy,' he said, his face wearing a mask of concentration that Bel found . . . cute. She went back to making the coffee and tried to ignore that thought. Moments later she placed his mug on the counter next to the open cookbook.

'Does this look pale and creamy enough?' he asked, tilting the bowl slightly.

Bel stepped in closer to get a good look but was distracted by the light brush of his arm next to hers. She self-consciously swallowed back the unexpected rush of butterflies that swarmed her insides. 'Uh, I guess so . . .' she said, looking up at him. His chin and mouth were so close. Her head only barely reached his shoulder, but at this range, she suddenly noticed the tan line on his neck, and the slightly lighter shade of the skin just under his collar. His beard, trimmed just longer than stubble, ran across his lower face, and for the first time she noticed that among the blackish hairs were flecks of rusty brown.

Her gaze slowly moved across to his mouth and she saw it turn up ever so slightly into a crooked smile. Her eyes shot to his in alarm, but instead of seeing the expected humour she found an intense expression that made her catch her breath. For what seemed an eternity they stared at each other, until one of them moved—she had no idea who. All she knew was one moment, she was holding her breath and the next, she was melting under warm lips. Her senses overloaded—the slight but not uncomfortable friction of his beard against her face, the smell of him, a line-dried scent of sunshine and clean shirts, a manly sandalwood-type fragrance mixed with vanilla essence and sugary butter. She heard a small groan and realised that it had come from her. The kiss deepened and she moulded against him, losing herself in the sensation.

It was too much and somehow also not enough. He broke away from the kiss momentarily to run his lips down her neck, setting off a new wave of longing. It was as though she had no control over her body. It craved him. His hands went to her waist and in one smooth movement, he'd lifted her onto the bench, bringing their faces to the same level. Her thighs opened automatically to allow him to step closer. His mouth returned to hers and she wound her arms around him as he pulled her forward to fit snugly against his torso.

At one point, she heard the clang of something hitting the floor, but it didn't matter. She felt as though she were on fire and the only thing keeping her from burning up was his kisses and his roaming hands sending quivers of unexpected delight throughout her entire body. Her own impatient hands went to the buttons on the front of his shirt.

'Bel?' She heard the question in his husky voice and continued until her hands found his heated skin beneath. She heard him let out a low sound close to her ear. 'Wait. We need to take this somewhere else.'

She impatiently nodded towards the hallway. 'My room.'

Without waiting for further instructions, he lifted her down from the counter and led her towards the bedroom. Once inside, Bel spent no time trying to talk herself out of whatever crazy nonsense this was, but pushed his shirt down over his well-defined shoulders. She didn't linger too long on the discovery of his naked torso—there was too much else going on. For one, the need to get out of her own shirt and kick off her boots.

In record time, they'd both disposed of their clothing. Bel drew in a ragged breath as they came back together again, the kisses more desperate than before, the urgency to get closer, to want to almost step into the other person's skin completely overwhelming. She had never felt like this with anyone before, and the nearly primal need that roared inside her should have scared her. But there was no time to try and analyse it—there was no time for any rational thought. All she wanted to do was feel the raging heat between them and lose herself in wave after wave of sensation.

There was a strange quiet in the room; the only sound was their harsh breathing, which had eventually started to slow. She could sense Dean's uncertainty. It was the same as hers.

'I wasn't expecting that at all when I came over here today,' he said, breaking the silence.

'No. Neither was I.'

'That was . . .'

'Yeah,' she said with a nervous chuckle. 'It was.'

'I don't usually do that, just for the record,' he said after an awkward pause.

Bel rolled her head sideways to look at him and felt suddenly shy. She wished she could pull the sheet over herself, but they hadn't even bothered turning back the covers. 'Do what?'

'Have spontaneous sex at my friends' houses.'

His reply overshadowed her earlier discomfort and she giggled. 'Not an everyday occurrence for you?'

'No. Definitely not.'

'Me neither. But if I'd known what would happened when you offered to help cook, I might have been better prepared. Who knew it would be such an aphrodisiac?'

He gave a strangled chuckle, but quickly sobered. 'I wasn't even prepared . . . we didn't . . . use anything,' he said, his concern and awkwardness making her heart soften.

'It's okay. I've got an implant. I also haven't been with anyone in a long time, in case you're worried about, you know, diseases and stuff.'

'Oh. No, I wasn't. I mean . . . I'm okay too. But I was more concerned about accidentally getting you pregnant.'

Bel's heart picked up speed at the thought, but then quickly crashed back to reality again. She knew that getting pregnant by mistake would not help her current situation, even as she felt a microsecond of disappointment. She didn't want kids . . . did she? No! Of course she didn't. At least not that she was about to admit out loud to his face. It seemed too embarrassing. She'd never felt the least bit maternal, not even when Em was having hers. She liked being the fun aunty and handing them back.

She shook away that weird train of thought and realised they were going to have to somehow deal with what had just happened.

'Bel, I—'

'Dean, I—'

They both stopped and shared a small grin.

'You first,' she said.

'I was going to say, I didn't plan on jumping you like some horny teenager—clearly not one of my coolest moves—but I can't say I haven't thought about it.'

'Really?'

'You haven't thought about us, like that?' he asked slowly.

'Well . . . no. Not really.'

As soon as she said it, she sensed him withdrawing and wished she'd kept her mouth shut. 'I mean, I know Em's tried to push us together a few times, but I didn't think you really liked me like that.'

'Why would you think that?'

'I don't know . . . I guess because I always saw you as the kid who was mean to me at school. And it's not like you ever asked me out.'

'When I came back, I couldn't believe my luck to find you still here and single. I thought it was a sign that I'd made the right decision. But when you'd barely give me the time of day, I began second guessing all my choices. Then Mr Tall, Blond and Handsome came to town and you left. You know, even then, I didn't quite give up hope. I figured you'd come back after seeing through him . . . but you didn't. I gave up after that. Then, the day I picked you up from the airport, you walked in through those doors, the sun streaming in behind you, and you were dressed in that white blouse and tight jeans, and you did this thing where you slid your sunglasses onto the top of your head as you looked around . . . it was the hottest thing I'd seen in a long time.'

'Seriously?'

'You looked like you'd just stepped out of some high-fashion magazine. And for a minute, I had no idea who it was until you looked at me and it hit me like ten thousand volts.'

'You're crazy,' she said with a soft laugh.

'I'm being completely honest. You terrify the hell out of me, Bel. I can't think straight whenever you're around. I never have. You used to have me tripping over my words and getting all tongue-tied whenever I tried to talk to you . . . and that was before.'

'Before?'

'Before you went and changed your hair and stuff,' he elaborated.

'You barely even said two words to me back then, when you first came home.'

'Because I was always so nervous.'

'Of me?'

'Yeah. I really liked you. You couldn't tell?'

'No, I thought you couldn't stand me.'

'I thought you couldn't stand *me*.'

'Only because I remembered how you used to tease me all the time at school.'

'I liked you back then, too,' he said with a shrug.

'Then why did you tease me so much?'

'I don't know. That's just what kids did, I suppose. I didn't do anything bad, though.'

'You laughed along with everyone else whenever they made fun of my glasses,' she said, then groaned inwardly. Why on earth was she saying any of this? It was a million years ago. Who the hell cared?

'I do remember that,' he said grimly. 'I'm really sorry, Bel. I wish I'd been brave enough to stand up to them the way you did. You never backed down from anyone.' He sighed, leaning back on the pillows. 'I took a while to grow up. In primary school I was always shorter than most of my friends. I think I used to feel self-conscious about it, and figured if they were teasing someone else, then they were leaving me alone. I know how shitty that sounds, but as a kid, it kind of made perfect sense.'

'I get it,' she said with a long sigh. 'Honestly, I do. I probably would have felt the same in your position.'

'I hope we get a reunion someday. If you like, I'll beat up every kid that made your life hell.'

'Not that I don't appreciate the offer,' she said, 'but I don't think violence is as sexy as you seem to think it is.'

'Thank God for that, because last time I saw Brian Phelps, he was built like a brick shithouse. I'm pretty sure he'd flatten me with one punch.'

Bel laughed and he smiled back at her. He had the nicest smile. 'You should do that more often,' she said impulsively.

'Do what?'

'Smile,' she said. 'I don't think I've seen you do that much.'

'I guess when you were around, I was always wondering if you were going to snarl at me.'

'I wasn't that bad,' she protested.

'You really didn't seem to like me much when I first came back to town.'

'I guess I wasn't in a particularly happy place back then.'

'You seem better now.'

'I am. I think. I'm not sure why, though.' She took a moment to find the right words. 'I mean, I still don't really know what I'm doing with my life. I have a great business and that makes me happy, but I just don't really know where I fit anymore.' She glanced up at him and saw he was listening to her carefully. 'I mean, I absolutely loved Perth. I never thought I'd leave here, but I did and it was . . .' She paused as everything she'd gone through rolled past her eyes in a succession of memories that almost made her dizzy. 'Well, a lot happened, good and bad I suppose. I came back here in such a hurry that I didn't give much thought as to where I want to go in the future.'

'You don't see yourself back here?'

'I'm not sure,' she said, wincing a little as she dragged out the words. 'I mean, this has always been home, but I think you were right earlier when you said that I was different. I am. I have changed and I'm not quite sure who I am anymore.'

'Maybe it'll take some time. It was the same for me when I came back. Once you leave somewhere, you're never the exact same person when you come back. That's why they call it change,' he said with a flash of a grin.

Bel had almost forgotten they were both lying side by side, completely naked. It felt weirdly . . . natural. *How strange.*

'I guess we should probably go and make a start on the kitchen mess—again,' Dean said reluctantly.

'Yeah. So much for baking.'

'I don't have any complaints. I'm more than happy to come over and bake with you any time,' he said, gathering up his clothing.

'The CWA ladies would be horrified if they knew what we'd done while supposedly following their recipes.'

'The CWA ladies have probably done a lot worse than that in their day.'

'My gran was in the CWA,' she said, eyeing him doubtfully.

'I'm just sayin','

'Well, don't. It's disturbing.'

'I think I can save this,' he announced once they were back in the kitchen, dressed and somewhat respectable again.

The damage wasn't nearly as bad as she'd expected. Only a few implements had clattered to the floor, and the bowl of eggs and sugar was safe. Dean opened the book back up and continued mixing in the ingredients. 'Okay. I guess we wait and see now,' he said after he slid in the last tray and closed the oven. 'I'll have to leave you in charge. I've got to get back.'

'Sorry that I kept you longer than you were planning,' she said, feeling the words suddenly thicken in her mouth like sugary toffee as his eyes slid across her face and down her body.

'It was my pleasure,' he said, lowering his head to kiss her.

'I think this is what started it before,' she said when they broke apart.

'Yeah. I know,' he said with a regretful sigh. 'I'll be working tonight and probably flat-out for the next few days. They say there's some bad weather coming, so I want to get as much in as I can on the off-chance the weather bureau is right for once.' He ended with a small grin but held her gaze. 'I don't want you to think I'm avoiding you.'

'It's okay. I know you've got a lot on.'

'But if you need anything, call, okay?'

'I'm sure we'll be fine. But thank you.'

They walked towards the back door and Bel felt another wave of shyness wash over her. This was so weird. In the space of no more than an hour, everything had changed.

Dean stopped at the top of the steps and turned back to face her, looking as though he wanted to say something, but then seemed to think better of it. He gave a brief wave before leaping down the stairs and jogging to his vehicle.

She watched as the dust tail plumed up behind him on the driveway until a loud buzz alerted her that the biscuits were done and she raced back inside.

Nineteen

Bel listened to the phone as it rang before Emma answered. 'Hey,' Bel said. 'How's things going?'

'Better today. He's saying a few words and the doctors are happy that he's got a bit more sensation in his feet and legs. They're going to move him to the rehab ward tomorrow.'

'That's great news,' Bel said, relief rushing through her.

'Yeah, it is. They've warned me he might relapse a bit for a while, in terms of being able to follow commands consistently, doing things today that maybe he won't do again tomorrow, that kind of thing. It's just the way it is with this recovery thing. It's going to be a long, slow process.'

'Are you doing okay?' Bel asked softly.

'Yeah,' Emma said, sounding weary. 'I mean, it's exhausting but I'm not even doing anything, just sitting beside his bed and holding his hand and talking to him non-bloody-stop to try and jog his memory. It's probably driving him crazy.' She gave a weary chuckle. 'I miss the kids so much, but I can't leave him yet. Even with his family here, I just can't do it. I have this feeling that he needs me to be here or he might just . . . give up.'

'Oh, Em. He's not going to do that. He loves you and the kids so much. He'll keep fighting to get through all this. The kids miss you too, but you have to do whatever you need to do. They know you're down there helping their dad. They're doing fine. I promise.'

'I know they're in good hands. And honestly, I don't want them down here, seeing him like this . . . If he keeps making progress, then I'll bring them down, but it's just too soon. He'd hate them to see him and get upset by it. It's hard enough for me seeing him this way, I can't even imagine how the kids would handle it.'

'Whatever happens, they'll accept it. Kids seem to adapt to things,' Bel said, thinking back to how well they'd accepted her moving in with them. 'But for now, just focus on you and Craig.'

Bel heard her let out a fortifying breath and imagined her friend straightening her shoulders and regrouping. 'So, what's new there?' Emma asked. 'The kids sounded better today. Happier.'

'Yeah, they're doing really well. They miss you both, but we've managed to keep them distracted most of the time. I think that's helping.'

'So I've been hearing. The kids are full of Aunty Bel and Uncle Dean stories.'

Bel automatically thought back to earlier and squeezed her eyes shut. It was all so new and unexpected, but she'd never kept anything from her friend before. 'I slept with him,' she blurted before clamping her lips shut firmly. *Oh God, why did I do that?*

'It's about time.'

'What?'

'Seriously, you two have been dancing around this whole attraction thing for ages.'

'That's not true. I could barely stand him before I left.'

'You told yourself that. Everyone else could see what was really going on.'

'How nice for you all to have such clarity about something I had no idea about.'

'Don't get all snitty. You clearly had to learn a few life lessons before you were ready to see the truth. But now you have and I am beyond excited for you both.'

'Calm down. We're not engaged. We had . . . a moment.'

'Everything will fall into place.'

'Or not. I don't want to make a big deal out of it.'

'But it is a big deal. I mean . . . how was it?'

'It was . . . pretty amazing,' Bel admitted. 'He's been so great with the kids, helping with everything. I'm not sure I could have handled all this on my own.'

'Sure you could. But I'm glad you didn't have to. I can't tell you how much of a load it's taken off me to know the kids are okay.'

'Just concentrate on getting that man of yours better. Don't worry about anything out here.'

Bel ended the call and stared down at the biscuits. There were other people with bigger problems than her. And to think she'd been stressing over something as mundane as baking.

'You should be on *MasterChef*, Aunty Bel,' Ayla said, reaching for her third biscuit later that afternoon.

'These are delicious!' Ben said around a mouthful of crumbs.

'I'm glad you like them,' Bel said, only feeling slightly guilty for not mentioning that Dean had actually made them, not her.

'We love them. Can you make some more?' Ayla asked.

Bel swallowed before mustering a confident smile. 'Absolutely. But maybe not today. I've used all the butter. Okay, now that we've done afternoon tea, it's homework time,' she said, rolling her eyes at the groans that followed. 'I know. Homework sucks. But we have to do it.'

'I wanna do homework,' Lucy said.

'You're in preschool,' Ivy told her. 'You don't get homework.'

'I wanna do homework,' Lucy repeated, her bottom lip beginning to tremble as she looked up at Bel with big, devastated eyes.

'You can do some homework too,' Bel assured her, clapping her hands at the small bodies slowly climbing off bar stools to retrieve their school bags.

It took a further thirty minutes to set everyone up with their books and find something to keep Lucy occupied, but eventually everyone was on task and the routine was back on track.

'Aunty Bel, I don't know what I have to do,' Ben said, his head resting in his hand as he dug a hole in the paper with his pencil.

'Let me see.' Bel took his book, suspecting he wasn't even really trying. She did feel bad for them—they'd been sitting at a desk in school all day and now all they wanted to do was run outside—but Em's chart on the fridge said homework until four-thirty.

She began reading the instructions at the top of the printed page Ben had glued into his book—crooked—and frowned. She read it again. *Okay, this is strange.* She tried reading it a third time and felt a flutter of panic. The kid was in kindergarten, it shouldn't be difficult! And yet, as she read through the rather detailed and long instructions, she found herself completely confused. How was a five-year-old supposed to understand these instructions when even she couldn't even make sense of them? *It can't be that hard.*

She glanced at the clock on the wall and felt sweat beads break out on her forehead. It was almost four-thirty . . .

'Okay!' she said in an overly bright tone. 'Pens down. We're going outside for a play. We'll finish homework later.'

Four little voices chorused happily as they slid off their seats. They were out the back door before she even had time to call out to be careful. Bel dragged Ben's book closer, trying not to panic. She was a grown adult. Surely Emma wouldn't have left her in charge of her children if she didn't think she could figure out something as basic as Year One homework.

Bel smiled as she followed the kids into Emma's room and watched them scramble up onto the huge bed. This was her favourite part of the day.

Ivy rubbed her face against her arm as she snuggled in. 'You smell like Dean,' she said.

'Really?' She decided to play dumb and hope for the best. 'Okay, where were we up to?'

It didn't take too much arm-twisting to get Bel to read a couple of extra chapters—she was enjoying the story as much as the kids were—but with Lucy struggling to keep her eyes open, she called it a night and hustled them all into their own beds.

'Aunty Bel, your shirt is inside out,' Ayla said sleepily as Bel walked into her room.

Crap! Really? 'I must have been in a rush to get dressed this morning. Silly me.'

She dragged her shirt up over her head as she undressed to take a shower and gave it a sniff. It *did* smell like Dean. A few images of the events which had taken place mid-morning flashed briefly through her mind. She'd done her best to stay busy and not think too much about it, but now, with no kids to distract her, it was difficult to keep the thoughts at bay.

It had been like something out of a romance novel—a moment of uncontrollable lust, in the kitchen of all places. She'd never even imagined stuff like that happened in real life, and here she was, living it, and with a wholesome country boy no less. Things like hot kitchen sex always happened with bad boys, not farmers. Or so she'd thought. Clearly Dean didn't play by the rules of stereotype.

Bel stepped under the stream of hot water, lathered up her hair and did her best to ignore the tiny little aches, lingering reminders of the day's events.

The next day, Bel's phone started to ding and ping constantly. She didn't have time for the distraction, with a number of invoices to send out and a few jobs she was working on. Irritated, she eventually put it on silent.

When she picked the phone up a few hours later, she shook her head at the crazy number of notifications lighting up her screen, and tentatively opened her Instagram app.

The numbers of shares on her post about Elvis had exploded. The Federal Police had also gotten in on the act, playfully bantering with other law enforcers and taking the whole tongue-in-cheek post one step further by tagging ASIO. *This is getting out of hand.*

That night, after Emma had spoken with the kids before bedtime, Bel took the phone.

'Bel, your post is all over the internet!' Emma cried.

'I know,' she groaned.

'What on earth is going on?'

'It started out as a bit of fun when I discovered someone had stolen Elvis. I had no idea it would go this far. I mean, who the hell would steal it? Although I bet Bob Baxter is getting a bit antsy with all this sudden attention.'

'What do you mean?'

'That it was probably him who stole Elvis.'

'Don't go saying that out loud, for God's sake. He'll sue you.'

'Well, it's something he'd do.'

'Maybe whoever took it will put it back now that there's all this attention?'

'Maybe. Who knows,' Bel said. 'Well, I better go and get these kids into bed. I'll talk to you tomorrow.'

Bel had been determined to master the whole biscuit thing once and for all, and finally had a win with a jam drop recipe she'd found online. The kids decided that Dean should try some and begged her to invite him over.

The night before, he'd called once the kids were in bed and they'd talked till late, but they hadn't seen each other since he'd left yesterday morning. Bel was annoyed to realise she felt like a nervous schoolgirl at the thought of seeing him. 'I think he might be a bit busy,' she hedged, feeling awkward.

'I'll call him,' Ayla said. 'Mummy lets me call Nanna on the phone all the time.'

'She does not. She said you have to ask first,' Ivy pointed out.

'Can I call Dean?' Ben asked.

'No. I'm the oldest,' Ayla protested.

'You're not the boss,' Ivy argued.

'I like blueberries,' Lucy chimed in without lifting her eyes from the drawing she was quietly doing at the end of the kitchen bench.

Bel gave a small sigh before picking up her phone and raising her voice. *'I'll* call him,' she said firmly. *It's like working in a freaking three-ring circus.* The phone rang but switched to a brief instruction to leave a message after the tone. 'He didn't answer, guys. He's probably busy. We can invite him over another time.'

'We can take some over and leave them at his front door? That's what Mummy does sometimes,' Ivy suggested helpfully.

'She does?' Bel asked.

'Yeah. Sometimes she cooks him dinner and drops it over there because you know what single men are like,' Ayla said, rolling her eyes. 'That's what Mummy always says to Daddy.'

Bel chuckled. 'Well, I suppose we could drop some over.' It was the least she could do, really.

After packaging up a number of biscuits into a container, they all bundled into the car and headed off.

Dean's driveway was less impressive than Emma and Craig's, just a rough dirt track and a few weeds. The house was white timber and could do with a new coat of paint but it had a rustic charm, with its bullnosed verandah wrapping around the square building. There were three enormous sheds across a wide clearing from the house, but nothing more than a few shade-giving trees scattered around the yard for a garden.

'Can I take the biscuits, Aunty Bel?' Ben asked.

'Can I?' Ivy piped up, followed by the usual protest from the others in the back seat.

'Do we have to do this every single time, guys?' she asked wearily. While she was still trying to play referee, a tap at her window made her jump.

'Hi,' Dean said when she opened the door.

'Hi,' she echoed. A flutter of butterflies invaded her stomach as she latched onto the smile that spread across his face, before remembering she had a car full of arguing children.

'We bought you bickies. Aunty Bel made them,' Ivy informed him.

'Oh, yeah?'

'They're surprisingly edible,' Bel assured him. 'The kids wanted to invite you over for afternoon tea but we thought maybe you were a bit busy.'

'So we brought some over to surprise you, like Mummy does with your dinner,' Ayla put in.

'Thanks, guys,' he said, smiling at the beaming faces behind Bel. 'I was working out in the shed. But how about we have afternoon tea here?'

The back doors were thrust open and four little bodies were scrambling out of the car before Bel even had time to agree. 'I guess that's a yes,' she murmured, then unclipped her seatbelt to slide from the driver's seat. She glanced up when Dean lowered his head to place a gentle kiss on her lips before moving back to allow her to walk past.

'This is a nice surprise,' he said. 'I've been trying to come up with an excuse to go over to your place all day.'

'You didn't need an excuse,' she said, suddenly shy but also happy that she wasn't the only one feeling this way.

'I haven't been able to stop thinking about yesterday.'

She opened her mouth to agree but didn't get a chance to reply as Ben came over and began jumping up and down like an excited puppy. Dean and Bel swapped a wry look before he herded the kids inside to organise drinks and jam drops.

Bel clicked her tongue irritably as her ringtone sounded during the chaos of breakfast the next morning. She searched for her phone, locating it under a hat on the bench. 'Put this in your bag, Ivy,' she said handing over the hat and answering the call in a breathless rush.

'Is that Bel Buckley?'

'Yes, it is,' she said, distracted by the twins arguing over a toy they weren't even supposed to be playing with.

'This is Peggy Armstrong from *Mornings with Georgia-Mae*. We'd like to organise an interview with you tomorrow morning.'

'Sorry, what?' Bel watched *Mornings with Georgia-Mae* most mornings. *Is this a joke?*

'Your story about Elvis the missing rooster has been gaining a lot of traction and we think it would be a great fit for our breakfast audience.'

'Uh . . . really?' Good grief. She'd never imagined her post would get this kind of reaction.

'Absolutely. I'll send you an email with all the details and get back in touch with you a little bit later today.'

Bel rattled off her email address to the chipper woman before lowering her phone to the bench. What on earth had she just agreed to?

After school drop-off, she parked up the road and took out her phone, opening it to find an email from the TV show waiting in her inbox. They were sending a freelance cameraman out from Dubbo early the next day to set up for a live interview.

'A live morning show appearance? That's . . . wow,' Dean said when she called him in a panic.

'It's crazy is what it is,' she clarified.

'Well, you wanted to raise some awareness. I guess this will do it.'

'Yeah, but now this missing rooster sounds dumb.'

'I hate to tell you, but it always sounded kinda dumb,' he said, chuckling. 'Okay, sorry, that's not being helpful. Look at it this way, you'll be promoting Wessex and the Big Rooster. Maybe this will give the tourism campaign a bit of a push?'

'Maybe,' she conceded dully. She just wished she wasn't the one who was going to have to talk about it. She already knew they wanted to use it as light-hearted entertainment, and she didn't particularly want to be the butt of the joke.

'So get the progress committee involved,' Dean suggested. 'They'll probably want to be.'

She'd already sent a message to Betty and forwarded the email. With any luck, Betty would step in. She was never afraid of being front and centre.

Bel had barely slept; she was way too nervous about the whole stupid interview. The kids were beyond excited, staying up past their bedtime to make signs to hold up in the background while she was being interviewed and, for once, they were ready even before Bel the next morning.

She shouldn't have been surprised at the crowd, which had already gathered in front of the statue of Elvis on the main street. Word of mouth spread news faster than any phone line and it seemed like the entire population of Wessex had turned out for their fifteen minutes of fame on national television.

Even Bob Baxter was there. 'The hide of that man,' Betty scoffed, staring daggers. 'Coming to witness all the ruckus over his crime.'

'Make sure you don't say that on TV,' Bel suggested weakly. She hadn't gotten out of the interview completely, but Betty had been more than happy to do it with her, and she had a feeling she wouldn't be needing to say much once Betty got started.

Chris the cameraman was a stout forty-something with a decided lack of outward emotion. After a brief run-down of how the segment would go, he handed Bel and Betty each an earpiece and hooked them up with microphones, which was apparently referred to as 'micing up the talent', as the email the day before had explained. Bel had never been referred to as talent before, so it was somewhat nerve-racking. Betty, on the other hand, was enjoying the attention and looked like she'd been born to stand in front of a man with a camera. The host of the show would be asking questions through the earpieces when they were given the cue. Bel wasn't sure if she wanted to throw up or run, but there wasn't time to do either because Chris the cameraman was suddenly counting them down and then they were live in front of the entire nation.

Fuck. For a horrifying moment, she thought she had sworn out loud, but then she realised the sound was the host, Georgia-Mae Bartlet, welcoming her to the show.

'Were you surprised by all the interest in the story?' Georgia-Mae asked Bel after giving the audience a run-down of where the town was and the story of her initial post going viral.

'Completely. I had no idea when I posted the story that it'd become this big.'

'In all seriousness, though, despite the light-hearted banter going on between the different law enforcement agencies, this is a bit of a mystery isn't it, this question of who stole the town mascot?'

Betty immediately cut in, angling herself in front of Bel. 'It's a crime is what it is. Elvis is the heart and soul of Wessex. He's more than a mascot. He's irreplaceable.'

Bel cringed a little at the overly dramatic response. Heart and soul might be going a little too far.

'Have there been any leads in the story? Do we have any further ransom notes? I mean, it seems like a good idea to bring in ASIO since this *is* their area of expertise, and they did respond on their official Facebook page to the Federal Police's post. Do you hope that with these extra resources you might be able to find out what happened to Elvis and get him back?'

'I would certainly hope so,' Betty said. 'It may seem like a joke to most people, but I can assure you, stealing from a museum is a very serious crime. And between you and me, I suspect the culprit is someone with very close ties to the town, with a vendetta against our tourism push.'

The show's host did seem to prick up at that little piece of scandal and Bel quickly jumped in before Betty could start naming names and getting herself slapped with a lawsuit.

'We are encouraging anyone who might have been involved, perhaps as a practical joke, to return Elvis. We're all after a peaceful resolution,' Bel said.

'That's all we have time for this morning. Thank you, ladies, for joining us, and let's hope Elvis is returned to his rightful place very soon.'

They said goodbye and their connection was cut. Bel felt her shoulders sag in relief. *Thank God that's over.*

'Did you see us waving, Mummy? Did Daddy see the sign we made?' Ayla asked excitedly as the children gathered around Bel's phone to talk to their mother.

'I did. Daddy loved the sign. That was so exciting!'

'And Aunty Bel was on TV. She's famous!' Ivy added.

'She certainly is.'

Bel noticed her friend sounded a little distracted. 'We have to get you lot to school so we'll let Mummy go and we'll call her this afternoon, okay?' Taking the phone back and turning away from the kids, Bel added in a low voice, 'Is everything okay?'

'Yeah. Just waiting for the doctor to finish with Craig and give us an update.'

There was a note of concern in her friend's voice and Bel knew she hadn't been imagining the earlier distraction. 'Are you worried it'll be bad news?' she asked cautiously.

Her question was greeted with a long pause, before Emma said, 'I don't know. Brain injuries can vary so much and they keep saying wait and see, but I just . . . don't know. The doctors have mentioned that recovery can stop at any stage and he's still barely talking. I've been trying so hard to stay optimistic and not expect too much too soon, but . . . I can't help it, Bel. What if he doesn't get any better than he is right now?'

Bel closed her eyes briefly at the thought. 'Then we deal with that if it happens. I think you've had to be strong for so long and it's only natural that you'd have moments where you feel overwhelmed. Maybe you need to come home for a bit and recharge your batteries. Have a break?'

'I've been thinking about it,' Emma agreed softly. 'I could only be away a few days, though.'

'Think it over.'

'I gotta go, the doctor's here. I'll call you tonight.'

Bel slipped her phone into her back pocket and hurried to catch up to the kids walking ahead with a few of their friends.

The school had sent a notice out letting everyone know they were starting twenty minutes later to accommodate all the fanfare the interview had stirred up. It felt more like a town parade than a normal weekday morning, with people gathering in small groups to catch up and others ambling along the street as they began to disperse and move on. Maybe this whole going viral thing did have benefits. There was a definite vibe happening in their small town.

Twenty

Over the next week, Bel did a total of five radio interviews and two more interviews with television shows. She'd expected the fuss to have died down by now, but it seemed the country, and even some other parts of the world, were invested in the whole #WhereIsElvis campaign. She'd been encouraged to do daily updates on her social media, which had included reposting a legion of supposed Elvis sightings, ranging from very *alive* versions of roosters that looked like Elvis from all around the world, to one gruesome, yet kind of funny, image of a pile of feathers in a what-was-left-of-Elvis photo. Her posts sparked a thread of why-did-the-rooster-cross-the-road jokes, along with some humorous alternative ransom notes. It was as crazy as it was confounding, and it came with an unexpected windfall: tourists. And lots of them. For the first time since their tourism campaign had started, the town was seeing results.

A steady stream of mobile homes and caravans had been rolling into town ever since that first morning show broadcast and they hadn't stopped. It was now almost impossible to get a park in the main street.

Bel smiled ruefully as she passed the supermarket window and saw the poster someone had put up with a cartoon drawing of Elvis the rooster captioned 'Who stole Elvis?' The signs had been popping up all over town as everyone got behind the push to find Elvis.

'The whole place has gone nuts,' Dean muttered later when they met for coffee. She'd been shopping when he'd messaged to tell her he was in town to pick up a part and had a few minutes to catch up. Lately, that was pretty much all they'd been able to do. Between the harvest and the kids, there wasn't a lot of alone time.

'I know, right?' she said with a chuckle.

'Whoever was behind this is a freaking promotional genius, though,' he added, looking over at her thoughtfully.

'What?' she said nervously.

'Nothing. It's just that you turn up in town and suddenly this whole Elvis thing goes off. If I didn't know any better I'd think maybe . . .' He let the words trail off sheepishly.

'That I had something to do with it? Well, Sherlock, there's one small flaw in your theory. He went missing *before* I came back, remember?'

'Oh. Yeah,' he said, sounding a little disappointed.

'I can't believe you think I'd resort to stealing as a PR stunt,' she said with only the slightest tone of indignation. Actually, she was more miffed that she *hadn't* thought of it. It really was next-level clever. Although, until she'd posted about it, nothing had really happened. It was all just a huge fluke.

'Stealing for a reason would be a little better than trying to figure out why someone would take a dusty old bird from a museum in the first place, don't you think?'

He did have point there.

'Well, well, well,' Larrisa said as she came to the table with their coffee order. 'I see maybe the rumour mill is actually right for once?'

Bel resisted the urge to squirm in her seat as she forced a smile onto her face. They hadn't really spoken about what this relationship was, and they certainly hadn't spoken about what to do when they appeared in public together . . . like now. *Rookie mistake.* Everyone in town knew they'd been helping out at Fernvale, and apparently already had them picked as a couple.

'Come on, Larrisa, you should know by now not to listen to rumours,' Dean said with a smile.

'Well, in certain cases, like with the ones that were going around about you and me a few months ago,' she tossed back. Bel hesitated, cup halfway to her mouth, glancing up at Dean.

'Uh, yeah. Like that.'

Bel wasn't sure, but it looked like he might have been blushing.

'I think it's great. I always thought you two would make a great couple,' Larrisa said, turning back to the counter to serve as other patrons entered.

Dean shifted a little in his seat in the short silence that followed her departure. 'So, you and Larrisa were an item?' she asked lightly.

'No,' he said, a little too quickly.

Bel lifted an eyebrow.

'I gave her a hand finishing off some of the renovations in here, so I was in the cafe a bit. That naturally started a few tongues wagging. We didn't date or anything.'

'Why not?'

'What?' He looked up at her, surprised by her question.

'You were both single. She's a lovely person,' she said. 'How come you two didn't get together? It's not like the dating pool is limitless around here.'

'I don't know.' He glanced down at his cup briefly before looking back up. 'She's great, but I guess . . . she wasn't you.'

She smiled. 'You say that. But we weren't dating before I left.'

'If that knobhead hadn't come to town, I'd like to think we might have.'

Bel looked at Dean across the table. 'I know Emma was trying to play matchmaker,' she said.

'I made a dick of myself trying to work up the courage to ask you out.'

'To think, I had no idea that was what you were after.'

'Do you really think I needed to come into the store as often as I used to just to buy a bag of chips?' he asked dryly.

Well, now that he mentioned it . . . she supposed that had been odd. She still coudn't believe she'd never suspected he'd been trying to ask her out. Then again, why would she have noticed? Her head had always been buried in a book.

'I sort of did ask you out, in a roundabout way. To the movie night. We were going to meet up there. But you met that Tate bloke.'

A trickle of discomfort ran through her. 'I didn't realise that's what you were thinking . . . I mean, I was going to be there with Em and the kids.' She winced a little, thinking how he must have felt when she'd left to go off with Tate.

'It was my fault. I should have told you I liked you. I guess I figured I had all the time in the world. It wasn't like there was much chance of any other competition moving to Wessex,' he said. 'But then that bloody wedding brought in all those Barbie and Ken lookalikes.'

Bel smiled slightly. 'If it makes you feel any better, he turned out to be a big mistake.'

'It doesn't make me feel better that you were hurt.'

'I think . . . he was supposed to enter my life when he did for a reason.'

'I'm not sure I believe in any of that destiny stuff.'

Before she'd left town, his easy dismissal of something she believed in would have made her more than a little defensive. Now, though, all she felt was kind of . . . sad. Her manifesting list hadn't exactly played out the way she'd thought it would, yet it *had* worked. Sort of. 'Really?'

'Nah. I think you make choices and those choices give you consequences. Good or bad, you either learn from them or you don't.'

'But you don't think that maybe something put those choices or whatever in your path for a reason?'

'Not really. It's the results of those choices that have a roll-on effect to other people.'

'Like how?'

'Take this whole thing with Craig. He made the call to get up on the tractor that day and as a result of that decision, he hurt himself. That decision, in some way, then changed *your* trajectory, bringing you back here, which then put you and me back on track. And it was all because of a wrong choice on Craig's part that had a wider effect on other people.'

'I guess you could look at it like that,' she conceded.

'As opposed to some higher power having all this mapped out ahead of time. If that was the case, then Craig got a pretty sucky part in this whole lesson.'

'Craig's lesson might have been something different,' Bel countered. 'Maybe he's going through this whole experience so he can use it somehow in the future?'

'I think I prefer to think of it as, I'm making my own decisions in life, not just being a pawn in some greater power's game of chess.'

Bel had never been particularly religious, but she liked to think that there were guardian angels and that some kind of universal karma system was watching over everyone, sending little signs to help guide the way now and then. Maybe she was too naïve.

Dean was right about one thing—Craig didn't deserve anything he was going through. He was a good guy and a great dad and husband. If the universe was supposed to be watching over them, why would something this horrible happen to Craig? And what lesson could be worth so much heartache and pain?

'How many more interviews do you have left to do?' Dean asked, interrupting her troubled thoughts.

'None. That was the last one yesterday. I think we've gone as far as we're going to go.'

'It's about time. I still don't get this whole social media hype thing.'

'That's because you aren't on it.'

'Yeah, I am. I just don't use it.'

'I didn't know that.'

'I've had it for a while, but I don't really look at it much. Em made me get on it. She used to show me your videos after you left. I can see why you have such a big following, you're a natural.'

'I don't know about that. It helps if you're interested in what you post about.'

'It's more than that. You aren't fake or following any stupid trends. You're just you. People like that.'

She wasn't sure what to say to that. It was one of the nicest compliments she'd ever received. 'Well, it's not always like this. I mean, the whole Elvis thing is pretty unusual. One of those things that had all the right bits to make it go viral, but social media is great for lots of other stuff too. You can find old school friends, and follow pages to do with farming and even your regen stuff. There'd be heaps of groups set up with people helping each other and sharing information.'

'I'm already in touch with any old friends I want to still be in touch with, and if I want information, I go out and search for it. How do you know any of these people in these groups even know what the hell they're talking about? They could be full of shit.'

'Hopeless,' she muttered, shaking her head in dismay. 'Seriously, for a progressive farmer, you're a dinosaur when it comes to technology. I don't know how you think you're going to stay up to date with everything going on.'

'The old-fashioned way. I watch the news and listen to talkback radio in the tractor.' He smiled and reached over to link his fingers through hers. 'And for everything else, I've got you.'

'Like I said.' She smiled softly. 'Hopeless.'

'I gotta get back,' he said, gently rocking their linked hands back and forth. 'But I'll come by later tonight?'

Bel nodded, already looking forward to seeing him. She felt only a flicker of apprehension when he leaned down to kiss her goodbye, hoping no one noticed, but by the time his lips lifted from hers, all she felt was regret that he had to go back to work. She didn't care who knew they were seeing each other. Dean Preston left her feeling a little giddy.

The chook pen was almost finished and not a moment too soon. Much to everyone's relief, Craig's progress hadn't stopped and he was slowly getting stronger. Emma was due home at the end of the week for a visit with the kids and a break from the hospital, and the pen would be a lovely surprise—something happy she could take back to tell Craig.

Bel let her gaze roam freely over Dean as he hammered a final piece of wire into place to make the enclosure safe for the assortment of black, red, white and speckled hens that scratched and pecked around their feet. He didn't have to be spending so much time over here helping. He had more than enough to do at his own place, but he'd given up hours and hours to help out his friends. She had nothing but admiration for him. She liked the way he did things without any fanfare or expectation. Like the other day, he'd noticed the kitchen tap leaking and went out to his car only to return with some tools to replace the washer, all without having to be asked. Nothing bothered him—kids running through the house, arguing or having tantrums. He took it all in his stride.

He looked up and caught her watching, giving her one of his brief side grins that she found more than a little distracting. A flutter of awareness raced through her as she thought about later this evening. It had been hard to find any quality time together lately, between his long hours harvesting and her duties with the kids. But tonight, he wasn't working. They'd planned to spend the whole day together, getting the house sorted for Emma's return tomorrow, and he was staying for dinner.

The kids were putting the finishing touches on the outside of the hen house, each painting their own sections, when Bel left them to fetch a bag of laying pellets from the shed so she could fill up the new self-feeders Dean had made.

It took a second for her eyes to adjust from the sunlight outside to the darker interior of the shed as she headed across to the stack of various feed bags neatly stored on pallets.

As she pulled one of the bags free, she noticed a timber box behind it that seemed strangely out of place. It looked old and had faded stencilled signage on the side, the kind that second-hand stores put eye-watering prices on to sell as vintage collectables.

Inside was a hessian bag. Curiosity well and truly got the best of her and she opened the bag, jumping backwards and letting out a startled scream as she revealed the stiff body of an animal. A stuffed animal or, more precisely, a very familiar stuffed rooster.

What the hell?

As she leaned forward to inspect the contents of the bag, she felt something drop behind her. In the split-second it took to turn and register what the noise was, her mouth had already opened in a silent scream, which suddenly turned into a shriek of utter horror when a fat, extremely long snake slithered across the floor.

Within moments, Dean was rushing through the doorway, and he quickly spotted her perched on top of the stacked feed bags she'd somehow scaled, though she couldn't recall how.

'What's wrong?'

'There's a snake,' she stammered.

'What kind?' he asked, carefully scanning the corner of the shed her shaky finger indicated.

'I don't know.'

'Well, was it black or brown? A red-belly?'

'I don't know!' she said, her voice raising frantically. 'It almost fell on me.'

'Fell on you?'

They both glanced upwards and Bel let out a startled squeak when they spotted a second snake, looped around the rafters above.

'It's just a python,' Dean said, sounding relieved.

'That's another one!'

'Its mate probably fell down while they were getting frisky. It's mating season.'

'It's still down here somewhere,' Bel said nervously, torn between keeping an eye on the snake above and searching for the one that had fallen.

'I got him,' Dean said, crouching down by some nearby equipment.

'You *what?*' Bel's eyes widened as she watched him reach under and withdraw the reptile. 'Oh my God. Are you insane?'

'He'll want to get back up to his girlfriend. There you go, mate,' he said, taking him across to the wall, where the terrifyingly large snake proceeded to cautiously navigate the rough timber walls as it made its way back up onto the exposed rafters above.

Bel gave a shiver of revulsion, scampering off the pile of feed and out of the dim shed.

'They aren't poisonous,' Dean said. 'He was probably more shocked than you were.'

'I highly doubt that,' she said as another huge shiver wracked her body. *So gross.* 'Are you just going to leave them in there?'

'They keep the rats and mice away.'

'And now me. I'm never going in that damn shed again.'

'You probably won't even see them after this.'

'That's not comforting at all.' *Not* seeing them was far more terrifying than seeing them, now that she knew they were there. Then she suddenly remembered the other thing she'd found.

'Dean, there's something else,' she said, pointing at the wooden box. She watched him retrieve it and bring it outside. He lifted the lid.

'What the hell is that doing here?' he asked.

Bel shook her head. 'I have no idea. But I know who will.'

Twenty-one

'Hey, I was just about to call you with my flight details,' Emma said, greeting Bel on the phone.

'Great. So, I was wondering, when you were planning on coming clean about the stuffed rooster in the feed shed?' Bel asked casually.

The silence on the phone was confirmation of what Bel had suspected.

'I was planning on getting rid of that when I came back.'

'Getting rid of it?'

'Returning it, whatever,' Emma said.

The shrug in her tone was annoying Bel. 'What are you *doing* with it in the first place?'

'It was a dare, of sorts,' Emma said, sounding a little less offhand and a lot more sheepish.

'What are you talking about?'

'Craig and I were out on our wedding anniversary, we were reminiscing about our youth and how much fun we used to have, and . . . how boring we've become,' she sighed deeply. 'There'd been a fair bit of alcohol consumed with dinner and we were walking past the museum. I don't know, I just had this crazy idea. I dared Craig to do something illegal and the least likely thing to get prison time for was to break into the museum. So he double-dared me and . . . we did it. Together.'

'The *least* likely thing to get prison time for? Good grief, Em, you're supposed to be a respectable parent. You're on the P&C committee, for goodness' sake!'

'The alternative was to have sex in a public place,' Emma said defensively, as though she'd made a much more respectable choice in breaking and entering.

'Oh my God.'

'Oh, stop it. You have no idea how depressing it is to remember how fun you used to be before you had to give it all up and become the strict mum and fun police.'

Okay, so maybe now she'd had a taste of losing her fun aunty identity to enforce Emma's guidelines, she could sympathise. And yes, it did hurt to be strict with the kids about eating dinner and doing homework, but still . . .

'I realised the next day how stupid it was, and I was planning on taking it back when I got a chance, but then Craig had his accident and everything . . . I'd forgotten about the damn thing until you made that post.'

The bloody post that had suddenly drawn attention to the missing bird that was currently in a bag at her feet.

'ASIO is involved, Emma! The freaking spooks!'

'Oh, would you relax. You're obviously getting all caught up in your own social media whirlwind. Everyone thinks it's a joke and a big publicity stunt.'

'Which means they probably think I'm behind it,' Bel groaned.

'It'll be fine. I'll take Elvis back when I get home and it'll all blow over.'

'Meanwhile, I have stolen goods in my possession.'

'Stash it under a bed somewhere.'

'I am not stashing poor Elvis under a bed.'

'I have to go, the insurance company are calling. I'll take care of it when I get home.'

So all Bel had to do was pretend she had no idea who the bird thief was or where Elvis was, despite using the hashtag #WhereIsElvis on every single post she'd been making. *No worries at all.*

'I can't believe we're doing this.'

'*You* can't believe it?' Dean whispered back. 'I've managed to survive thirty years without committing a crime and I'm breaking into a museum to *put something back*. If we get caught, it's not even for something cool.'

'If Emma wasn't already going through hell, I'd . . .' Well, there wasn't much point worrying about what she'd do. They had to fix it. Now, before this whole thing went any further.

'She probably wouldn't be too thrilled to know we'd brought her children along,' Dean said.

Bel's gaze went back to the four-wheel drive parked nearby in the shadows. They'd had little choice there, considering they couldn't very well get a babysitter in while they smuggled a stolen artefact back to the museum, Indiana Jones–style. Instead, they'd decided to use the treat of going out to dinner as their alibi. Once the kids had fallen asleep on the return trip from Toormanlee, they planned to slip Elvis back under the cover of darkness. 'She wasn't too concerned about her kids when she considered committing Wilful and Obscene Exposure,' Bel said under her breath.

'What?'

'Doesn't matter. Let's just get this over and done with.'

They stopped beside the back door of the old church and Dean took out his pocketknife. 'Keep watch.'

'For who?' she asked scathingly.

'For . . . I don't know, the police? Someone coming?'

'It's *Wessex*.'

'Do you want to explain to anyone what we're doing here?'

'Fine. I'll keep watch. But hurry up.'

She heard him mutter something but didn't bother asking him to repeat it. This whole thing was a gigantic shitshow.

She turned once she heard a small click and exhaled a rush of air when the door opened and no alarms went off. Not that she was expecting there to have been a high-tech security system installed over the last few days, but she'd never handled stressful situations very well.

Dean picked up the hessian bag and silently led the way inside. The museum was morbid enough in daylight, with its creepy old mannequins dressed up in vintage fashions, without the almost total darkness adding to the horror-movie effect.

Bel followed Dean, rationally lecturing herself that this was no different to being here in daylight and trying not to knock anything over.

On reaching the glass cabinet, they had a problem.

'It's locked,' Dean whispered incredulously. 'Why would they lock an empty case?'

Oh, for heaven's sake. 'Just leave it beside the case.'

Dean hesitated briefly and then removed the rooster from the bag and sat it on the floor. 'Okay. Let's get out of here.'

They retraced their steps through the old church faster than they'd come and slipped through the back door and out into the cool night air once more. Bel felt better the further they left the case behind. Her heart was racing as though she'd just completed a jewellery heist instead of simply returning a stuffed rooster.

Back in the car, with the kids still sound asleep, she let out a long sigh.

'Glad that's over,' Dean said, starting the car and driving away without switching on his headlights, as though he'd been committing illegal activities his entire life.

'How did you know how to pick a lock?' she asked, suddenly remembering that small detail.

'I may or may not have had occasion in my youth to open locked gun cabinets to go shooting without my old man's consent.'

'You know, this whole break-and-enter thing is actually kind of hot,' she said. She saw a twitch of a smile touch his mouth.

'Yeah?'

'Kind of.'

'Maybe we can reenact it later.'

Not a chance in hell. She hoped they'd never have to relive any of the last few days ever again. She was well and truly sick of Elvis the bloody rooster.

Emma's return felt like Christmas, only a thousand times better. The kids were excited to have their mum home. But Emma had lost weight and, despite the cheerful front she put on for her family, Bel could see the dark circles under her eyes and the exhaustion beneath her smile.

Sitting on the lounge together after the kids had finally gone to bed, the two women drank wine and talked quietly.

'How are you, really?' Bel asked.

'I'm wrecked,' her friend said with a sad smile. 'We've had some stressful times in our life, but nothing compares to this. The physiotherapy and rehabilitation he'll need is *a lot.*' She shook her head slowly. 'I don't know how we're going to get through it all. They say he's going to have to learn how to walk all over again, and at this stage, they aren't even sure how much mobility he'll actually regain,' she said as her eyes filled with tears. 'I don't know how he'll cope, Bel. If he can't walk, he won't be able to work the farm. We can't afford to hire anyone. It's going to kill him.'

Bel's heart dropped. She couldn't think of a single thing to say that would ease her friend's misery, so she did the only thing she could—cradled her in her arms and let her cry. Bel suspected Emma hadn't been able to let her guard down around Craig's family, and she was constantly putting on a brave face for her children. Tonight, she needed to let it out.

The next evening, Bel left the little family to have some time alone after being invited to Dean's place for dinner.

She and the kids had been over there a number of times, mainly to get them out of the house and as an excuse for the two of them to see each other when he was working long hours, but tonight was the first time she'd been here alone. She was more than a little excited by the prospect.

While Dean's driveway was a still rough dirt, his paddocks were impeccable. He'd worked hard to bring his property back from the slow decline it had been on over the years when his father had been unwell—the yard and driveway would obviously be the least of his priorities.

The sight of the property made Bel even more impressed by Dean's generosity over the last few weeks, with all the time he'd donated to helping with the kids and keeping Fernvale running. It wasn't as though he didn't have a million things here he could have been doing instead. *He really is a good guy.*

Her arrival was met with loud barking from Dean's two work dogs before a sharp whistle split the air and the noise ceased. Dean appeared, pushing open the screen door to greet her. He always kissed her as though he hadn't seen her in months instead of mere hours. She smiled as he pulled reluctantly away from their kiss.

'Dinner smells good,' she said, catching the scent of something delicious wafting in from the kitchen.

'I put a leg of lamb in the slow cooker this morning.'

'I'm starving,' she said, almost drooling as she followed him inside. 'Can I help with anything?'

'Nope, all under control.' He was so confident in the kitchen, and she'd never realised how hot that could be in a man. It had never been part of the whole Jax Lexington thing—cooking would have been far too mundane for Jax—and while Tate had cooked the odd breakfast and the occasional barbecue, it was never like this. When he'd been home, he had preferred eating out.

'How's it going over there?' Dean asked.

'The kids are still so excited about Em being home. They've barely left her side.'

'It's been tough on them. On Emma, too.'

Bel had blinked away tears more times than she could count since Emma had arrived as she'd watched the love between mother and children unfold before her eyes. Emma had taken over reading the bedtime stories and doing the rounds of tucking in each child at night, and Bel had realised what a poor consolation prize she had been for the kids. Nothing could replace a mum's hug. 'It's going to be so hard for them all to say goodbye after the weekend.'

'I can imagine. Hopefully when she goes back, they'll get some good news from the doctors about when Craig can get home.'

'I hope so,' Bel said. 'It's so quiet here. I'm resisting the reflex to go and see what mischief the kids are up to.'

'Stand down, soldier.' Dean grinned. 'You're officially off duty tonight. But yeah, it does get quiet out here. Why do you think I always take up Emma up on an invite to dinner?'

'That's one extreme to the other,' she said, smiling. The house certainly wasn't the sterile motel room that Tate's apartment had been, but it still lacked a personal touch that branded it as Dean's. There were some photos on the walls, but they were old ones, of grandparents maybe, although there were a few smaller ones gathered on top of a china cabinet that she walked over to now to inspect. In one of them, two people stood behind a small boy. She could already tell the boy was Dean, dressed in a football uniform and about seven or eight years old. A man and a woman were in the next one, which had been taken in front of a church on their wedding day, and she guessed they were his parents. A third photo was of a woman in her late forties, sitting on the front steps of this house and patting a small white dog. She was smiling brightly at whoever was taking the photo. 'Is this your mum?' she asked, holding up the photo in its brass frame.

He glanced up and nodded, a soft smile touching his lips. 'Things were better when she was around.' He dropped his gaze and turned away to put the tongs he'd been using into the sink.

Bel swallowed as her throat tightened. She understood too well how grief could creep up on you sometimes. It often caught her unawares. It never went away; you just learned to move forward with it.

'I like the noise and chaos at Fernvale. I never had it,' he said, turning back to face her before searching in the cutlery drawer and retrieving a spoon.

'Being an only child? Yeah, I get that. It's one of the things I love about being part of Emma and Craig's crazy life too.'

'For a long time, it was just Dad and me out here, and he wasn't a great conversationalist at the best of times.'

'Did you two never get on?' she asked, curious about a topic they hadn't really discussed much.

Dean quietly stirred the gravy before answering. 'It wasn't that we didn't get on. I mean, we had farming in common, but we never really talked. He'd grunt here and there and tell me what I had to do the next day, but we wouldn't talk about our days or anything. Dinner was always silent with the news on in the background. At breakfast we'd have the radio, local news and weather.'

Bel couldn't help but feel for the younger Dean. The picture he'd painted sounded incredibly lonely.

'He was of that generation where men were stoic and worked until they dropped dead out in the paddock. Which he did, quite literally.'

'Was it a farming accident?'

'Heart attack. His doctor had been telling him for years to change his diet and had tried to get him to take medication, but Dad didn't have time for any of that. He was a stubborn bastard,' Dean muttered, shaking his head. 'I guess part of me feels guilty that I wasn't here when it happened.'

'Feeling guilty is understandable, but even if you were here, what you could have done?'

'Yeah, I guess. He never really forgave me for not coming back to work this place. I wish now that I'd come back sooner. Maybe it wouldn't have changed anything, but I'll always regret not making things right between us before he died.'

Bel closed the gap between them and slipped her arms around his waist. The hug seemed to surprise him, and he initially remained stiff before relaxing against her and hugging her tightly back. She wasn't sure there were any words to take away the regret he felt—she only knew she wanted to ease some of the pain he was carrying.

They stood quietly like that for a long time before he let out a muffled expletive at the scent of smoke and released her to grab a set of oven mitts and retrieve the charcoal-encrusted garlic bread from the oven.

The meal had been delicious, despite the extra crunchy bread, and Bel found herself comfortably satisfied with a full tummy and a warmth inside that continued to grow as she spent more time with this man across the table from her.

The next morning, Bel kissed Dean goodbye as they left the house together.

'Stay in bed longer,' he'd told her as his alarm went off.

'No. I have a few things I want to do in town this morning anyway,' she'd said, reaching up to kiss him lazily.

She could certainly get used to waking up beside him every day. She pondered that thought. She honestly could. She was beginning to hate the time they spent apart and counted down the hours until they saw each other again. Luckily, he didn't have an employer to explain his rather late start that morning when they'd finally gotten out of bed and dressed. She looked back in her rear-view mirror and saw him standing where she'd left him in the driveway, still watching her, and a happy smile broke out on her face.

She wasn't sure what the immediate future held in store for her, but she was going to have to think about it soon. She wasn't going to be able to stay at Emma's once Craig came home, and even though that might still be some time away, it was going to happen. She had Gran's house, but it was currently being rented out and she was worried about what her return would mean for her tenant. She swore silently. She was definitely not cut out for the landlord business.

She'd dropped by one morning when she'd first come back, seeing Bert out in the garden and stopping to have a chat. He'd been so grateful she'd rented him the house and he clearly enjoyed living there. The garden had never looked better. She felt a small pang of emotion as she thought about how happy Gran would be to know someone was taking care of her beloved flowers.

She pulled up in front of the house now and let out a long breath. She had to at least let Bert know there was a possibility that she may need to move back into her house, to give him some warning. She hated the thought of doing it to him.

She knocked on the door but there was no answer. It was possible he'd gone into town or something, but then . . . Bert was elderly. What if something had happened and he couldn't get to the door?

'Hello, dear. Are you looking for Bert?'

Bel turned and spotted a familiar face over the low side fence. 'Hello, Mrs Vernon. Yes, I was. He's not answering the door though.'

'No, he's in hospital. Poor man had a fall a couple of days ago. I called his son to check on him and he said Bert was waiting to have an operation. I haven't heard anything since. I didn't like to bother the family. You know how it is, dear,' she added, clearly concerned for her neighbour.

'I hope he's okay.'

'I can give you the son's number, if you like. If you find out anything, do let me know, won't you?'

'Of course,' Bel assured her.

'It's a worry, when you get old and a bit shaky on your feet,' Mrs Vernon said as she led Bel to her house to get the phone number. 'I'm very fortunate that I have my two daughters nearby, and my grandchildren. They keep an eye on me. Poor Bert, his children don't live locally. Luckily it happened outside in the garden or he may not have been found as soon as he was,' she tsked.

Bel could only imagine how scary living alone could be for older people. Her thoughts briefly went to Dean's father, and how horrible it would have been for him as well, dying alone out there, and she felt how the burden of that knowledge must weigh on Dean's shoulders. Not that all the blame could rest on Dean—his father was a grown man who at any point could have tried to reach out to his son. Pride was a terrible thing when it stood in the way of happiness.

The town was busy. The excitement hadn't really stopped since the whole Elvis fiasco, although it had settled into a more manageable bustle now that the media circus had moved on to a new scandal somewhere else.

There'd been one update about the mysterious return of Elvis the rooster on morning TV. They hadn't come out to Wessex but had interviewed Betty via videocall, which showed how much the story had fallen from public interest.

'Betty, it's a miracle,' the female co-host announced as an opening. 'Elvis is back!'

'Yes, he most certainly is and we're all very relieved,' Betty, crossing from the museum, confirmed.

'Do we have any idea who was responsible? Were there any clues? We know the rooster-nappers left a ransom note when they stole him, but do we have an explanation about where he's been or, more importantly, who took him?'

'No,' Betty informed them quite seriously. 'There was no note when they returned him. We still don't know who took him or why. It's a big mystery to everyone.'

'Well, on the upside, if there was anything good to come from this tragedy,' the male co-host said with a completely straight face, 'it's that the town of Wessex has seen an unprecedented rise in visitors. How are the locals handling their newfound fame?'

'It's been very busy in Wessex, and we're all extremely grateful for everyone's well wishes. There's been plenty of celebrating since Elvis's return and we look forward to continuing to welcome visitors to our little town and now being able to showcase our very special mascot.'

'Well, we're all extremely happy Elvis has been returned home where he belongs, and we wish you all the best.'

The segment ended and Emma burst into uncontrollable laughter beside Bel on the lounge, where they'd been watching on the TV.

'There is nothing amusing about any of this,' Bel told her friend, eyeing her with a narrowed gaze.

'Oh, come on, Bel. I've said I was sorry a million times. But even you have to see the absolute genius, albeit unintentional genius, of the whole thing? It's put us on the map.'

'Dean and I could have been caught putting that stupid thing back. Can you imagine the uproar that would have caused?'

'Stop being so dramatic. Betty would have nominated you for Citizen of the Year next Australia Day ceremony,' Emma said dismissively.

'Betty would have been devastated that her theory about Bob Baxter being the criminal was wrong,' Bel corrected.

Bel had been concerned that once the whole social media thing had died down, so too would the unexpected tourist trade, but her dire predictions hadn't proved true. All the hype had alerted people to another 'big' thing to add to their sightseeing list. Word of mouth was sending a steady stream of people out to see this part of the country, and everyone in Wessex was reaping the rewards.

Emma's departure was every bit as sad as Bel was expecting. When Dean came to pick her up and drive her to the airport, the kids cried as they waved her off. Bel spent the rest of the afternoon sitting with them quietly and coming up with ideas for the welcome-home party they would undoubtedly be having once their father was well enough to return to Fernvale. It may have been a little premature, but it helped to distract and cheer them all up somewhat.

When Dean came back, he brought ice cream; having four children on a sugar high right before bedtime was deemed okay, just this once.

As Bel and Dean sat together on the lounge after a *very* long bedtime tuck-in routine, wine in hand and listening to nothing but the sounds of nightfall outside, Bel was finally able to let out a long breath.

'I hope they let Craig come back soon. The kids have been through so much upheaval. They need to have their dad back home, in whatever capacity that turns out to be.'

'Emma reckons he's making progress. At least she sounded positive when she was talking to me about it,' Dean said. His arm around her felt solid and she buried herself closer into his side.

'They're still going to need his family's help for a while, though. I think we need to be prepared that it's going to take a long time before he's back to where he was before the accident.'

'He'll get there,' Dean said.

'I hope so.'

'He's a tough bugger—always has been. You'll see. He'll do whatever needs to be done and probably in half the time the doctors reckon he will.'

Bel latched onto Dean's words and held them close to her heart, praying he'd be right. Emma and the kids needed him back.

Her phone beeped on the lounge beside her and she gave a small groan as she read the text.

'What is it?' Dean asked, lifting his head from where he'd dropped it back against the head rest.

'I've been summoned to dinner tomorrow night at Glentoberon. Aunt Lois just texted me.'

'I thought they were still away?'

'So did I. Apparently, they're back.' She'd thought she'd been saved from family duties for a while. *Great.*

'It's not like you'll have to say much. You won't be able to get a word in edgewise with your aunt.'

Bel sighed. Larkin must have passed on the news that Bel was back in town. In typical Larkin fashion, she'd gotten over her earlier huff about Bel not cooperating by going to the reunion. She never stayed angry long and besides, she'd had too much tea to spill about the week *not* to give in and call when she got back to Sydney. Apparently Tate had been a no-show and two others had pulled out at the last minute—namely Niki and Kelly, when they found out that Oliver had been up to his old tricks again, this time with Gigi—so it had been a complete disaster.

It would be fine. It was just dinner. How bad could it be?

Twenty-two

'Bel, darling, how lovely to *finally* see you,' Aunt Lois crooned as Bel stepped up to kiss the cheek of her impeccably made-up face. Her aunt's tone, as usual, felt like a reprimand. How *she* was at fault for not catching up sooner when *they* hadn't even been in town, she wasn't sure.

'It's been a while,' Bel agreed, holding her smile in place. 'How was your trip overseas?' *Where you've just spent the last three months.*

'Absolutely divine. Europe is to die for. I didn't want to come back to all this dust and heat.'

And the rather sumptuous mansion you live in. Despite the fact she found the place to be more like a museum, she would never understand why her aunt always seemed to consider it less than impressive simply because of *where* it was located.

'Bel!'

Bel's gaze shot to the top of the staircase to discover her cousin gracefully gliding down towards her.

'Larkin? I didn't know you were home.'

'Just got here this afternoon. I heard you were coming for dinner.'

Bel eyed her cousin cautiously, searching for any lingering animosity, but was greeted with a smile. At least dinner wouldn't be the awkward experience she'd been dreading, trying to make uncomfortable small talk with her uncle and aunt.

They moved into the living room, and Bel felt a flash of old memories briefly return as she thought back to the last time she'd been here, with Tate during the wedding. She could see him standing at the back of the room, drink in hand as he laughed with the other groomsmen on that first night he'd noticed her. She was relieved she no longer felt any sort of yearning, the way she had back then.

She found her uncle and Tristan sitting on the lounge, talking golf techniques. Both men stood, and Bel was quickly handed a tall glass of champagne.

Larkin slid her hand around her husband's waist and grinned up at him. 'We were going to wait until dinner to make the announcement, but I'm just too excited. We're expecting!'

A loud and somewhat undignified squeal erupted from Aunt Lois as she threw herself at the happy couple, pushing Uncle Stan out of the way in her excitement. 'I'm going to be a grandmother!' she said, dabbing at her eyes with a lace-edged handkerchief.

Bel watched on with a touch of bemusement. Larkin was going to be a mother.

Then, a sudden rush of unexpected emotion ran through her. She'd never wanted kids of her own . . . well, at least she hadn't before she'd come back and let herself fall into the somewhat faux family she and Dean had created. She felt a trickle of warmth flow through her as glimpses of snuggling up for bedtime stories popped into her head, and of sharing amused glances with Dean at dinner as they listened to the silly jokes Ben and Ivy had taken to entertaining them with lately.

What was she even thinking? She prided herself on being so responsible and grown up. She needed to stop living in a fantasy world. She hadn't let her mind run away like this since . . .

Her stomach dropped slightly. Had she been blindly falling into the same trap with Dean that she'd found herself in with Tate? Surely not. She'd vowed she'd never again allow herself to get caught up in an unrealistic romance. Yet here she was. Dean had somehow swept her off her feet.

She felt a little dizzy as something suddenly occurred to her and she sank down onto the lounge. The hot kitchen sex . . . the constant distraction of his body, his heart-melting acts of kindness. *Oh God.* She'd gone from a Jax Lexington-style romantic suspense hero to a hot boy-next-door, enemies-to-lovers trope.

'Bel!' Larkin said impatiently.

She looked up quickly.

'Are you okay?'

'Absolutely.' She smiled, hoping her face didn't show her rapidly growing panic. 'Congratulations,' she added, and stood up to hug her cousin. She refused to acknowledge the ridiculous chaos unfolding inside her. Dean was not Tate, and she would not have fallen for something fake after everything she'd been through. It wasn't possible.

And yet . . .

Later that night, after she'd managed to sit through the endless chatter about baby plans and then her aunt's relentless Europe stories, Bel found herself returning to her unexpected reaction.

There was no way her relationship with Dean was anything like the one she'd had with Tate. Dean was . . . perfect. Not in the dreamy, over-the-top way Tate had been. He was perfect in a forever kind of way. A father kind of way. Bel's mind began to replay all the times Dean had stepped up to distract the kids and made them feel loved during one of the most unsettled and scary periods of their young lives. He was the decent, good man that Emma had been telling her he was. She'd simply never understood it before now.

But did she want that? And if she did, why was the thought so terrifying?

Craig's progress was frustratingly slow. This was expected from a traumatic brain injury, but that didn't make it any less discouraging. The endless game of wait-and-see over the next month took its toll on everyone—none more so than Craig and Emma, but it flowed on through to the kids and to Bel as well, with life pretty much on hold for all of them.

As the time dragged on, Bel began to notice a change in the children's behaviour. Ben was getting into trouble at school—nothing terribly serious, but enough for Emma to be receiving calls from his teachers, which only added to her worries. Lucy had started going backwards with her toilet training, suddenly having accidents when previously she'd had none. Ayla had been having nightmares, and would only settle if she was allowed to climb into bed with Bel. It didn't take long before the sleepless nights began catching up with Bel. As a result, she found herself becoming tired and irritable throughout the day.

Adding to all of this, Bel's business had begun to suffer, with the loss of some larger clients who weren't happy with her reduced hours and availability. She'd expected her income to take a bit of a hit for a while, of course, and she was still making enough to survive. It just went against the grain, and everything she'd been working so hard for, to have to turn away big clients with deep pockets.

She'd just made one such difficult decision, having to refer a client to another service, when Dean called to let her know he wouldn't be able to pick up the kids from school like they'd arranged earlier, so Bel could have a full day working.

'Sorry,' Dean added after he'd explained his predicament.

'Fine. Don't worry about it. I've got it . . . as usual,' she muttered.

'I didn't plan on driving into a bloody bore drain, Bel,' he snapped. 'I could do without having the stuff-around of walking back to the house to get the tractor and pulling it out.'

Bel instantly felt a ripple of guilt. She knew he'd been putting in long hours at his place on top of helping her out with the kids. 'I know. I'm sorry. I've just had a frustrating day.'

'I hear ya,' he agreed. 'Mine's been pretty shit as well.'

'I get it,' she said, trying not to let her irritation show, but fearing she wasn't succeeding.

'I'll try and make it over there after dinner.'

'No, don't worry. I think I'll have an early night. I haven't been getting much sleep lately.'

'Righto, if that's what you want,' he said somewhat stiffly.

They hung up and Bel pushed herself out from the table and grabbed her purse and the car keys. By the time she had the kids safely home from school, she'd lost her earlier irritability with the world. Who could stay cranky with an adorable three-year-old retelling the misadventure of the daycare turtle that had escaped from its enclosure and subsequently recaptured by Miss Judy, who was now Lucy's idol?

However, by the time Bel had negotiated a peace treaty between the three older kids, who were fighting over whose turn it was to feed the chooks, confiscated a packet of sugary snacks Lucy had apparently *found* and decided to eat before dinner, argued about bathtime and then sat through the ordeal of having all four kids decide they didn't like the sausages and mashed potatoes she'd laboured to cook them, she was at breaking point again.

When she climbed into bed, feeling like it must be at least midnight, only to discover that it was eight-thirty, she was too exhausted to even feel disheartened.

Her phone vibrated to indicate an incoming call. She glanced at the screen and saw that it was Dean. She turned on her side and ignored it. She simply couldn't adult another moment longer, today.

'I tried to call last night,' Dean said. He was waiting for her at Fernvale when she returned from dropping the kids at school the next morning.

'I told you I was going to bed early.'

'I wanted to catch you before you went to sleep. I'm sorry I let you down yesterday, but it really was out of my control.'

'I know,' she said wearily. 'It was just a really crappy day.'

'Is everything okay? Between us, I mean?'

Bel shut the driver-side door and stepped around him, taking the three bags of groceries from the back seat, which he automatically took from her to carry inside. 'Yeah. I'm just tired.'

'And you have every right to be. You've taken on a huge job stepping in to be here and taking care of four kids. Which is why I felt so bad having to cancel on you. I promised to help out and I know I haven't been much help lately, being caught up with my place and everything else going wrong.'

'I know it wasn't your fault. I shouldn't have snapped yesterday. I just . . .' She ran a hand through her hair, absently noting she probably needed to go to the hairdresser at some point for a trim, but who the hell had time? 'I seriously have no idea how Em does this. It's *exhausting*. All the arguing, crying and meltdowns—and that's just me!' she said with a weary smile. 'Kids take it out of you, mentally, physically . . . emotionally.' She shook her head. 'It's more than a full-time job and she just seems to take it all in her stride. Plus do all the charity work and the farm stuff. I feel like I'm winging everything. What if I'm stuffing these kids up while she's away? What if I'm doing some actual damage to them?'

'You're overthinking it. You're great with the kids. You're not going to damage them,' he said gently, putting the jug on as she slumped at the bench, defeated.

'I feel like a terrible friend for wishing she'd come home and take over.'

'I bet there's days when Emma probably wishes someone else would come and take over for her too. I've heard her complaining to Craig about her day and the kids, and how the house has been a disaster zone all week. It's a tough gig and you are doing great, especially since you were pretty much thrown in the deep end. Not many people get lumped with four kids all at once,' he said, placing a coffee in front of her. 'Why don't you take tomorrow off and go and spend it in Toormanlee? Go shopping or take your computer to a cafe and work, away from all this? I'll stay the night and take the kids to school and pick them up.'

'You can't take the day off to do that,' she said wearily.

'I'll make it work.'

She was instantly struck by his gesture. It was almost heroic, something that Jax would do, if he were an everyday, average guy. Bel shook her head quickly. 'I really appreciate the offer, but I'm okay. I snapped yesterday, but I had a decent sleep last night.' He was just as tired as her, if not more so, with all the pressure he was under to get his crops harvested and the next lot ready to put in. She felt bad about her little dummy spit. She wasn't special. Everyone was tired.

'How was your visit with Larkin? How far along is she now?' Dean asked.

'Yeah, good,' she said, taking a sip of her coffee. 'She's four months now.'

'Do they make designer maternity wear for socialites?' he asked, taking a seat beside her.

Bel chuckled. 'I have no idea.'

'It's great anyway. I'm happy for them.'

'Yeah, me too.'

'Do I detect a "but"?' he asked, taking her hand in his.

'Not at all,' she said, putting her cup back down. 'I guess . . . I was surprised when I first found out. That child will be the most fashionable baby on the entire North Shore of Sydney.' She pulled her hand free to pick up her cup once more, shifting a little uncomfortably in her seat as she did so.

A silence fell between them before Dean spoke. 'I get the feeling something's changed. That it's more than just being tired.'

Bel stood up and carried her cup to the sink. 'I'm still trying to figure out what I want to do after this. Where I belong.'

'You . . . don't feel like you belong here?'

'Part of me does.'

'I heard Tom was planning on moving into Fernvale to take over for Craig,' Dean commented.

'Yeah. Emma mentioned it the other day.' Craig's younger brother, Tom, and his father, Mick, planned to share the load until Craig regained his mobility and was strong enough to resume work. There was still no certainty that he would make a complete recoveryy, but his slow and steady progress so far had been impressing his doctors even if Craig and Emma felt frustrated.

'It'll be getting a bit crowded here,' Dean said.

'I'll move out once Emma and Craig are back,' she said. 'Back to Gran's.'

'You could move in with me,' he suggested lightly, although she detected a slight nervous energy underneath his casual demeanour.

'At your place?'

'Why not?'

Bel's first instinct was to consider the idea, but then she shook her head and gave a weak smile. 'We've barely gotten to know each other. I think it's a bit soon to be moving in together.'

'We've known each other all our lives,' he pointed out.

'Not like . . . this.'

'Bel, I know what I want.'

'What do you want?'

'I want you,' he said simply. 'And I want a family.'

That's what she'd been afraid he'd say. 'It's too soon.'

'I'm thirty. Most blokes my age already have their kids.'

'No, I mean it's too soon to know if I'm the right one for you to have a family with.'

'I've always known you were the right one.'

'How could you always have known that?'

He shrugged. 'I told you I had a crush on you back in primary school, and that it was still there when I came back to town. All I know is we're great together and I want it to be permanent.'

'We've only been together a couple of months,' she said, shaking her head at his adamant tone.

'Sometimes, you just know.'

That's what Tate said. The thought set off an unpleasant reaction inside her.

Unaware of her inner turmoil, he continued, taking her hand back in his. 'Move in and let me prove it.'

'I've got Gran's place sitting there,' Bel managed, still reeling from his unexpected offer.

'What's *really* stopping you?' he asked quietly.

'God, Dean, so many things,' she said, putting a hand to her forehead and briefly closing her eyes as she tried to make sense of the storm inside her. 'I don't want to make another mistake.'

'The mistake being us, I take it?' he asked in a quiet, clipped tone.

'I jumped into a relationship with Tate, thinking I knew exactly what I was doing, and it turned out I had no idea. I'm afraid of jumping into something else too fast. I didn't come back here to find a relationship.'

'Sometimes we find what we want when we least expect it,' Dean said matter-of-factly.

She opened her mouth to reply but was interrupted by her phone on the bench, ringing. 'It's Em,' she said, picking it up. 'Hey—' she started before being cut off quickly.

'We're coming home!'

For a while, she'd been able to delay deciding on her plans, with no firm end date on when she'd be able to leave Fernvale. Now, suddenly, the sand of the hourglass was beginning to run, counting down. And she still didn't know where she went from here.

Twenty-three

Things started moving fast once Craig was given the okay to come home. Ramps had been rapidly built for the wheelchair access he would still be needing for a good while yet, and there were renovations to the bathroom and changes to the bedroom. Bel helped Emma as much as she could, taking on the painting and whatever else needed doing before Craig's arrival. Underneath the excitement, there was an air of apprehension lingering. For Emma, Bel suspected it came from worrying over how her family was going to adapt to this new dynamic, and maybe even how their marriage would change.

Bel knew nothing would ever break the two of them up—there had never been a more perfect couple created—but life as they knew it had been shaken to its core, and things were bound to have changed.

For Bel, the apprehension came from the knowledge that she could no longer put off facing her own dilemma—what did she want to do with the rest of her life?

Her concern about giving Bert his notice had thankfully resolved itself when his son had called her, asking to terminate the lease. The fall had impacted Bert's ability to live alone and the family had decided he should move closer to them. Bel assured his son she didn't want him to pay out the remaining time on the lease; she was just relieved she didn't have evict an elderly man.

She should have been happy that everything seemed to be falling into place. Her house was now vacant, which gave her somewhere to move so she could get out of Emma and Craig's hair, but she found herself inexplicably annoyed. It felt like the universe was trying to funnel her in a certain direction when she wasn't even sure she wanted to go that way, which made no sense at all.

'My offer still stands. Move in here, with me,' Dean said after they'd finished dinner and were sitting on his couch half-watching a reality show one night.

Her heart thudded a little more heavily against her ribs at his words. Part of her desperately wanted to accept, but another part of her was remembering the parallels between this situation and the Tate disaster, which she'd first seen that night at Glentoberon with her family. A flutter of panic began to rise again, dulling the excitement.

'You don't want to,' he surmised after the silence stretched between them a little too long.

A small throb began to build behind her temples, and she massaged her fingers against them. 'I've been putting off figuring out what I want to do ever since I got back here. Now, suddenly, there's all this pressure to make a decision.'

'But you've liked being back here?'

'I have.' She'd found herself seeing her hometown through new eyes and falling in love with it, maybe for the first time. Growing up in a place, you sometimes took it for granted, and never really learned to appreciate it as outsiders did. Coming back, she'd realised how special this town really was.

'You can't deny that these last few months, taking care of the kids and being together . . . it's been good. Right?'

'It's been great,' she said, smiling gently.

He gave a slight nod. 'I don't want that to end. I want kids of my own . . . with you.' He held her gaze steadily.

She knew he did, and it scared her that, deep down, she wanted the same thing. Only . . .

'No,' she blurted nervously. She shifted on the couch and moved away, getting to her feet. 'I can't. I don't know anything about being a mother.' All of a sudden, everything felt claustrophobic, like the walls were beginning to close in.

She saw confusion slide over his face. He stood up and opened his hands, palms up, inviting her to explain. 'You've been awesome with those kids. You'd make an amazing mum. We made a great team.'

'But it *wasn't real*,' she stressed. Just like her stupid manifesting list of her perfect man hadn't been real. 'We were just playing happy families. It wasn't reality. Before all this happened, I was starting to live my own life. I had a business that was flourishing, that I'd been working hard to build.'

'You can still have your business. You said it yourself, you can work from anywhere.'

'You don't get it. I'm back where I started. I was supposed to leave and *do* something with my life . . . but here I am, back in Wessex.'

'There's nothing wrong with Wessex. Coming back doesn't mean you've failed.'

'It doesn't mean I've succeeded either.'

Dean stepped back. 'I'm sorry this town isn't enough for you. That *I'm* not enough for you.'

His words hit her with unexpected force, but not enough to make her take back what she'd said. She wasn't even sure what it was she was feeling—her emotions were jumbled and chaotic. She needed some space and time to try to sort through them. 'I can't do this right now.'

'Okay,' he said, sounding almost defeated, which made her feel even sadder. 'Let me know when you can.' It was impossible to miss the sarcasm, but she knew that underneath it he was hurt.

Bel blinked rapidly as she stared through the beams of her headlights on the narrow road back towards Emma's. Everything was unravelling.

Craig's welcome home was set to be as heartwarming as a welcome home could get. The kids had slaved for days over a huge WELCOME HOME, DADDY banner and enough cards to put a Hallmark display to shame. The chook pen had had its final coat of paint and was ready for its grand unveiling. Emma had returned to Sydney two days earlier to bring him home, and the house was alive with anticipation.

It had been three days since Bel had seen Dean and so far nothing had been resolved. Part of her wanted to call him and say yes to all his crazy ideas—yes, she wanted to move in with him and yes, she wanted to have his babies—but another part kept throwing up reminders of her past mistakes, the disasters that had resulted from listening to her heart instead of her head. All those stupid giddy feelings she'd had with Tate and the way she'd been so sure he was the manifested man of her dreams. *What an idiot.* She couldn't trust those kinds of emotions when making a life-altering decision. This was too important to mess up.

Bel heard Jack barking at an approaching vehicle and knew even before the kids' announcement that Dean had arrived. Although she'd braced herself to see him, her pulse still gave a little leap of excitement when he appeared at the front door. Proof of how much she let her hormones influence her judgement, she tried to tell herself. Still, a rush of sadness flooded through her when he looked at her before quickly turning away and beginning to play with the kids.

When the next car pulled up, everything the kids had been practising for the big surprise was forgotten. Instead, all four of them ran outside, down the new ramp Dean had built, and circled the car like a school of excited sharks.

Emma and Bel had taken them to see their dad after he'd been transferred to rehab and, as children did, they had absorbed it all with beguiling innocence. Not afraid to ask the questions adults probably wouldn't pose up front, the kids had quickly and completely accepted that this was still their dad and got on with their business. The only thing they really cared about was the fact they missed their father. And now he was finally home.

It was both sobering and heart-wrenching to watch the kids taking in this new version of their dad at home, where he'd always been so capable and strong. They'd been talking about this moment ever since the accident, and Emma had been preparing them the last few weeks for when Daddy would come home and how different things were going to be, but nothing could truly prepare them.

Bel watched as Emma went to the back of the car to retrieve the stowed wheelchair, which Dean effortlessly lifted out, setting it up under Emma's instructions and bringing it to his friend's door.

Craig positioned himself carefully, with Dean supporting the chair, and slid from the car to the chair smoothly, if a little slowly. He declined Dean's offer to push, taking over with a smile for his kids, who, after a brief hesitation, were jumping around the chair excitedly, wanting a ride.

'Come on, you lot,' Emma said, gathering them to her with a smile. 'Give Dad some room and let him catch his breath.'

'Can we have a go later, Daddy?' Ivy asked. In typical kid fashion, they didn't see the chair as an intrusion, but as another form of transportation they could master, like a quad or a farm bike.

Craig chuckled. 'Sure, kiddo. Later,' he said with a gentle smile.

It was almost like old times. Craig was maybe a little quieter than he used to be, and his speech was noticeably slower, but he looked better than when Bel had last seen him, on the visit with the kids. He looked healthier, his body having gradually recovered from its initial deterioration. He seemed happy to be home. She knew from Emma he'd suffered terribly with bouts of depression, but he'd worked through that and come out the other side a lot more positive than Bel had been expecting. She was glad she could move back to Gran's, at least until she figured out what she wanted to do. The family needed their own space to reconnect and adjust to their new life.

Her gaze turned to Dean and she gave a small sigh, which Emma heard, thanks to her uncanny ability to always appear at the most inconvenient time.

'What's going on with you and Dean?'

'Nothing.'

'Sure. That's why he's moping about over there and you're on the other side of the room, looking like you just lost your best friend.'

'He wasn't thrilled about me moving back into Gran's.'

'How come?'

'He wanted me to move in with him.'

'And why aren't you?'

'Because I . . . don't know if that's what I want to do.'

'You two have been practically inseparable ever since you got back. Why would you have to think about it?'

'Maybe I want to do something else other than settle down and have kids.'

'He wants to have kids with you?'

'Would you keep your voice down?' Bel said with a scowl.

'And you need to think about it?' Emma continued, doubtfully.

'Emma, I came home right when everything was beginning to take off. I want to keep making a career for myself. I never planned to come back and get married and have a bunch of kids.'

'You might not have planned it, but is it really so bad that it could be an option?'

'It's not bad,' Bel started, then made a frustrated sound in her throat. 'I just don't want to be pressured into making a decision like that. He surprised me.'

'But you *are* thinking about it?' Emma probed.

'I don't know,' Bel snapped, then felt bad. 'I don't want to end up in another situation like the one I was in with Tate. Like I don't have any control.' *Why couldn't anyone else understand this?* 'I need some space to figure out my options.'

'I get that you might be worried, I do, honestly. But Dean is not Tate.'

'I know,' Bel conceded wearily. 'It's the situation, not the guy, that feels the same.'

'You aren't the person you were back then either. You were wishing for something exciting to happen in your life and Tate suddenly appeared and you ran with it. You aren't like that now.'

'What if I still want adventure and excitement?'

Emma gave a small smile. 'I don't think you'd be lacking in excitement being around Dean every day. I've seen how you light up when he walks in the room, and I know I've never seen that man happier in the whole time I've known him. Sometimes, the excitement and adventure are found in the little everyday things. You just have to know where to look for them.'

Bel thought over Emma's words as she left the party early, saying her goodbyes and slipping out without speaking to Dean. Yes, she felt like a coward, but she'd barely slept and she was definitely not in possession of the kind of emotional fortitude she'd be needing when she spoke to him again.

Bel had been cleaning since coming back from the welcome-home party and it was now dark. The beauty of having rented the house out furnished was that nothing had needed to be stored, other than her personal items, which she'd kept in the shed. After a bit of a clean, everything felt like home again. Only . . . not quite. Even home, despite looking the same, didn't feel quite the same. Like it too had somehow moved on and changed in some infinitesimal way.

She put down the last box she'd carried in from the shed and opened it to find the remaining bits and pieces from her bedroom. After a brief hesitation, she removed the pink and gold hardcover journal that sat on top. She ran her fingers across the beautifully embossed cover and felt a strange tingle moving through her fingers. Opening the book, she found the torn-out page and let out a fatalistic sigh at the title: 'My Soulmate List'.

It had been nearly two years since she'd sat down to write her list, pouring her heart into that one desperate wish to find her soulmate. What a disaster that had turned out to be.

Against her better judgement, she allowed her gaze to skim over the handwritten list, bracing for the disappointment to emerge. At first glance, the requests she'd made seemed simple enough . . . even if she'd had the fictional character of Jax Lexington in mind when she'd written them out. Only she hadn't gotten Jax; instead, she'd gotten Tate. After allowing a brief interlude of self-pity, though, Bel felt an unexpected calmness settle around her.

Her eyes narrowed slightly as she sat in thoughtful reflection, and she reviewed the list once more, a lot more slowly this time. Her heart began being in a weird, out-of-kilter rhythm.

Brave. Tate hadn't done anything that could be called bravery. Jax could parachute from a plane and rescue a socialite heiress from a kidnapper in South America. Pretty extreme. And yet, there was Dean, snake handling and willingly putting himself in danger—being part of the RFS and SES to help others in need? *That* was brave.

Chiselled jaw. It had been one of the first things she'd noticed about Tate, but an image of Dean's strong jawline, emphasised by the sexy stubble he now preferred, flashed through her mind.

Intelligent. Tate had obviously come from a good school and he had a degree in management. Listening to him explain his job, though, had bored her silly within minutes, while listening to Dean talk about farming and how technical the whole thing was nowadays had really impressed her.

Someone who understands me. Tate didn't have a clue about what made her tick, not even with all the time they'd spent together. Not once had he ever asked what was important to her, what she was passionate about. But she and Dean had talked about their dreams for hours. She knew that he wanted to expand his crops within the next few seasons and was excited to experiment with regen farming. He knew about her love of reading and how important books had always been to her, and how much she valued her newfound independence with her business.

Loves excitement . . . hero qualities. Tate *had* played the chivalrous hero at the cocktail party, saving her from an embarrassing wardrobe malfunction, but when it came to real hero qualities, there hadn't been many of those. Dean, on the other hand, was a man who was out on the front line when his community needed him. The guy had committed break and enter to return a rooster to the museum . . . for *her*. It didn't get much more exciting than that. He really had been not only *her* hero but a hero to the kids as well, building the chook pen of their dreams, stepping in to be the father figure they'd needed while their own had been fighting to regain his life. Not to mention helping her bake biscuits . . .

Handsome. Tate had certainly been that, in a skin-deep way. Dean, meanwhile, may never be on the cover of a romance novel, but her heart fluttered every time she saw him. He was compassionate and caring. He would do anything for his friends and loved ones and that made him even more attractive.

Beautiful eyes. She had a memory of Dean's green-grey eyes as they stared down into hers, caught by the glimmer of moonlight as it shone through the bedroom window . . .

The book fell from her fingers. *How could I have been so blind?*

She'd been *so* sure back then that it had been Tate. Tall, handsome, charismatic Tate, who had come along and swept her off her feet. She'd been so fixated on finding her very own Jax Lexington that she'd allowed herself to see only the parts of Tate that appeared to be like Jax. And if they hadn't been there, she'd somehow either ignored them or *forced* him to fit into this image of the man she'd thought she wanted.

And this entire time, he'd been right here under her nose. She'd been a complete idiot.

It *wasn't* Tate. It had *never* been Tate. She *had* manifested the man of her dreams—and he'd come back to town after years of being away.

She'd manifested Dean.

No drive had ever invoked this quantity of nervous butterflies in Bel's stomach. Her mind had been rehearsing a million different ways to explain the chaos that had been unfolding within her ever since she'd made the connection a mere two hours earlier.

It had suddenly become clear *why* Tate hadn't worked out. Rushing into things with him had been the dumbest thing she'd ever done, yet maybe that had been part of the universe's grand plan too; some vital lesson in life she'd apparently needed to learn.

The lack of trust she had in her own judgement because of her previous decisions suddenly cleared up. She *could* trust her heart. Falling for Tate had never been about her heart—it was simply a hard experience she had to undergo in order to recognise what *real* love was supposed to feel like when it eventually showed up. *It was supposed to feel like Dean.*

She'd paced her bedroom floor anxiously before coming to the only logical decision: she needed to tell him she'd been foolishly focused on all the wrong things.

Now, she sat in the car in his driveway, gathering her courage. The outside floodlight came on as she walked towards the house, then the front door opened and Dean appeared in the doorway.

'Bel?' His surprise proved he'd obviously been expecting *anyone* but her. 'What's happened? Are you okay?'

She almost smiled at his immediate concern, only she feared she might vomit due to the sudden nausea she was feeling as her nerves rolled about in the pit of her stomach. 'I'm fine. I should have called,' she started, then wondered *why* the hell she *hadn't* simply called him. *Too late to go back now.* 'I was unpacking at Gran's.' She stopped once more. *Don't tell him about all the woo-woo stuff.* 'I made this list,' she blurted, and immediately groaned inwardly.

'A list?' he echoed, obviously still trying to work out if she really *was* okay.

'That's not really important right now,' she said quickly. 'The thing is . . . I thought I knew what I *wanted*. And, it turned out, I had no idea what I actually *need*.'

'And what is it you need?'

Bel swallowed and let out a shaky breath. *Just say it.* 'You,' she said softly. 'I want to be here with you.'

She watched as his shoulders almost sagged in relief and his face lost its guarded expression, melting into a smile. He reached out and she immediately stepped into his embrace.

'I'm sorry I've been acting like such a moron. I'm clearly a slow learner,' she said, and she could almost picture her guardian angels nodding their heads in agreement.

'You're perfect,' he said, pulling back slightly to look down at her. 'You've always been perfect to me—glasses, no glasses. Comfy jeans or model-like glamour. I love all of you. I always have.'

Bel swallowed over a hard lump of emotion. Someone seriously needed to write this man into a romance novel of his own—a love story about real people and real love. 'I love you too. Anyone who could have put up with the amount of indecisive crap I've been throwing at you lately is definitely worth holding onto.'

'If that's as bad as things get, I reckon we'll be okay,' he said with a grin before kissing her. 'Let's go and get your stuff first thing tomorrow. I don't want you changing your mind on me.'

'No need. I brought it all with me, it's out in the car,' she said, grinning as his eyes crinkled and his smile grew wider. 'I wasn't planning on changing my mind.'

She'd always thought she'd known what home had felt like, but not until this very moment had she realised the *real* meaning of the word. And she had finally arrived.

Acknowledgements

Thank you to Tina, Jess and Mandy, who taught me that the making of very important manifestation lists should probably *not* involve copious amounts of wine—although, it certainly makes it more fun! Who knew at the time, but that night was where this story was born!

Sharna Schafer, Raelene Watson, Kym Kirchner, Louise Langley, Bronwyn Stuart and Joel Donkin, thank you for answering the odd, crazy call for information. Britt Ramsey, journalist extraordinaire, thank you for your help. A big thank you to Kaitlin, Lyn and Milly for the brainstorming sessions that often helped me out of a bit of a hole.

Todd Jones for your helpful input and possible great idea for a future story! And my son, Rourke, for always being on hand for brainstorming some extra ideas and scenarios that usually have to spill over into a whole new book.